"Jillian Weise is a troublemaker. We need more writers like her, more novels like her hilarious, deeply moving, sexy, scary novel *The Colony*, which is about gene therapy, Watson and Crick, excessive alcohol consumption and cigarette smoking, mortality, finding love, finding a home, finding family, and all the other doomed experiments we conduct in the hope of making a better human." —Brock Clarke, author of *An Arsonist's Guide to Writers' Homes in New England*

"*The Colony* is howlingly funny and deeply sad. It is touching and toweringly angry. It is melancholy and lavishly sexual. It is unique—but it speaks with graceful force to everyone. I read many novels and forget many, but I will never forget what Jillian Weise has so brilliantly set down. Neither will you. Please try it. You will thank me." —Fred Chappell, author of *Shadow Box* and former poet laureate of North Carolina

"Part Wellsian dystopia, part medical mystery, part Hawthornian allegory, and part reality show, *The Colony* is a potent exploration of ethics in the Age of the Genome. But Weise's novel is not merely an exceedingly smart and formally elegant novel of ideas—it is also a deeply compelling character-driven drama. Anne Hatley's voice is irresistible—witty, assured, sexy, righteous, wounded. *The Colony* is a tremendous success, one of the most exciting first novels in recent memory." —Chris Bachelder, author of *Bear v. Shark* and *U.S.!*

"A debut that should be cause for much rejoicing . . . it's a coming-of-age tale, a razor-sharp comedy of eros, a meditation on 'disability' and the misguided ways in which we purport to 'fix' it, a scorched-earth denunciation of eugenics. And Anne Hatley—vulnerable and strong in equal measure, delightfully cranky, conflicted—is one of the most memorable protagonists in recent American fiction . . . Weise's grace, wit, and imaginative fearlessness mark her as a writer to be reckoned with for the long haul. *The Colony* is clever and playful, yes, but there's no mistaking this for whimsy—Weise's is a playfulness backed by steel." —Michael Griffith, author of *Spikes*

THE Colony

a novel

JILLIAN WEISE

Soft Skull Press
New York

Library of Congress Cataloging-in-Publication Data

Weise, Jillian Marie.
  The colony / Jillian Weise.
  p. cm.
  ISBN-13: 978-1-59376-267-4 (alk. paper)
  ISBN-10: 1-59376-267-4
  1. Young women--Fiction. 2. Human experimentation in medicine--Fiction.
  3. Genetics--Experiments--Fiction. 4. Cold Spring Harbor (N.Y.)--Fiction. 5.
  Conformity--Fiction. I. Title.
  PS3623.E432474C65 2010
  813'.6--dc22
      2009040421

Cover design by Lynn Buckley
Interior design by Neuwirth Associates
Printed in the United States of America

Soft Skull Press
An Imprint of Counterpoint LLC
2117 Fourth Street
Suite D
Berkeley, CA 94710

www.softskull.com
www.counterpointpress.com

Distributed by Publishers Group West

10 9 8 7 6 5 4 3 2 1

Dear B.L.,
When you thought we weren't talking anymore, I was telling you this story.

—JILLIAN

————

The Colony

WE CAME FROM all over. We taught in Durham. We bartended in Madison. Our parents were dying in Houston. We packed duffel bags, station wagons, and U-Hauls. We flew into New York and took a van to Cold Spring Harbor. Some of us had partners who helped us move cross-country and flew back to places like Fargo. In return for their couriership, we gave them mix CDs and bear hugs. It was what we always wanted: a roof over our heads and a check twice a month. We were picked for our renegade genes. Five of us. Five types. In return for housing and money, we would submit DNA. Meanwhile, we could do whatever we wanted. No obligations to grade papers or pour shots. No families looking over our shoulders; no consequences for staying out or sleeping in. Some of us had even demanded these things before. I need space, we'd said. I need time. We were free to relax in the cavernous lounge, watch flat screen, play Ping-Pong in the auditorium, walk the dunes, and drink at Sandy's Bar. Our relatives were suspicious: "You'll be doing what exactly? Who pays for all this? What happens to your DNA? Why would you want to live in the middle of Long Island for three months?" We reassured them with the same phrases: once-in-a-lifetime opportunity, three months isn't that long, I love you. "You'll be fine," my folks said. "Keep your legs closed and your Bible open."

First Impressions

———

I LANDED AT JFK and was bumped in the head by an elbow while trying to retrieve my luggage from the conveyor belt. The man didn't say anything. He was too busy. I'd been once before to the city. It was a lot of rushing around and stairs and ruts in the sidewalk and dogs on leashes and people walking into you. It was an obstacle course for anyone, but especially someone wearing a fake leg. My fake leg had a computer inside it and was very smart, but I didn't like to test it for fear of falling on my face. It was infinitely more reliable than humans, or human parts, but still I regarded it with suspicion. I wasn't the only one. A boy, maybe five or six, tugged on the bottom of his mother's shorts and said, "What's wrong with that lady's leg?"

Outside, I was just about to light a cigarette when I saw a man holding a sign that read COLONISTS. He looked out of place in his overalls. He told me he was Simon and I was his last passenger. As he loaded my luggage into the back of a white Astro van, I looked in my purse for cash. I came up with $2 and a stick of gum. If they wanted me to tip the driver, they should've said so. I settled into the front passenger seat. Simon pulled a small clipboard down from the visor and asked me to sign a form. My photo was affixed beside the Colony seal. At first glance, the seal looked like the common medical symbol, two snakes intertwined around a rod.

The rod belonged to Hermes, Olympian god of boundaries and conductor of the dead. Homer calls him "a robber" and "a thief at the gates." I'd always thought Hermes a perverse choice. The Colony seal featured the spiral of a genome in place of the snakes. I signed on a line above the word *arrived*.

Getting out of the city was hell: Simon never honked. He preferred to keep his foot on the brake and his hands in his lap until some kind soul let us on the interstate. Signs pointed toward the Long Island Expressway, the LIE, which seemed absolutely right for a road that did not take anyone expressly anywhere. We got off at Exit 41, Oyster Bay, looped around onto Route 106, and drove through the town of Jericho, flat and sparsely treed, with factories and parking lots. As we left Jericho, parking lots turned to fields, fields guarded driveways to palatial homes, and homes boasted four-car garages, three-story top-to-bottom windows. We passed estates with tennis courts, private ponds, and swimming pools. We passed Brookfield Road, Windsor Road, Bella Sonia Road, and I was feeling regal in the front seat of the Astro, my head back, thinking of Grayson going down on me in a mansion. Who was I kidding? We could never afford a mansion. Besides, Grayson had never quite figured me out in that regard. I was always left on the ledge, like make your tongue stronger, honey. I started thinking of a pool boy and a float.

I'd forgotten all about Simon when he pointed out Muttontown Preserve and said it was named "Best Nature Walk of Long Island." I didn't hear the rest of his spiel. I was stuck on the word *mutton* and why on earth someone would name a town after sheep flesh, stew, prostitutes. The leaves of the trees had just begun to turn yellow at the tips. One tree seemed to have said *fuck it* and gone dying yellow before the rest. Several large birds, with patches around their eyes, circled the preserve. To make Simon feel useful,

I asked, "What are those birds called?" Sea hawks, he told me, and other things concerning the wildlife of Long Island. Just when I thought I'd seen the biggest palace, a bigger palace appeared, mocking the one before it, with additional wings and gardens.

Around East Norwich, the houses got smaller and closer together. We passed a high school, and I thought of Durham Prep, where I taught, and of Mrs. Snodgrass, the incapable substitute who was standing behind my desk, writing on my chalkboard, and requiring my honors students to read *Our Town*. "I think I'll teach *Our Town*," she said, in that monotone of hers, punctuated with long *mmm* sounds as if she were enjoying a bowl of mutton. "Mmm, I've taught it so much I could teach it in my sleep." How was Gabe Fink or Erin Truitt or Adam McLane going to learn anything from Mrs. Snodgrass? Didn't she realize she was competing against pills, inhalants, handhelds, and hormones for their attention? And she was going to do this with *Our Town*? We passed signs for Pine Hollow Country Club.

A convertible cut in front of us with a bumper sticker that read PREVAIL THROUGH KNOWLEDGE. More and more boats parked in driveways, more and more tackle shops. Everything I knew about Long Island came from Emily Smoak, a transfer student who rose to popularity at my own high school. She lived in Westchester, before moving to Durham, and had this to say about Long Island: "People want to go to the Hamptons. I don't like the Hamptons because I think they're overpriced and annoying. I'm not into it at all, but all the stars go there during the summer. Long Island is full of people who have no class but have a lot of money. If you're from Westchester, like me, then you're old money. Either place, people take the train, everyone takes the train, nobody drives. People mostly go to their pool."

We turned right on to the turnpike, passed a golf course, more mansions. My family is lodged squarely in the middle class, two thousand antebellum square feet in Hickory, North Carolina. Maybe the Colony would be a restored estate. We approached the harbor, and Simon pointed out Bungtown Road, home to the laboratories at Cold Spring Harbor. The Colony was situated across the bay, opposite headquarters, in Cold Spring Harbor State Park. Just as we were about to cross the bridge, a police officer stepped in front of the van with a stop sign. Behind him, people were running back and forth carrying stacks of something in their hands.

"Petri Plate Relay Race," Simon said, shifting the Astro into park. "Happens every fall."

A small crowd lined either side of the street, rooting for one of three teams. The teams wore shirts with the Greek symbols alpha, zeta, or omega. A girl close to my window dropped her ice cream cone. She looked up at her parents, who were chanting *go, zeta, go*, and picked the cone from the ground and resumed licking it. I wanted a cigarette. A woman on the alpha team dropped her Petri plates. So the alpha team would not take home—what—the Bacteria Trophy? Finally, a man on the omega team reached the other side of the street with all his Petri plates stacked. Race over. We crossed the bridge. I had to pee. Maybe my apartment, my suite, my chalet, would have a bidet. Simon turned down an unmarked road, heading away from the water. We curved to the right, to the left, to the right again, on black asphalt with trees on both sides. We were obeying the fifteen-miles-per-hour speed limit. Simon didn't look like a man who ever gunned anything. We turned into a gravel parking lot. "Here we are," he said.

Check-In

———

THE SECRETARY GAVE me a folder with a handout on the participants, the history of the Colony, a map of the property, and my room assignment. I was assigned to Bungalow North, an A-frame with two windows, one on the front door, one on the back wall, a view to trees and a view to the other bungalows. The place was sparsely decorated; no one had bothered to paint the wood. It felt like being at camp minus the bunk beds. It was one big room. I couldn't even locate a closet. I walked out to the quad and asked Simon if there was a secret shed of furniture. There wasn't. I ran into a guy who said he could help move the bed. Back in Bungalow North, I called Grayson.

"How am I supposed to live without walls? And the bed sitting smack-dab in the middle of the room?"

"What a travesty. Did you eat lobster yet?"

"I don't like lobster. I like walls."

"Lobster's great up there."

"Lobster's in Maine. I'm in New York."

"I bet they have great seafood."

"Where am I going to put the bed?" I surveyed the room, about forty by twelve feet, and focused on where to put the bed. The kitchen had a table and chairs, shelving over the sink, pots stored in the stove. The bathroom was hidden behind the refrigerator.

It had a regular toilet and a tub, beige towels. The living area was not any more dignified. The bed was in the middle of the room flanked by a blue chair and ottoman. The pillows were tan, the sheets brown, the comforter beige. A flat screen hung from the eaves. The ceiling of the bungalow was lowest around the perimeter of the room.

"You'll figure it out," he said. "Did you go to the beach?"

"There's an alcove. I'll stick the bed in the alcove."

Someone knocked at the door. "Help's here," I said.

"Help?"

"I asked one of the guys to help move furniture."

There was an awkward pause. It looked like a hawk flying backward into a closet. Just then, overhead, a voice: "Please remember to attend the ceremony tomorrow afternoon, four o'clock, in the quad. The word of the day is *allele*."

"Annie, are you there?" Grayson said.

"I'm being bombarded from all sides. I have to get the door and there's a voice speaking to me from the ceiling." I told him I'd call him back.

The guy at the door wore a straw hat, tipped to the side, and a shirt with red piping. I'd met him in the parking lot. His sleeves were rolled up to his elbows. Underneath the rodeo shirt, he wore a long-sleeved thermal. He looked ready to fix a tractor. I'd forgotten his name, but remembered his gene from the handout—suicide. He was going to kill himself, so said science.

"Cool place." He removed his hat and set it on the kitchen table.

He told me he was the last cowboy from Madison, Wisconsin, he liked cold weather, he was hoping for a blizzard, and yes, he would try some sweet tea. I poured him a glass. As he took it, I checked his wrists. On the first sip, he grimaced. "I make it very sweet," I said. I told him I liked his hat, I was from Durham, North Carolina, I was hoping it stayed warm. I told him the bed sitting in the middle of the bungalow bothered me. The bed needed to go in the far corner, in the alcove. He pushed his sleeves up and moved the bed.

"It's not going to work under here," he said, lying down on the bed.

"I think it will." It was cozy. I planned on hanging a curtain.

When he sat up, his head bumped the ceiling. "Nope." He stood and latched his thumbs on his belt buckle. "Leave it be if you want, but that bed won't work under here."

"What's your name?"

"Nick."

"You don't look suicidal."

"I'm not suicidal."

"You have the gene."

"I have the gene."

"Is that even a gene? Shouldn't it be depression or something?"

"They found a gene," Nick said with pride. I hadn't heard of a suicide gene, but I figured if they were going to label mine *mutation* and call it a day, then they might as well call Nick's *suicide*.

Ceremony in Honor of James D. Watson

People say it would be terrible if we made all girls pretty. I think it would be great.

—JAMES D. WATSON

MY SECOND DAY at the Colony, I woke at six, terrified I'd forgotten to prepare a lesson plan, then thrilled not to have to teach, then terrified again that I'd forgotten something, like an appointment, morning roll call, did the Colony have roll call? I checked the folder. The schedule for the first week included a ceremony in honor of James D. Watson and an appointment with the Geneticist. The ceremony was at four in the afternoon. That meant only ten hours to kill. Ten hours! By noon, I'd read the *Messenger*, the local paper delivered to our doors. Front page: Karen Kilcotti, a nice if unremarkable resident of Cold Spring Harbor, moved to the Florida Keys. Page two: Cops were called about a large barrel outside Sandy's Bar. Turned out to be grease. I started reading an anthology to see if I wanted to teach it in the spring. I walked to the grocery store for a carton of Winstons. It was farther than I expected. On the map, it looked like it was right around the corner. As I was leaving the store, Simon pulled up in the Astro. "You can ask for a ride anytime," he said. I drank a pitcher of tea.

At three thirty, I changed into a cotton calf-length dress, black and plain and simple, and walked out to the quad. I hate being early for things, especially when I don't know anyone, but also when I do. I walked through the quad, where a dozen people stood, including a guy from the Petri Plate Relay Race. I walked to the door of the lounge. A bearded man sat with a journal, next to a skin-and-bones blonde flipping through a magazine. "Have you guys heard of Watson?"

The bearded man said nothing.

The blonde looked up from *Cosmo* and said, "Does he write mysteries?"

At the ceremony, Watson peered at us from posters. The posters hung on tree branches under a banner that read PREVAIL THROUGH KNOWLEDGE. The group gathered around the Geneticist, who was not Watson. Judging by the way the Geneticist said Watson's name, he wanted to be Watson, had wet dreams about Watson. The Geneticist shielded his face from the sun. We stood around him and waited. The blonde wandered over from the lounge; the bearded man followed. He seemed terribly sad or lost. The night before I'd discovered *am lost* in *almost*. Did everyone already know? I'd asked Nick while we rearranged furniture. He'd said: "Your teeth remind me of Linda Ronstadt, the whole package, you have that deer-caught-in-headlights look, Capitol Records 1971; I ain't always been faithful, there's women in Madison who wish me run over by eighteen-wheelers. Baby, where would you like the bed? Who's that guy on your Frigidaire? He looks all right if you go in for business, a bit pinched, collared. I myself was raised by an Indian who married a Jew; I've got the bed now, don't you worry."

I looked for Nick at the ceremony. He stood beside a poster with a beer in his hand.

The Geneticist, whose name was Engel Deeter, which I refused to call him, for obvious reasons, began his speech. Nick kept catching my eye and making faces at me until he ran out of faces to make and got on his hands and knees and crawled to me, between the legs of the audience, with no respect for the Geneticist's speech.

"What are you doing? Stop it."

The Geneticist paused and pointed to me.

"Anne Hatley," he said.

"Yes." I tried to step forward. Nick had me by the ankles.

"Is something wrong?" the Geneticist said.

"No."

He pulled a ledger from his pants pocket. "Allow me this opportunity to introduce you to the rest. Anne Hatley is from Durham where she teaches English. She's twenty-five with a rare genetic mutation. We're wondering how you're alive."

The blonde looked me up and down. When she saw Nick by my ankles, she shifted from one high heel to the other and pushed her shoulders back.

"How are you alive?" the Geneticist asked.

"I'm not sure." I felt my face blaze. It wasn't fair for him to single me out and introduce me to everyone. It was Nick's fault. I'd have a talk with Nick.

"Modern science," he answered.

Modern Science
(Some Things I Know about It)

———

GOD CREATES MAN. Allah creates man. The big bang creates amoebas that become man. Woman happens out of a rib. Out of a pair of goddesses. Out of amoebas oozing in the ocean. God, God, more God for many, many years. Enlightenment. The microscope. Finch, finch, Galápago. Charles Darwin signs letters to his wife, Emma, "Believe me." We do. Evolution. We go to war. We get out. We go with better weapons. Hand to club to spear to gunpowder to chemical. The doctors say, "Due to the use of toxins in a sandstorm, which planted themselves in your father's genes, you will die a child. You're just not meant to be." I don't die. "Okay," they say. "You will not die a child. We were wrong. Now we have determined you will be in a wheelchair." I'm not in a wheelchair. They are shocked, disappointed, they discuss it at the water cooler: "I'll be damned. Bones grew where no bones were. I think that Hatley girl intends to walk." I schedule appointments. I spend months traveling up and down in elevators. "Okay," they say. "You will not be in a wheelchair, but neither will you walk on your own two feet. Your leg has no knee. For walking, we will allow you a leg with a computer for a knee. You can plug it into the wall like a lamp." I do.

Goal of
Cold Spring Colony

———

OUR GOAL IS to allow individuals to gain deeper insights into their ancestry, genealogy, and inherited traits and, ultimately, the option to work together to advance the overall understanding of the human genome.

Goal of
Springs That Are Cold

———

OUR GOAL IS to open the earth, form pools, flow and overflow, make rivers, run down mountains, carve caves, and, ultimately, reach negative degrees, freeze, fossilize bones, provide safety for life on Mars.

Nick's Place

AFTER THE CEREMONY, Nick introduced me to Mercedes, who was talking on her cell phone, and Leonard, who was polishing his Harley.

"What are you in for?" Leonard said, standing up and using his rag to wipe sweat from his forehead.

I looked at Nick. Nick and Leonard were both looking at me. "I have a faulty gene," I said.

"Yeah, we all do. I'm bipolar. Name of the gene is ANK3. What's yours called?"

"PRX1."

"Sounds like a dirt bike."

Mercedes walked toward us. "Sorry—that was my boyfriend. So you're Anne Hatley. Now about me. My mom, bless her heart, weighs two hundred and eighty-five pounds and has tried every diet known to man. Turns out there's more than Irish-German in our blood. There's FTO. The Fat Gene. I like to think of it as the Fabulously Terrific Om. They found it involved with every other fat-causing gene. So I'm going on viral vector therapy. You know what they say: If you can't beat it, beat it before it gets to you." Mercedes turned on the ball of her foot to face Nick. "Are we still on for tonight?"

"Sure," Nick said. He put his hand in his back pocket.

Leonard returned to polishing his Harley.

"I know where to find you," Mercedes said and walked off.

What the hell Nick saw in Mercedes I did not know. It bothers me when people I like like other people I would never like. Nonetheless, I followed Nick to his place. He lived in Bungalow South. His place was about a hundred feet from mine, a straight line, except the main office was in the center of the Colony. The main office, octagonal in shape, housed the front desk with switchboard and secretary, the maintenance man's shop, the lounge, auditorium, mail room, and examining rooms. The Colony was an extension of Cold Spring Harbor Laboratory, established in 1890 and occupying 110 acres across the harbor, according to the literature in my folder. The folder contained a sheet on celebrities of the lab—Alfred Hershey, Martha Chase, Max Delbrück, Salvador Luria, Richard J. Roberts, and my favorite, Barbara McClintock, pictured holding a stalk of corn. She discovered jumping genes, the process by which corn sexes itself. Cold Spring Harbor Lab received annual contributions of more than twenty million, which they did not spend on furniture, judging by the condition of my bungalow. James D. Watson kept his office in Cold Spring Harbor proper and had not been present at the opening ceremony in his honor. The Colony was an Eden of large oaks; ten acres of land, the oaks taller than the bungalows and main office, the state park on three sides. The fourth side bordered the gravel lot leading to the road. A right turn led to the town of Cold Spring Harbor, the Long Island Sound, and the Atlantic Ocean; a left turn led through the park and toward Huntington Bay. The Geneticist hopped in a sports car with doors that opened up rather than out. Nick pointed to his car, a station wagon with a cracked windshield.

Nick's place had walls and hallways. The front door opened to a living room–kitchen combo, with windows to the right and above the sink. A dozen clay pots, filled with flower and fern, lined the perimeter of the room. It was like someone had died and bequeathed to him a plant kingdom.

"I don't like being called out at ceremonies," I said. "You have a lot of plants."

"It's a hobby."

I opened his refrigerator—a suitcase of Pabst, some sausages, chicken, eggs, and a small carton of goat cheese. I was impressed with the last item. It suggested the presence of refined taste: eggs are improved by goat cheese, and so Nick sought to improve breakfast. He asked if I wanted gefilte fish. It smelled awful. I'm not sure if Nick actually ate the stuff or if his heritage required him to keep them for the First Coming or if his mother smuggled them into his suitcase to remind her son of home.

"You want something to eat?" Nick raised his eyebrows. It was his face's trick. He used it drinking the tea, crawling across the lawn, and looking up at me.

"What was your angle on the lawn?"

"You can't be upset about that." Nick sidestepped me at the fridge, pulled out a beer, and popped the tab.

It tasted too cheap for five in the PM. "I think we should be friends before you grab my ankles."

"I moved your bed."

"Plus, I entirely missed the point of the Geneticist's speech."

"Long and boring."

"I'm still confused about who James D. Watson is and why we honor him."

"He's a big shit." Nick paced around the kitchen inspecting plants.

"Revelatory." There was a back door beside the stove. I went for it to smoke a cigarette. A plastic grocery bag hung from the doorknob. I stepped onto the porch and nearly ran into a ficus. "What else do you know about him?"

"He's got his hands in this place from inventing DNA."

"You can't invent DNA."

"Whatever."

"He found it?"

"He's a molecular biologist. Won a Nobel."

Nick was smarter than he let on. I was wearing Grayson's shirt and it fit like a moccasin. I heard Grayson's voice: "Don't kiss any dudes." I was only smoking a cigarette on a dude's porch. Though granted, I had already imagined this dude in his straw hat, slow-mo, with his hands on my ankles in a violent manner, the type of manner Grayson could not provide, having graduated summa cum laude, poli-sci and art history, and so knowing the whole story from Margaret Sanger to Guerrilla Girls. He could not say *suck my dick* or its compatriot phrases that tend to pitch me from cool beans to hot damn the world is ending. When I'd begged it of him, he'd added *please* with a vigilance that made me, during my turn, fake an orgasm. It had been nice to imagine Nick spared of an education.

"You want to Jimmy Watson me?" Nick asked.

"What's that mean?"

"Discover the prurient pleasures of my helix?"

I blushed. Nick caught me blushing and bit his lip. I put my cigarette out in the ficus pot.

"Eliot seems all right," Nick said.

"Who's Eliot?"

"Has a beard. I think he's Alzheimer's."

"How do you know?"

"Everybody knows. We're on the handout." Nick pointed to the handout which he'd hung on his refrigerator.

NAME	GENE	SEX	AGE
Eliot Fitzpatrick	Alzheimer's	M	33
Leonard Carroll	Bipolar	M	42
Anne Hatley	Mutation	F	25
Mercedes Minnow	Obesity	F	36
Nick Burkowitz	Suicide	M	30

He started cooking dinner. "I had one of the most amazing moments today."

"You got laid."

"No, no." He handed me an envelope from the side table. "My uncle sent me his medals from the Middle East."

I opened the envelope and pulled out three tan pieces of paper. "These aren't medals."

"Are your hands clean?"

"What are these?"

"Those are certificates; the medals are in my bedroom."

"So what, you bring a woman back, if she's cute she gets the certificates. If she's really hot, she gets the medals."

"You can see my medals."

"Say sorry about the ceremony."

"I'm sorry."

I lit a cigarette inside. Nick complained. I finished the smoke and lit another while he cooked. He talked about winning the Madison Award for Gardening Excellence. He wore boots with tight jeans. He had a date later with Mercedes. He listened to Clay Walker and Merle Haggard. I just had to hear Haggard and Wilson's version of "Poncho and Lefty." Nick used to play banjo, but not since undergrad. He used to garden for the mayor, but not since he made more bartending. He used to attend synagogue and study under a renowned rabbi, but not since his parents started getting along. In light of these interests, wildly pursued and flippantly dropped, I was skeptical. I did not bring up his suicide gene. While he was talking, I kept thinking, fuck, you're going to kill yourself. Then I started wondering how he'd do it and when he'd do it. We ate. He was dedicated to eating, thick chest, broad shoulders, evenly proportioned over the plate. His elbows were on the table. When a piece of chicken got stuck in his teeth, he picked it out with his thumbnail. He spoke of other women who had loved him, one in particular, a nurse in Verona.

If he wanted to do me, this was not the way to it. I got tangled up once in a triangle where I was the one left out and lied about. I was not going back there. The man I loved had mentioned—not a nurse—but a similar attachment. We didn't talk much about her, hardly at all, three or four times. He said he liked my toes, compared them to those on a statue in Italy, and I was embarrassed. My toes are unattractive, so what was he doing looking at them? *Callisto* he called me, when he was still calling me things. Let this be a lesson to womankind: Don't let anyone see some part of yourself you shrink from, spin that into myth, smite you with affections, and keep you in hiding. Leave that to your Doric order, your Delians, your Athenians, your ancient Parthenon.

Nick gave his case for and against God; it took five minutes. Under the table, he stretched his legs. He called me *baby*. Occasionally he called me *girlie*. I told him it reminded me of porn. "What's a God-fearing girl like you watching porn for?" he said. He scraped rice to one side of his plate, chicken to the other. The man liked garlic, big time.

Ways That Nick
Might Kill Himself

———

IN MY BUNGALOW, I concocted a list of ways that Nick might kill himself.

5) First-degree burns from roasting s'mores.
4) Double suicide with horse.
3) Asphyxiation during rough-and-tumble sex with cowgirl.
2) Shoot-out with self.
1) Jump from saloon roof.

Jump seemed most likely. One second Nick was a tall, straw-hat-wearing guy, the next he was on his knees going for my ankles. It would be that way, I guessed, when he died. It would be impulse, standing with his boots on the edge of a roof and, on whim, on woozy, what would happen if—

Calling Durham

———

This "telephone" has too many shortcomings to be seriously considered as a practical form of communication. The device is inherently of no value to us.

—Western Union memo, 1878

TO NOT CHEAT, not in the first week, I talked to Grayson every night. I told him to make the drive. I told him about the ceremony, the posters hung from trees, the Geneticist, the codes of others, such as Nick. I put Nick's name in with a lot of other names so as not to draw attention. Grayson had been suspicious of the Colony.

"Why are you doing this?" he kept asking. "Are you doing this for me?"

"I'm doing it for me."

"But why?" he said.

"It's easy money." That wasn't a good enough answer for Grayson. My doctor had mentioned it to me at the end of an annual checkup. "And here's this," he said, handing me an advertisement from one of his medical journals. "Thought you might be interested." I tacked the ad to my bulletin board—The Colony at Cold Spring Harbor, Fall Lab, September 15–December 15,

$5,000/month. It stayed there for a few weeks before I sent an email. My doctor sent my files and a letter of recommendation, and then I didn't hear anything for a while. The invitation came, embossed in fancy font, with the endorsement of the Public Health Association, the president, and a plea from a mother whose son was born with birth defects. I majored in English at Duke. What did I know about cellular biology?

Earlier in the day Engel Deeter explained, "The problem with using human cells is this: If you take them away from humans, they die. So the only cells we can study are live ones in the body." Then he complimented my left leg, the real one. "Look at this leg. It's anatomically superior. Consider the support it's had to provide your entire body through years and years of physical work."

"It sounds like you're introducing me to my own leg. Do you think I don't know my own leg?" It was a pet peeve of mine that doctors, upon meeting me, presumed it was as monumental a moment for me as it was for them. They had never seen my particular configuration of bones, nor did they understand my particular birth defect, because it was granted to only one out of fifteen million of us and I was its only survivor. Everyone before me who had it died of pneumonia, respiratory failure, or cardiac arrest. They suffocated. Their rib cages were too small. Their bones were stunted. It always happened in the first fifteen months. So those first fifteen months they were waiting for me to die. Then they took more X-rays and saw that bones had grown, out of chaos into order, and the only bones that never grew were those in my leg. My gynecologist at college actually asked, "How did you get in here?" He'd seen my files before seeing me and was in awe that I could walk, and he expected me to be in awe too, except there was nothing awesome about him.

Engel glared at me. "It's just a finely toned specimen of a leg.

Now imagine an identical leg, regenerated on your body, to match the left. Can you imagine?"

"Regenerated?"

"Made of your own cells."

"I didn't ask for whatever you're implying, you're asking it of me."

"I just imagine two legs," he said. "Both real."

I didn't want him imagining anything. I wanted to tell him that it wasn't my fault his folks named him Engel, and for this he jogged after work, buffed his hair, wore potent cologne, and wrote with a Montblanc. No amount of accoutrement could rid him of the name Engel Deeter. I wanted to tell him I was there for the money and the expenses-paid bungalow, and while I would deliver the cells for observation, there'd be no regenerated leg.

I came out of curiosity. Who were the others and what were they putting on the line? I came to get away from the latent impression I'd been having that Grayson wanted to hitch me and that I would say yes and that this would become our life—a back-and-forth of "do you want to" and "I do." In recent weeks, he'd begun staring at me for no reason at all. He would sit there and stare until I said, "What are you looking at?" I understand that once you get familiar with someone, once the strange is no longer strange, new games have to be introduced. This is why Cleopatra spoke thirteen languages and the *Hustler* adult-toy store was invented. I walked around the Colony annoyed that I was the only one whose gene manifested itself physically. I expected someone to have a hook for a hand or a patch over an eye. I checked out a book on sign language in case there were any deafs. I knew how to sign *hello* and *you're pretty*. Grayson was afraid that one day I'd run off with another amputee. "What if you just fall in love on principle?" he said. "What principle would that be?" I said.

In my first meeting with the Geneticist, I refused to sign for anything other than tests and X-rays. The Geneticist was telling me that I would keep the rights to my cells and helix. I thought that was kind of fucked up, like do I need this guy to tell me I'm in possession of my cells and helix? He explained that I was giving him permission to work with my cells as he saw fit in the lab. I hoped, at the end of my tenure at the Colony, to have a healthy savings and a settle-down mentality. If I wanted to split in a month, I'd split.

"I imagine two legs," Engel said. "Wouldn't that be ideal?"

I couldn't even think about it. I'd been disappointed before. I'd been, age six, to a healing ceremony at an Evangelical church in downtown Durham. After I was chanted on and shouted at, the pastor stuck a plastic crucifix down my dress and pushed me on the forehead. This had not resulted in a second leg of identical length and knee. I'd been, age seven, to Düsseldorf for the best orthopedic surgeon in the world. He recommended affixing a metal rod to my femur bone. He wanted to go in there and fuse metal to bone, and leave the metal sticking out of the skin, all of which sounded ugly and painful, besides being ineffective, since the metal would not grow along with me. I learned to say no adamantly, and I learned that in order to say no to the most accomplished orthopedic surgeon in the world, I had to come up with reports, reasons, lists, objectives, goals.

I used the time, when my peers were in gym, to research in the library. On my behalf, Holt Elementary School subscribed to LexisNexis. I found the leg I wanted. It had a computer in it and plugged into the wall. It was better than a metal rod fused into bone with skin grafted. It was better than a spiritual healing. It would lengthen my leg and give me a knee with which to jump rope and skip. My doctors and parents agreed. The Geneticist, who was sitting before me, inspected the computer leg — upgraded through the years, cosmetically refined—and found it lacking. "This leg versus the one you could grow is the difference between a wheel on a buggy and a tire on a Lamborghini."

Was that a compliment?

I left our first meeting with a stomachache. Grayson asked how I felt.

"It's not like I'm calling from a test tube," I said.

"I know," he said. "Just don't let them get you."

"Dear God, Grayson. What do you think's going on up here?"

"I'm just saying."

This was typical of him. He always wanted to blow things out of proportion. Once when a van from the telephone company sat in front of his apartment, he called the cops. He thought someone was spying on us. The cops said, "It's the telephone company."

"No one's out to get me."

"Not you, in particular, but—"

"Grayson, honey."

"Sometimes I get the feeling you don't think of consequences."

"I think of consequences."

"Do you?"

"You're starting to piss me off." I pictured Grayson, in his living room, sitting in front of his microwave dinner, doling out consequences with his plastic fork. He was a security guard at the North Carolina Museum of Art. He usually locked the doors to the museum at eight, drove his hybrid home, and left his tie on the counter. He'd stick a frozen dinner in the microwave and stand there, watching seconds tick down. He stared at the microwave the same way he stared at me. I told him the microwave beeps when it's finished, so he didn't have to stare at it. I'd meant it as a joke. "I'm watchful," he'd said with a tone that divided the night in half.

On the phone with him, I looked out the window. Nick was crossing the quad toward the lounge with Mercedes.

"I have the woolies," Grayson said. That was his word for sadness. The first time he used it, he'd gone into a description of an unemotional state. Like Kafka, he'd said. No, I'd said, Kafka weeps on the page. The first time he used it, he'd said I had eyes the color of carelessness. My eyes are light brown. I knew how to cut them just right, at the right moment, to make Grayson nervous. He'd said I had better put my eyes away. He veered into one of his philosophies of woe and ended the speech with an experience he'd had in the museum guarding a Rothko. He said things weren't in focus. There was fuzz on his canvas. "I'm probably just tired," he said.

"Then don't call if you're tired."

"I want to talk to you."

"Right, because talking to me puts you in such a good mood."

"Do you not want me to call?"

"Not if you're going to start shoving consequences around the plate."

"I better let you go."

I got off the phone and lit a cigarette. I didn't have an ashtray, so I ashed in the kitchen sink. I leaned against it. When Grayson and I first got together two years ago, the sink was one of our prime locales to fool around. Also highly ranked: the doorframe, the living room floor, the patio, the shower, the chair, the table. Was I simply fascinated by thresholds, carpet, concrete, water pressure, and finished oak? Was it possible Grayson wasn't actually involved in the act? Could I have been seducing a brown couch? The novelty wore off and it became the bed, the bed. I bet the bed causes many a break. Volumes are dedicated to avoiding such a break: *Ars Amatoria*; *The Lost Works of Elephantis*; *The Perfumed Garden for the Soul's Recreation*; Nerve.com's *Position of the Day*; *Aqua Erotica*; *Fork Me, Spoon Me*.

The Bricklayer, the Mortar, and Love

———

THE PROBLEM, BEYOND the bed, begins at first touch, when a bricklayer enters the room. "You are touching her," the bricklayer says. "I am here to build an extensive labyrinth between the two of you."

Then comes the mortar, a nice layer of misunderstanding. Someone says, "You go ahead without me. I want to stay home tonight," and the other person hears, "I prefer loneliness to your incessant droning. I don't enjoy your company. I never enjoyed your company. I've only been pretending to enjoy your company." Walls go up. Pigeons alight on walls and shit on heads. The bricklayer brings out his spirit level. Someone says, "My ex lives in Alamance," and the other person hears, "Where her beauty is comparable only to the sun setting over the ravine." Someone says, "Are you really going to wear *that*?" and the other person hears, "I want to change the core of your being. I want to shapeshift you into an entirely new person, beginning with your green shorts." It becomes even more complicated when talking sex. Someone asks, "Are you always in the mood?" and the other person hears, "You're desperate. You're a slut." Someone asks, "Are you still hard?" and the other person hears, "Your dick is so inconsequential I can't even tell if it's erect."

Grayson had a fantastic dick. Not too big, not too small,

somewhere in between. I've surveyed a variety and I prefer the 'tweeners. They possess an acceptance of their average size that is much more tolerable than the arrogance of big ones or the shame of small ones. There is nothing at all wrong with an average dick. On the speed dial of dicks, it moseys along. Grayson liked to keep his dick dry, was the problem. He vetoed lube. He called it "fake-feeling" and "artificial." I said, "Are you kidding me?" and I was wide-eyed when I said it, waiting for him to say, "Indeed, I am kidding. I'm being ironic." My palm was open below the KY, and he flipped the bottle closed, so that was the end of that. He wasn't having any help in that department, which meant our foreplay was limited to what prepared us for getting the job done naturally and efficiently.

I put on a pair of heels and called him back. "Are you awake?"

"Going to sleep."

"What are you wearing?"

"Boxers."

"Ask me what I'm wearing."

"What are you wearing?"

"The peekaboos." I bought the shoes at Nine West. The wedges were two inches tall, the maximum height I could wear; I had to adjust my leg at the ankle, and it wouldn't crank more than two inches for a heel. The shoes were dark brown with polka dots and the essential peekaboo feature: the cutout toe. I wore them as a signal that I wanted to get off. I leaned against the sink.

"Annie."

"What? Are we going to play?" The sink had a counter on either side. I put my palms on the counter and lifted myself up. From this height, I could see dust in the eaves of the bungalow. Grayson had a fantastic dick six hundred miles away and now he was—

"Seriously?"

—protective of it. Did I consider consequences? What was wrong with him? The first time we had phone sex, I fell off the bed laughing. We had never been talkers. Then, we were. Grayson hesitated on the phone and started breathing heavy.

"You're faking it," I said.

"Are you always in the mood?" he said.

"Yes. I'm a slut."

How Good Are You
at Phone Sex?

You are between the ages of:
    a. I am immortal.
    b. 18 and 39
    c. 40 and 59
    d. 60 and 100

You make the following salary:
    a. I live hand-to-mouth.
    b. < $30,000
    c. > $30,000
    d. Call my accountant.

You have compared yourself to:
    a. Dracula
    b. An ant
    c. The Man
    d. Saint Teresa

If we recorded you in conversation, and removed the words, we would hear which of the following sounds:
    a. *ahhh, ahhh*
    b. *ugg-a, ugg-a*
    c. *a-hem, k-chew*
    d. *zzz, zzz*

First Visit
from Charles Darwin

———

MY SECOND WEEK at the Colony, Darwin visited. He wore a top hat and his beard dragged the floor. A trail of sand followed him. He put the sound track from *The Jazz Singer* on the flat screen. I gave him a beer and joined him in the living room. He didn't say anything. I didn't want to stare, but he was Darwin and he was sitting in my blue chair. I sat on the ottoman in front of him and lit a cigarette. We sat there listening to Al Jolson.

"You're ashing in my beer," he said.

"You want one?" I slid the pack of Winstons over to him.

"I shouldn't." He held out his hand. "I'm dying."

"You've been dead."

"It takes a while." He motioned to his mouth. For a second I thought he wanted me to kiss him and I was leaning in for it. I could smell his breath.

"Emma, give me a cigarette."

"I'm not Emma."

"For now."

I placed the cigarette between his lips. "What are you doing here?"

"I'm tired of walking the sand trap." He took a deep drag. "And you?"

"Free room, and money."

"What's shaking in this town?"

"It's whale season." I expected him to leap to his feet and bum-rush the ocean.

"Aren't there any strip clubs?"

"It's quiet."

"There must be something."

"A grocery store, a pharmacy, and a pub."

"Bloody hell."

"Tell me about it."

"I guess you better sport the red miniskirt."

"Too cold."

"You could lose your mind otherwise."

"Thanks." We sat there, face-to-face, smoking my cigarettes. He tilted his head back and closed his eyes. He was probably thinking of his glory days when he traveled by *Beagle* and measured beaks. He was probably thinking of all the salt in the world, all the salamanders, all the giant sloths. Or maybe he was just thinking of one species, one animal, he personally mapped and charted, on repeat. Emma, for example. Maybe he was not thinking at all, just listening to "Blue Skies" and liking his top hat.

"We lost the paradise parrot," he said. "1927."

We Found the Secret of Life

———

—FRANCIS CRICK TO JAMES D. WATSON, 1962

Interview
with the Geneticist

Did I solicit thee / From darkness to promote me?
— Paradise Lost, Book X, lines 744–745

ON WEDNESDAY OF the second week, the Geneticist came to
my place with his briefcase. He was wearing a lab coat over khakis
and a shirt embroidered with COLD SPRING HARBOR LABORATORY
in gold thread on the pocket. He told me he wanted to meet "on
my terms." I decided to wear a bra for the occasion. I sprayed the
room until it smelled like a jasmine smokestack.

"What do you like to be called?" he asked.

"Excuse me?"

"Disabled, handicapped, or . . . ?"

"I like to be called Anne."

"I only ask for the paperwork." He passed a clipboard to me.
"We have a high success rate. Last year, in a case I personally
oversaw, we saved a girl from anorexia."

"Do you have money for a couch?" I said. I fixed him tea in a
mason jar and left him standing in the kitchen. I sat down on the
one chair in the living room. I was primed from birth to take what
doctors say and transform it into fantasy. If we want to be Freudian,
my first physician replaced The Father, his gaze sexed me into the

world, six months in the baby ward, and at age three I learned the masturbatory techniques on my own polymer leg. Then physicians, with their digi cams, snapped nude photographs, slipped them into envelopes with X-rays, licked and sealed, delivery confirmation, sent me to their colleagues. Every nanometer of my body has been seen, studied, flagged, magnified, and qualified.

The Geneticist sipped the tea. I thought of what to call him. Engel wouldn't do and neither would Deeter. "Mind if I call you the Gee?" It reminded me of the Bee Gees. They were born on the Isle of Man. So that was about right.

"The Gee?"

"Take it like a term of endearment."

The Gee wanted to get down to business. He pulled a chair from the kitchen and read clauses from his clipboard. The Colony was not liable for this or that. The Colony assumed no responsibility for lost property in the case of fire, accident, theft, or natural disaster. The Colony was under no obligation to cover any tabs accrued at local eating establishments. The Colony would pay me every other week. Here was my check, but first would I kindly sign the agreement.

The Agreement

This Agreement is entered by and between ANNE HATLEY, an individual, and THE COLONY, a Limited Liability Company.

In consideration of the mutual promises set forth hereunder, the sufficiency of which is hereby acknowledged, ANNE HATLEY and THE COLONY agree to the following:

ANNE HATLEY, having been chosen from among 23,374 applicants, having desired three months' internment at THE COLONY, agrees to the following: Attendance at THE COLONY functions, scientific and social, including, but not limited to appointments with Dr. Engel Deeter, fund-raising ceremonies, professional lectures, and press junkets;

Blood, cell, helix, and hair donation; permission to show images on the Cold Spring Harbor Channel to foster a team spirit; X-rays at no expense to ANNE HATLEY; various treatments as determined by Dr. Engel Deeter, supervised by James D. Watson and approved by the Czar for Progress of the Food and Drug Administration. Treatments are subject to approval by ANNE HATLEY.

THE COLONY agrees to the following:

Above all, to do no harm to ANNE HATLEY; act in the best interests of ANNE HATLEY with consideration of his/her economic, social, and historiographic background; compensate

ANNE HATLEY in the sum of $5,000.00/month, to be paid in two monthly installments, in weeks two and four of each month; provide room and utilities at no expense to ANNE HATLEY.

This agreement may be terminated as follows: Either party may terminate this contract at any time.

Time shall be of the essence in the performance of this agreement.

If any part of this agreement is held unenforceable for any reason, the remaining portion of this Agreement shall remain in full force and effect, and shall be carried out in a manner which is consistent with the intentions of the parties hereto.

If any legal action or proceeding, including any arbitration of disputes, arising out of, or relating to, this Agreement is brought by either party, the prevailing party as determined by the Court or Arbitrator, shall be entitled to receive from the nonprevailing party, in addition to any other relief that may be granted, reasonable attorney's fees, costs, and expenses incurred in the action or proceeding by the prevailing party.

This agreement is entered in the City of Cold Spring Harbor, the County of Nassau, State of New York.

_____

Anne Hatley   Date

_____

Dr. Engel Deeter, President and Lead Geneticist   Date

I signed. The Gee put the check in an envelope on the kitchen table. He walked back into the living room and sat down in front of me.

"How familiar are you with stem cells?" he said, looking me in the eyes.

"Not. At all."

"I understand. They have a bad rap. But if you can forget the jargon—right-wing, left-wing, up-wing, down-wing, whatever wingbat you are—" He waited for me to laugh; I gave him a smile. "You know that stem cells are the directions for life."

"Why's that?" I said.

"Stem cells contain DNA," he said. "The directions for how to build proteins. Which is how human life works. Proteins repair things, transport things, and communicate things. They're like body traffic control."

"You mean like one cell calls over to another, 'Hello. We're making hemoglobin.' The other cell replies, 'Ten-four.'"

"Sort of." He sat back in the chair.

"Hey, don't look at me like that."

"Pardon?"

"The way you look at people. Do you want another glass of tea?" He had drunk the tea down to the ice. I stood up, bumping into his knee, and walked to the kitchen with his glass.

"As I was saying," he continued. "We want to use your stem cells, combined with a select pool of micro RNAs, to grow your leg."

I handed him the tea. "This is interesting stuff. Really," I said. I wanted to make up for telling him that he didn't look at people right. But he didn't. He looked people too much in the eye and someone should have told him by now. "So you want to grow my leg in the lab? My boyfriend thinks you're going to grow my leg in a test tube."

"Well, we could grow it in the lab, we could do that, and then attach it surgically, but this has drawbacks. For one thing, we would have to wait for your leg to develop from infancy on up to your twenty-fifth year. For another, we would have to hope that your body would accept the leg. I want to grow your leg one part at a time on your body. Using your stem cells. I want to keep the part of your gene that stimulates rapid bone growth. That's a valuable gene. You will hear your fellow Colonists talking about viral vector therapy. We're not interested in viral vector therapy for you. We're dealing with stem cell therapy. Essentially, stem cells resurrect dying cells and regenerate things. They self-renew. They can be used to correct a disorder or grow an organ or, in your case, a limb. We already have your stem cells. We've been working with them for years."

"Where did you get them?"

"From your doctor."

"Where did he get them?"

"From you. He had the foresight to collect a sample. And he sent them to us. Perfectly preserved."

"Then you already have what you need. I thought you said you could only study cells live from my body?"

"I understand. You're skeptical. In 2000 a research team headed by Cavazzana-Calvo completed the first successful treatment of a genetic condition. They cured human severe combined immunodeficiency disease. And when I say cured, I mean they fully corrected the genetic disorder. But it came at a price. When they changed one part of the DNA sequence, they accidentally changed another. Three of the patients developed cancer. We've come a long way since then. I joined the lab in 2010, and I've overseen several clinical trials of this kind. I work with stem cell and viral vector therapies. In either case, you can think of me as a postman who delivers a letter that will change your life."

I could tell by the way he spoke, emphasizing certain words, pausing emphatically between sentences, that he had stood in front of a mirror, practiced when to smile, when to look serious.

He had recited it, to patients, doctors, financial backers, and yet he had managed to tell me nothing about what, specifically, he wanted to do to me.

"I don't know if I want you to change my life right now. It's Wednesday and I'm in the middle of reading a book. So unless your therapy intends to deliver the good-luck gene to me or the young forever gene, I think I'll just get back to my book, if you don't mind."

"I love my job," the Gee said. It seemed to surprise him as much as me. He was veering from the flash cards of his speech. "I love my job and here's why: If you truly think about what I can do for you, if you truly consider it, I know you will give it a chance."

I stood from the chair and crossed to the window. I opened it. Outside was a beautiful, clear-skied day.

"Listen, Anne. Your gene is invaluable. When you were born, your bones were either stunted or nonexistent. When you were born, some extremities, your left hand, for example, contained no bones at all. It was a sack of nerves and tissue. Then, almost overnight, bones grew. Look at your left hand. How did that happen? Do you realize what kind of implications such a gene holds? I want to use your stem cells to grow your leg in a matter of days."

"I'm fine with you studying me. I'm fine with you using whatever samples you have for whatever they can do. But I don't want to grow a leg."

"You should at least consider germ line therapy, so that you can have children."

"I can have children."

"Certainly you wouldn't be that socially irresponsible. Naturally, if we offer to do something for you, to make you more equal in life, then we expect you to show us, and future generations, a modicum of generosity."

The New York Times Responds
to the Declaration of Independence

———

DoI: We hold these truths to be self-evident, that all men are created equal.

NYT: Boop! Not true. It's very hard to believe that all human beings are equal. It takes a profound moral case to defend the proposition that the youngest and the oldest, the weakest and the strongest, all of us, simply by virtue of our common humanity, are in some basic and inalienable way equals.

The Young and the Old

———

LAST SUMMER, FOR a little extra cash, I worked in the mainte-nance department of a senior citizens' community called Golden Oaks. I answered the phones and radioed the maintenance men. They took breaks at ten, noon, and three to smoke Pall Malls and talk soap operas. I had a soft spot for an older man, Vic. "I know everything there is to know about computers," he said. When a resident called with a computer problem—she wanted to play a DVD or the computer wouldn't turn on—Vic was dispatched. Usually, the solution was simple. Sometimes residents had what Vic described as "a real technical issue." On these occasions, Vic returned to the office and delivered a blow-by-blow of how he removed a very serious bug using Norton.

Golden Oaks had three complexes: A for independent living, B for assisted living, and C for the nursing home. Once a person moved into Golden Oaks, they were likely to go through all three complexes, unless they died first. A resident named Margaret, who lived in Complex C, called every day.

"I have a note here says call Anne," she whispered into the phone. "Says call Anne, she knows Vic and the men. She's your friend. Are you Anne?"

"Yes, that's me."

"Because I want to speak with Anne."

"Speaking."

"Anne, let me tell you." The first week I worked at Golden Oaks, someone died in Complex B. We got the call from housekeeping. B217 hadn't opened his fridge in twenty-four hours. There were censors inside the fridge for just this purpose. People have to eat. I went over to Grayson's place after work. I picked up tilapia thinking we'd have an old-fashioned meal. I thought fish was the easiest thing in the world to cook. I hadn't cooked it long enough. Grayson put his hand on the back of my neck and kissed me. We called for pizza. I said, "We'll be all right in Golden Oaks. They have a cafeteria. They have karaoke. And poker. I know you love poker. It wouldn't be the worst place to die." He rubbed my neck.

"Anne, let me tell you about my television," Margaret said. "I have a beautiful television. When it first arrived, Vic and the men came to install it. They were so excited, like how most men are with a new engine. Now I called about my television and no one has come. I have a very elegant and beautiful manual here, with pictures and figures of all my parts."

The Red Button

————

COMPARED TO GOLDEN Oaks, the Colony was an administrative disaster. It would have profited from an employee with an MBA. The Gee's title was lead geneticist, and while he had a few research assistants running around, most of his help stayed across the harbor in labs we never saw. The Gee drove back and forth between these labs and the Colony. Teams of scientists worked on each of our cases well before we arrived; we never met them. Public relations, fund-raising, accounting—all on the other side of the harbor. The totem pole at the Colony featured the Gee at the tippy top; followed by Patricia, the secretary who scheduled our appointments and delivered our mail; followed by Simon, who made sure our bungalows were equipped with working smoke alarms and fire extinguishers, mowed and watered the quad, changed lightbulbs, fixed leaking faucets, and gave me and Eliot rides to the store.

In our third week, the Gee called a meeting to discuss the control panel in each of our bungalows. I'd already familiarized myself with the control panel. I figured out how to turn the speaker down so I wouldn't have to hear the words of the day. To reach me, any announcement would have to come by email, post, phone, or house call. In addition to a volume knob, the control panel had a thermostat, a black button, and a red button. We were instructed to push the red button only for a true emergency.

"Like my commode's overflowing?" Mercedes said.

We were gathered in the Gee's office. It was only the second time we'd all been together, and Grayson had told me he thought that was weird. Grayson thought the Colony should've provided a meet and greet, daily, or every Friday. He thought I should become a "more active part of the community." Grayson liked people more than I did. He was one of those who believed every human being had something to offer. So he couldn't understand why I wasn't taking the Colonists up on their offers. "No one's really offering anything," I'd told him. "We're only here for three months. What's the point of getting to know people?" Grayson gave everyone the benefit of the doubt, even Luther, a guard at the museum, who swindled Grayson out of money each payday with a story about his wife and kids and the economy. I was sitting beside Nick, and I wondered if he was a swindler. He glanced at me and smiled. Probably. I waited for him to look away and then looked at his knees, a rip in the denim, and up to his lap. He hung left.

"If my commode's overflowing, I'm pushing the button," Mercedes said.

"Is that an emergency you typically have?" the Gee said.

"No, but it's a pain in the ass, and I don't do plungers," Mercedes said.

"Maintenance is the black button," the Gee instructed. Then he yelled to Simon, who appeared with his hands on the edge of the door.

"Yes, sir?" His hands were rough and covered in grime. Perhaps he'd been cleaning a toilet.

"These are our guests: Mercedes, Nick, Anne, Leonard, Eliot. I trust you'll help them as needed," the Gee said.

"Yes, sir, I met them," Simon said, and with a tilt of his head, disappeared behind the door.

"He's an affable individual once you get to know him," the Gee said.

"When do you turn on the heat?" Nick said.

"I'm freezing. I've got my thermostat at eighty-five and nothing," Mercedes said. She lived in a perpetual-summer land. One got the sense that all her dreams came true.

"Please use the space heaters for another week, let's say until October 15, and afterward keep the thermostat around seventy." The Gee spoke like a business letter and enveloped himself with his arms across his chest.

"I'll keep the thermostat wherever I want," Mercedes said.

"I don't know where my thermostat is," Leonard said. The Gee rose from his chair and we followed him through the hall, past Patricia, and toward Leonard's bungalow.

"We're all going in?" Leonard said as we stood at the top of his stairs on a wooden platform.

"Is that a problem?" the Gee said.

"I'm kind of private about my space," Leonard said.

Eliot spoke. "I don't want to go in." Everyone turned to look at Eliot, who cracked a pistachio with his teeth and dropped the shell on the platform. Eliot left a trail of pistachio shells wherever he went so he could remember how to get back. I didn't know much about Eliot other than what Nick told me. Nick was outgoing, like Mercedes, and while I was holed up reading books, the two of them were making friends in town, or with each other, or with Eliot. Nick said Eliot didn't make friends. Eliot's mind was a mess. Nick described a run-in where Eliot talked about a camping trip: "Rinding woads, stridges over breams, all that." Eliot's belongings were labeled. He was picking at the label on his long-sleeved shirt, the rest of us standing by, while the Gee walked in with Leonard to show him the location of the control panel behind the mirror. The platform was small and we stood close together. I was the shortest, so everyone looked gigantic to me. Mercedes leaned against the rail at the top of the stairs and said to Nick, "I like your hat."

"Thank you," he said.

"I want a hat like that. Where do you get a hat like that?"

"I'm not sure why I'm standing here. I already know where my mirror is," I said.

Eliot said, "I know where mine is too." His voice was soft. I looked down at his shoes, checkerboard canvas, beside a pile of pistachio shells.

The door to Leonard's bungalow opened out, crowding us, and I took one step back. Nick's hand went behind me and I felt his thumb against my spine.

"Here's the mirror," the Gee said. "Swing up for the thermostat, maintenance, or an emergency. Is that clear? Everyone recognize this?"

My mirror was hanging by the coatrack in Bungalow North.

The Gee had the mirror in his hand facing us. In the mirror I saw Mercedes smirking at Nick who was looking at himself in the glass. Then I realized he was looking at me, not himself, and instead of smiling, like a normal person, I rolled my eyes.

We walked back to our respective bungalows. I gave my mirror a cursory glance and half suspected it of being a two-way contraption. I took it off the wall and scratched the back of it with my fingernail. It was a regular mirror, now with a scratch mark in the center.

Eliot pushed the red button the very next day. Nick and I were at his place, eating lunch, garlic pork chops and mashed potatoes. Nick thought it was the end of the world.

"Do you think the end sounds like a siren?" I said.

"Turn on the flat screen," Nick said. "The networks will be playing a song if it's the end of the world."

"What song?"

"A hymn or something."

I flipped to CNN where no hymn was playing. "Fire alarm," I said, as I stretched my arms. Outside, Leonard and Mercedes were talking in a whisper as Eliot stood near the flagpole.

"I did it, okay, I did it," Eliot shouted.

I walked over to him. "What's the matter?"

"I pushed the red button."

"What's wrong?"

"I thought it was a doorbell."

I looked at Eliot and tried to empathize.

"Didn't it say *emergency* next to the button?"

Eliot was shaking, so I gave him a hug.

"What are you doing?" he said.

"I'm hugging you." He relaxed a little and gave my left shoulder two taps with his palm.

"It'll be all right, Anne," he said. "They're spelling *emergency* like *doorbell* now, and *doorbell* like *emergency*."

"But, Eliot," I said, "Why did you want to push the doorbell from inside your house?"

"Because the phone was ringing. I had to answer the phone."

"I know how you feel." I walked with Eliot over to Nick and Mercedes and Leonard. Eliot didn't want to talk about it. We waited with him to tell the fire truck, the ambulance, and the Gee to go home.

Later in the afternoon, with the pork chops on our plates like we'd left them, Nick said, "I wish you'd hug me like you hugged Eliot." He took his plate to the door and scraped the remains of his dinner into the plastic bag hanging from the knob.

"You need a trash can," I said. I followed Nick to the plastic bag. I was standing there, scraping rice into it, when Nick kissed me on the ear. It was quick, almost like an accident, and Nick fidgeted with his fork and knife in one hand and his plate in the other. I looked at him, down at his pants, left, definitely left, then back at his face. I put my hand on my ear where he'd kissed it.

"What?" I said.

"Nothing," he said. He took my plate and walked to the sink.

"I don't know why you'd do that anyway. If you think I'm going into this, into this or whatever's next, then you've been seeing too many women from Madison and not enough from the South. I think maybe we're two birds of different flocks. Whereas you lead the way, honking, I'm usually flying backward and not toward the horizon. So if you think I'm just going to sit on your dick." I stopped to take a breath.

"You've been wanting to talk about my dick all night."

"I have not."

"And yesterday too."

"I have not."

"I saw you in Deeter's office."

I didn't have anything to say to that because I'd never been caught checking someone's dick out, or if I had, it wasn't discussed, and Nick calling me out made me uncomfortable, like things were galloping and I was liable to fall off my horse. Nick had his back to me at the sink. He turned the faucet on. I saw him messing with his belt, and then I saw the belt disappear through one loop, two loops, until he was holding it out to his side in one hand, his back to me, and I thought, here's a man who's confident even when I'm rebuffing him, here's a man who's about to do something with a belt, here's a man who's into whipping or humiliation or what is he doing with the belt? Not to be outdone, I pulled my shirt up, over my head, and dropped it on the floor. I looked down to see what bra I was wearing: faded black, front snap, rhinestones on the straps. I felt a rush of adrenaline and I worried Nick wouldn't go through with his side of the bargain, whatever bargain that was, and I'd be standing there topless. When he turned around, his pants were unzipped. I walked to where I'd left my purse next to the couch and got a cigarette.

"Don't smoke," he said.

"I'm full. I need a cigarette." I stayed arched over the couch, lighting the cigarette, dropping the lighter back into my purse, and I hoped Nick could see that other than the fake leg, the ankle of which he'd already grabbed during the ceremony, I had a real silhouette, a real pair of breasts, nicely affected by gravity, bending over something. I was wearing a gray cotton drawstring skirt, with DUKE on the rear, sleepwear, loungewear, a holdover, a skirt that had been thought of as nothing-else-is-clean, and was now thought of as too short to be wearing while bent over a couch, and suddenly the perfect skirt for a tryst. I propped my real knee on the cushion of the couch and pushed my hair behind my ear. I looked Nick in the eyes, and the adrenaline was like moments I've imagined, watching crime docudramas, moments between murderer and victim, are you going to kill me? am I going to kill you? is someone getting killed? things can only go one way or another, dead or alive, left or right, swindled or spared, and I needed to ash my cigarette, so I straightened up from leaning over the couch and walked to the trash bag on the doorknob. When I stood, Nick leaned back on the sink. I was no longer rattled with adrenaline. It was as if my walk to do something as mundane as ash a cigarette had broken the spell, and now we were just two people finishing dinner, exposing themselves to each other. I couldn't tell if this was a thing Nick had seen somewhere, or if it was all his own. I couldn't tell if it was a thing he did for all women, any woman, or just me. Maybe it was stolen from somewhere in his past, originally choreographed with the nurse in Verona, something they did once, the first time, the last time, and he wanted to recreate it. People will do that to you: stick you in their patterns. I couldn't tell what I truly thought since I was thinking about Nick, and his nurse, and I asked myself, what do you think, and I was turned on with Nick turned out. I ashed the cigarette.

"Show over," he said, zipping his pants. "Put your shirt on."

"No."

The water was still running over the plates.

"Tomorrow," Nick said. "I'm going to pick you up proper and take you to the movies."

Bonding with Mercedes

———

You have to care for your body.
—Xenophon, *Memorabilia*

Lubricate your eyelashes.
— *Cosmopolitan*

THE NEXT DAY I ran into Mercedes Minnow, the skin-and-bones girl, at the grocery store. She whisked me by the elbow through the checkout and walked me back to the Colony where we bonded over Cheez-Its in her bungalow. She lived in Bungalow West. Leonard lived above her. He revved his Harley in the parking lot.

"I feel sorry for him. He came here to save his marriage. His wife sent him here. He's always asking about my wild adolescent years. So sweet. Now check out this closet," Mercedes said.

There were four stand-alone clothes racks in the living room with hanging compartments for hair bands, headbands, banana clips, barrettes, necklaces, scarves, bracelets, belts, and doohickeys the likes of which I know not the names of. And she had a couch. I sat down. She tuned the flat screen to the Cold Spring Harbor Channel.

"If we're lucky, you can see my lab report. Have you given a lab report?"

"No, and I'm not going to." I didn't even know what a lab report was. Nick hadn't mentioned it. The Gee hadn't mentioned it. No one had said anything about a lab report to me.

"It's fun. You sit in the lab and talk about your feelings, your progress, whatever you want to talk about. I always end mine with PTK. You know. Prevail through Knowledge. Being in a confessional box on live TV makes me feel like I'm really accomplishing something. Plus it's good for morale."

I turned my attention to the screen. It showed an image of a brain. "Oh look! There's Eliot!" she said. "I'm after Eliot. We've got time." She opened the box of Cheez-Its. "You have to be really careful about these," she said, popping a cracker into her mouth. "They will sneak up on you and punch you in the stomach with five hundred calories."

She walked to the kitchen and poured two shots of tequila. Her skirt bounced. The skirt was a black-and-white striped number with pink toile peaking from the hem. She returned with the shots. I took a sip.

"So which leg is it? You can tell me." She was working an asymmetrical long-form bob. It looked like one side of her head weighed more than the other.

I wondered if Mercedes was pretending not to know. Sometimes people did that. They said, "I had no idea. You don't look the least bit disabled." They smiled and waited for me to take the said thing as a compliment. The only thing more annoying than the you-don't-look-it comment is the we-are-all-disabled comment. The latter usually prefaces an extended monologue about how we all have our problems, our afflictions, our trials and tribulations, our *disabilities* to deal with. Fork me.

"Do you mind?" Mercedes said, stretching out her hand. I nodded. I hadn't met a toucher in a while. The last toucher I met was a friend of Grayson's, a guy at a political rally, back when I still went with Grayson to those events. The guy wore suspenders over his belly. He assumed we were connected since he too wore a prosthetic. Here is a generally accepted law of body parts: yours is fake, mine is fake, we are obliged to be friends. We were sitting at a table, and he said, "Can I see?" He started with his hand on my ankle, then calf, then knee, then farther up. Enough. I went to the bathroom. Grayson came looking for me and we left. In the car, Grayson said: "It happened so fast I didn't even know what was happening. What happened?"

"It really sucks for you," Mercedes said, pulling her hand back. "I had a recruit at my sorority with one of those, what do you call it, lip things, like a lip-hook-um-a-jig, oh c'mon, you know what I'm talking about, the charity."

"Cleft lip."

"Right, and this girl was really normal otherwise, I mean a sweetheart, and I felt we really connected. But, at the end of the day, it's a unanimous vote, and some of my sisters didn't think the girl would feel comfortable in our house." Mercedes talked as quick as a sneeze. She stopped to take a deep breath. "That's top secret. I'm really surprised I told you that."

I didn't say anything.

"I mean what's it like for you? Are you totally stoked about treatment?" None of the Colonists had asked me about treatment. There seemed to be a consensus that we shouldn't talk to each other about the ins and outs of genetic engineering. In that respect, we were like the rest of the country.

Mercedes continued, "Because I'm really excited about mine. They're giving me a vector that corrects my fat gene. I was hoping for Xanax, to be honest. I asked the Gee if he could hook me up with some good shit. But no. We're supposed to stay clean. If it means I don't have to worry about size twenties and my arteries, I'll do it. Do you think we're going to be famous? Can you imagine, me, on the cover of *Cosmo*? It can't happen any sooner. I feel so bloated." She put her hand to her stomach.

"You're very skinny."

"That's the thing about genes though, you never know when they're going to fuck—you—up."

I looked at the coffee table where a book on yoga was open facedown.

"Look—it's me, it's me," Mercedes said to the screen. She turned the volume up. The screen filled with her face. "Next time I will know how close the camera is." She said hello to her family and friends back in Portland.

"Will they ever see this?" I asked, suddenly paranoid that the broadcast was nationwide.

"I'm YouTubing it. Just for my blog. I had fifty unique visitors last week."

On the screen, she winked and sent love to her boyfriend and said PTK.

"I'm so glad I ran into you in the supermarket. I feel like you're going to be a real inspiration to me. I feel it. We have to stick together because we're the only girls. Cheers! I got dibs on the Suicide by the way. We went to dinner and then back to his place. He played Merle Haggard for me. How hot are his blue jeans? So hot."

Prelude to the Movies

———

I BOUGHT COMET at the store and I was giving the bathroom a thorough cleaning when Grayson called. There'd been a death at the museum.

"You just don't think of people dying in front of a Youssef Nabil painting," he said. I heard him take a drag. He only smoked when he was around me or stressed.

"I just don't think of people dying." I placed a towel on the bathroom floor, knelt on the towel, and dowsed the toilet in Comet. The phone beeped.

"You just don't think Grandpa is going to keel over on a painting."

"I don't think I'd take Gramps to the museum if he's that old."

"He's a dedicated member."

The phone beeped. "Member of what?"

"The museum. You sound distracted."

"I'm scrubbing the toilet."

"It must be pretty bad there if you're cleaning the toilet. I miss you."

"I miss you more than Gramps misses life."

"Maybe he doesn't miss it. Maybe he's in heaven. That's your prerogative, right?"

"What do you mean my prerogative?"

"Convince me heaven exists."

Beep. "Right now?"

"Why not?"

"My head is in a toilet bowl."

"You never want to convince me there's a heaven." Beep. "If you're right, we'll be separated eternally."

"Yep."

"You don't want to be with me eternally?"

"Of course I do. I'm cleaning. You know how I get when I'm cleaning."

"Can we try Skype again?" Beep. "You keep cutting out."

"I don't want to Skype. It's weird."

"Skyping with me is weird but relinquishing your stem cells is common practice. Does this make sense to you?"

Grayson said he'd call later, how much later, I asked, and then he wanted to know why it mattered how much later, it's not like I was doing anything. "Actually," I said, "I'm going to the movies."

"With who?"

"Mercedes."

The Movies

———

"WHEN YOU CALL someone, and you know they're home, and they don't answer, do you ever think they might be on the phone with someone else and they'll call you back?" I said to Nick. He was turning left on Harbor Road. Garth Brooks crooned from the tape deck. Nick was wearing yesterday's belt with a Western shirt that had pearly buttons. He'd probably been looking forward to the movies since the night before. The last thing I needed was to get involved and naked and confused and compromised at the Colony. The last thing I needed was some guy who took his dick out for anyone who happened to be in his bungalow, than called maniacally the next day.

"I called one time."

"Bullshit."

"One time. Do you wish I had called more?" Nick said.

The closest theater was in Huntington Bay. Nick checked the listings and we didn't recognize any of the movies. "Art flicks," Nick said. We settled on one from France; of course it was a love triangle, man leaving wife to sleep with prostitute, but a good prostitute, one who was doing it to put herself through school, and I thought I knew where that was going. Nick kept his hands on his knees. In the middle of a steamy scene, I heard what sounded like actual steamy voices in the theater and sat up in my seat. I looked straight into the eyes of a woman who was sitting on a man's lap with her elbows on the back of his seat. I ducked down and pulled on the sleeve of Nick's shirt. I had made sure to sit to his right, so that my real leg would be beside him, and maybe he wasn't putting his hand on my leg because he wasn't sure if it was the real one. He swatted my hand.

"Have you done a lab report?" I whispered to him.

"You mean those things Mercedes does?"

"Yeah."

"No. I'm going to watch this here movie, though."

I tried to concentrate on the movie but I couldn't; the dark cover of the theater made me feel better about asking dark questions.

"Do you want to die?"

"What?"

"Do you want to die?"

"Don't know. I've never tried it." He looked over and smiled and looked back to the screen.

"Nick—"

"Baby, I'm the happiest guy I know. Now let's watch the movie before your skirt gets us kicked out."

"How would my skirt—"

"I'm trying hard not to remove it."

Our elbows were touching on the armrest, nothing more.

On the drive home, Garth Brooks picked up where we'd left him with the song "More Than a Memory."

"Do you know the story behind Garth and Trish?" Nick had his hands on ten and two. The lights on his dash were busted.

"They're married." I lit a cigarette and cracked the window.

"Yeah, but do you know the story?"

"What's the story?"

"They met in Nashville when they were nobodies. Garth Brooks made Trisha Yearwood who Trisha Yearwood is. She opened for him on tour, sang backup. Here's the catch. He was married to Sandy Mahl at the time. He met Sandy when he was a bouncer at a bar. She got in a fight and punched her hand through the wall and couldn't get her hand out. Garth helped her and drove her home that night and asked her on a date. They were together for fifteen years."

"He was probably sleeping with Trish the whole time."

"Ain't you just a ray of sunshine?"

"From what you're saying, they were on tour together, romantic cities, hotel rooms." I flicked the cigarette out the window. "This song is depressing."

"Break it off with your man."

I was stunned. I felt the muscles in the back of my throat tense. I felt disoriented. Where were we? We were passing some consequences. I wasn't going to break up with Grayson for a hat-wearing, cocksure guy from Madison just because he looked good in a pair of jeans and surpassed any man I'd met in spontaneity.

"You better leave that alone." I may have been talking to myself.

"I'm not interested," I said, because it sounded like a more definitive thing to say, and as soon as I said it I got chills down my spine straight down to where Nick's thumb had been while we stood outside Leonard's.

Nick turned off the music. "Look, I know you think I'm not sincere. This is the most sincere I've ever been. I had a talk with my friend Ronnie Woodruff and he told me absolutely not to do what I'm doing. He said, 'Nick, you are perpetuating a cycle of getting tangled up with these women who are already taken.' But you're not taken, you're took. Taken is when you're blown away by somebody. Garth by Trish. Trish by Garth. You're sassy and closed up as hell in a way that's near to unfair. So I'm going to try and take you, but it would be better if you'd get untook first."

"Were you listening? I'm not interested."

Nick turned down Harbor Road. We drove for a while in silence. People get silent with you when you've said something that pisses on their ego. They are then forced to zap you with silence until you submit. Whoever speaks first loses. I wanted to get home and call Grayson. He didn't give me the silent treatment. He preferred to say, "I'm mad at you, but we should sleep together and figure it out in the morning." He had his priorities straight. I was always doing something wrong. Sometimes it was *really* wrong, like lying, and other times it was only wrong because of Grayson's suspicion that I'd done the *really* wrong things. I skipped town for a week without telling him. I was only visiting my great-grandmother, but I told him I was visiting an old friend, a guy friend. I told him nothing happened. I did that because he'd been saying he was busy and couldn't hang out, and worse, he'd been ending phone calls with "Take it easy." Yes. "Take it easy." I felt I was being demoted, so I had to pull the outside-threat tactic. What can I say? I'm an excellent girlfriend.

"I don't want this to get weird," I said.

Nick popped his neck.

"I think you're a really good friend"—no, not that—"and while it's true we had, well, what was that, the top-off night—"

"Afternoon."

"Right, afternoon. I just hope it doesn't get weird or anything."

"I read you loud and clear," he said, pulling into the Colony.

Getting Charted
Week Four

---

1. Name of Examinee (Last, First): Hatley, Anne

2. Date of Birth: 11-07-1990

3. Place of Birth: Hickory, NC

4. Sex: F

5. Social Security Number: A05-19-0071

6. Name of Health Plan: The Colony at Cold Spring Harbor, LLC

FAMILY HISTORY

RELATION	AGE	STATE OF HEALTH	IF DEAD, CAUSE	AGE AT DEATH
Father	59	Good		
Mother	54	Good		
Brothers	None			
Sisters	None			

HAS ANY BLOOD RELATIVE (PARENT, BROTHER, SISTER, CHILD) HAD:

Allergy	No	Heart Disease	No
Diabetes	No	High Blood Pressure	Yes, father
Glaucoma	No	Cancer (Type)	No
Emotional Disease	No	Stroke	No

Examinee's Statement of Present Health: Good.

Medications currently used and for what purpose: Necon 1/35, birth control.

Has examinee ever had any significant illness or injury not noted elsewhere? 2° limb, see X-rays.

Has examinee ever been a patient in a mental hospital or sanatorium or been treated by a psychiatrist or psychologist for illness? No.

Has examinee ever been denied life insurance? No.

Race: White   Height: 5'4"   Weight: 110 lbs.   Pulse (Sitting): 96

Hearing: Right Ear: Normal   Left Ear: Normal   Blood Pressure: 112/77

Does the Examinee have now, or has Examinee ever had, symptoms noted below? (check each item)

Y	N		Y	N		Y	N	
	X	Frequent or severe headaches		X	Frequent indigestion		X	Recent gain or loss in weight
	X	Epilepsy, fits, or fainting spells		X	Stomach, liver, or intestinal trouble		X	Malaria or amoebic dysentery
	X	Eye trouble or visual defect in either eye		X	Gallbladder trouble or gallstones		X	Stutter or stammer habitually
	X	Skin disease		X	Rupture or hernia		X	Jaundice or hepatitis
	X	Ear, nose, or throat trouble		X	Piles or other rectal disease		X	Nervous trouble of any sort

Y	N		Y	N		Y	N	
	X	Severe tooth or gum trouble		X	Blood in stool or black (tarry) stool		X	Depression or excessive worry
	X	Asthma		X	Frequent or painful urination		X	Any drug or narcotic habit
	X	Shortness of breath		X	Kidney trouble, stone, or blood in urine		X	Excessive bleeding after injury or tooth extraction
	X	Chronic cough		X	Sugar or albumin in urine		X	Any reaction to serum immunization or medicine
	X	Tuberculosis, or close association with		X	Diabetes		X	Tumor, growth, cyst
	X	Pain or pressure in chest		X	Painful or "trick" shoulder or knee	X		Does examinee use alcohol?
	X	Palpitation or pounding of heart		X	Recurrent back pain; wear a back brace	X		Does examinee use cigarettes?
	X	Swelling of feet or ankles		X	Rheumatic fever	X		Does examinee use protection?

ALL TESTS REQUIRED UNLESS OTHERWISE SPECIFIED		
Hematology	Chemistry Profile	Urinalysis
Hematocrit 39.9 %	Blood Glucose 42	Specific Gravity
Hemoglobin 13.8 gms	Cholesterol 137	1,020
WBC 8.3 /cmm	Creatinine 0.7	WBC 75
	Uric Acid 3.9	
Differential:	SGPT 17	
Granulocytes 58.3 %	SGOT 10	
Lymphocytes 35.6 %	Alk Phos 48	
	Billrubin 0.4	

Cranios

———

ONE MONTH DOWN. I was the rogue Colonist who would not go into treatment. The others had signed on for theirs and went into the lab with the gusto of kids going to the bathroom to smoke dope. They acted nonchalant, nothing added to them, just something subtracted. I learned more about genes than I ever cared to know. The Cold Spring Harbor Channel was a mix of documentaries and slides, X-rays and tissue samples, images of the brain and the DNA sequence. And lab reports. They were voluntary. I was pretty sure Eliot did a lab report without knowing what it was. He sat there pulling the strings of his hoodie. He pulled the string on the right so the left string shortened. Then he pulled the string on the left so the right string shortened. After five minutes of this, he inspected the lens of the camera. He leaned in close until he was eyeball-to-lens, a large eyeball of white and green with long lashes, then he backed up and scratched his head. Mercedes was the only one of us who did lab reports knowingly. "This is my face time," she said.

I tuned into the Cold Spring Harbor Channel when I was bored. It didn't hurt to learn something. I learned that it took a lot of work to get here: a lot of scientists across a lot of different fields and continents. In the beginning were Watson and Crick in Cambridge. They sat down at the Eagle Pub, and Crick said to

Watson, "We found the secret of life." I imagine they gave each other high fives. To its credit, the Cold Spring Harbor Channel featured an array of opinions—from that of the pope to Peter Singer, professor of bioethics at Princeton. Since the days of Watson and Crick, scientists had pinpointed specific variants, on specific genes, on specific chromosomes. And it was these variants they sought to change. In Mercedes, the FTO that promised to grow her to a size twenty; in Leonard, the ANK3 that accounted for his "strange behavior" back home in Fargo; in Eliot, the SORL1 that caused him to forget; in Nick, the SUI that wanted to off all the genes and his whole body. I was less certain that my PRX1 was bad. It caused me no impending fat, no strange behavior, no forgetfulness, and no suicidal thoughts. How bad could it be? The Gee told me it was complicated, as if that weren't apparent; I'm not even sure how electricity works, so I understand genetics is complicated. He told me my gene was "problematic" but "potentially useful" in that—along with the stunted limb—it triggered blood production in triple-time. I gave him my usual: "I'll think about it." I called Nick and asked him to come over.

"Three days ago you weren't interested, remember?"

"Don't be weird," I said.

He walked in the door, took his boots off, and shoved his socks in his boots with the confidence of a man used to walking barefoot in women's homes around pictures of their boyfriends. We read together. He skipped around in long, sprawling biographies— General Custer, Stonewall Jackson. "I should be able to pick up in the middle and drop off when I like," he said. We were sitting in the living room. I sat in the chair and he sprawled on the floor with his feet on the ottoman. Around nine, I asked him to leave so I could call Grayson. He looked up from the floor, raised an eyebrow, and returned to his book.

"Seriously," I said, taking his hat and dropping it on the floor beside him.

I started playing with his hair while I dialed Grayson. Nick's hair was dark brown and long and thick. It had patches in it. Bald patches. Had those always been there? I said to Grayson, "Honey, I'm not with anyone. I'm all yours." I felt something near the bald patches on Nick's head, round and hard, the size of a tack, and I pulled my hand back. I turned from Nick and walked to the kitchen. What was on Nick's scalp? I tried to keep cool with Grayson on the phone and Nick on the floor with his head like a corkboard. I said I was tired, and Grayson said he was tired, and we hung up.

Nick said, "You just told your first lie."

"What's on your head?"

"Those are my cranios."

"Your what?"

"My cranios."

"What does that mean? What is it?"

I must've raised my voice. Nick said, "*Shhh*, I just got a craniotomy."

"You did? When?"

"Yesterday. I got some cranios on my noggin." Nick rubbed his head above his right ear, his left ear, and on the top.

"I don't understand. You get a haircut or you get hungry, but you don't just get a craniotomy. What's a craniotomy?"

"Deeter opened my noggin and left these little guys here, my cranios, so he can plug in and check my cellular activity. I didn't tell you because we weren't exactly speaking, and besides, I knew you'd freak out."

"I'm not freaking out." The way he kept saying *noggin* freaked me out. He was talking about the most complex organ in his body, an organ I happened to have a lot of admiration for, Nick's brain—for its swashbuckling, its country-music loving, its picking up at one battle and dropping off before the next, its love of driving and garlic-saturated recipes, and even its nurse in Verona (what's a brain without someone haunts it?)—and to tinker with it, to open it and cap it like a tube of toothpaste—

"You're freaking out."

"They went into your brain and you didn't tell me?" I sat down on the floor in front of him.

"Give me your hand." He took my hand in his and we moved our hands around his head. The hair around the cranios had been buzzed. The cranios themselves were small and flat, receptacles for something to snap into, and I didn't want to hurt him.

"Shouldn't I wash my hands?"

"Where've you been putting your hands?"

"Nick, seriously. Shouldn't I sanitize them?"

He said there was a seal. His brain wasn't exposed. A tiny bit of bone had been removed.

"What did they do with the bone?"

"Beats me," he said.

The Gee replaced the bone, that tiny bit of bone, with a synthetic seal, but I still wanted to know where the bit of bone went and what was snapping into Nick's brain.

"Look, baby," he said. "This is common procedure for these guys. I had a neurosurgeon and six nurses around me. I went to sleep thinking of ten acres and a barn, then nine acres and a barn, and by the time I got to eight acres I was out flat. I woke up looking for the barn. I was tired and hungry. They checked me for double vision, numbness, and all the other risks. They checked me for the sense of smell. I can smell you right now and you smell like a ray of sunshine. Deeter looked around and said there's nothing abnormal about me. How's that?"

"If there's nothing abnormal about you, why did you have the procedure?"

"Would you ask a mechanic to wear a blindfold while he diagnosed your transmission?"

"I guess not."

"Would you?"

"No."

"All right."

"Is anyone else doing it?"

"Doing what?"

"What you had done."

"Not far as I know. They can see what they need of Eliot's brain from CAT scans. Leonard, well, he's dosed most of the time. He calls it 'the juice.' Mercedes gets her vector in the rear end. Says it makes her feel light-headed. And me, I'm the wild card. They didn't know what they had until they opened me up to take a look."

Nick had been pacing the length of my room, from front door to back window. He described his procedure nonchalantly, as if he himself had spent time in med school, had practiced on cadavers, and had weighed the cost-benefits of genetic treatments.

"But what made you do it?" I asked.

"I have the suicide gene. That's a fact." Nick said.

"How do you know you have it?"

"They tested me for all sorts of things when I was a kid. They wanted to know my genetic disposition. Gave me a test. Didn't you have one?"

"I may have."

"Well, the suicide gene was located right next to some other inane gene. Just my luck. So while the lackeys were determining that I would never be good with numbers, they saw that I would be good at killing myself."

"Are you good at numbers?"

"I'm not bad at them."

"Then what makes you think they know what they're talking about?"

"It's not like genes are a rumor, Anne."

I could tell Nick wanted me to believe in genes as much as he did, as if genes were a belief system, and you had to get on board.

The Cave of Common Origins

———

THE CAVE OF Common Origins shows displays from the present to the ancient past. Meet Timmy, the E-Skin Child. Compare your face to the face of an ancient ancestor. Witness the advances of today, the marvels of yesteryear.

The Common Origin of Caves

––––––

IN ORDER TO be a cave, you need one of three things: (1) the flow of lava from a volcano, (2) gradual erosion by waves from a shoreline, (3) dissolution by limestone or glacier. Limestone caves are the most common.

Field Trip

———

Every living organism is a cell state in which every cell is a citizen.

— RUDOLF VIRCHOW, FATHER OF PATHOLOGY

MERCEDES ORGANIZED A field trip to the Cave of Common Origins. The cave was located in the state park, a mile east of the Colony. Mercedes led the way, speed walking in a pair of silver boots that matched the silver stripe on her aquamarine velour sweatpants. Leonard tried to keep up. When that failed, he stopped and opened his fanny pack for a package of beef jerky. Nick and I had been trailing them by about twenty feet. Leonard looked back and waited for us. Mercedes kept walking. She was hell-bent on seeing the Cave of Common Origins. Her bottom bounced ahead of us. She had so much enthusiasm that I figured she was getting it from somewhere.

Nick was naming off plants: American columbine, Allegheny foamflower, bayberry, spicebush, fringed bleeding heart, shadblow.

"I think you're making shit up," Leonard said.

"I know plants," Nick said.

"Shadblow," Leonard said. "Isn't that a guy in the Bible? Shadblow and some other dipshit."

"I bet you're thinking of Shadrach, Meshach, and Abednego."

"Got ourselves a Bible scholar."

"Torah scholar."

"A regular Bible scholar is what we got."

I was tired of walking. Nick took his hat off and put it on my head.

"Are you two getting groovy together?" Leonard said.

"I have a boyfriend."

"Getting groovy with a Bible scholar who has big holes bored into his head while I can't even get Mercedes to go for a spin on my Harley."

Nick's hat kept sliding down over my eyes.

"Mercedes," Leonard yelled. "When are you and me going for a spin?"

"You're married."

"Can't I give a ride to a lady?"

"I don't ride bikes, Lenny."

"I don't own a bike. I own a Harley-Davidson Ultra Classic Electra Glide." He stopped to take a breath.

"Hurry up," Mercedes said. She was doing stretches against a boulder next to the entrance of the cave. When she looked at us, she pouted. "That's my hat," she said, taking Nick's hat and putting it on.

As soon as we entered the cave, a woman's voice said, "We are all ninety-nine percent alike." There were platforms built into the walls. The first display featured the statue of Timmy.

"Sweet Jesus! He's so cute. Isn't he so cute?" Mercedes said to Nick. She looped her arm into Nick's. "What do you think he's made of?"

He looked like he was made of flesh. Light flooded the right side of his uniform, blue knee shorts and a button-up collar.

Mercedes walked arm in arm with Nick to the plaque on the wall beside the boy.

"That's a mannequin. That's not a kid. I know a kid when I see one. That's a mannequin. I've seen those at JCPenney," Leonard said.

Mercedes toggled a lever next to the plaque and the statue's head bobbed. "My name is Timmy," the statue said. His lips did not move. It sounded like the voice was coming from overhead. "My skin is made of transistor-based circuits and semiconductors. Touch me."

Mercedes dropped Nick's arm and stepped to the edge of the platform. Nick walked to where I was standing, close to the entrance of the cave. We watched as Mercedes reached out and touched Timmy's arm. He jerked his head and she gasped.

I bolted out of the cave and searched for a cigarette. Nick followed. Mercedes was trying to talk to the boy. She and Leonard came out of the cave. "He's not saying anything. Besides, his skin was cold," she said.

"Yeah well, it's sixty degrees," I said. "My skin's cold."

"I mean he's not real, Anne."

"Define *real*. He really jerked around when you touched him." Mercedes and Leonard gave their case for going back into the Cave of Common Origins. Nick said he would stay outside with me.

Mercedes said, "Either we're all going in, or we're all staying out."

They went in without us. We could hear the woman's voice start up again from the speakers.

"The nucleotides in our DNA account for our sameness. Nucleotides are structured like letters in a sentence. Six billion letters make a human. In 2007 a team led by Sam Levy published the first complete human genome. The DNA is Craig Venter's.

You can view it on the Human Reference Genome Browser. It was sequenced using the shotgun method, developed by the Institute for Genomic Research. The shotgun method uses computer algorithms to assemble millions of fragments into a continuous stretch resembling each chromosome. To sequence the DNA of a human manually, without this method, would have taken one hundred thousand years." The woman's voice stopped.

Craig Venter introduced himself over the speakers: "A doctor can save maybe a few hundred lives in a lifetime. A researcher can save the whole world. Over the next twenty years, synthetic genomics is going to become the standard for making anything. The chemical industry will depend on it. Hopefully, a large part of the energy industry will depend on it. We really need to find an alternative to taking carbon out of the ground, burning it, and putting it into the atmosphere. That is the single biggest contribution I could make."

On the walk back, Leonard and Nick got into a discussion on the origin of life. Leonard was asking Nick questions about Judaism and Israel and the migration of his people from one place to another and whether or not Nick had relatives in the Holocaust. He asked it as if the Holocaust were a movie one's relatives starred in. Nick said no, not that he knew of.

Leonard said, "Jews are all right. Church of Christ, on the other hand, those are some wackos."

Mercedes pulled me off the path and into a gap in the oak trees. "Time out," she said, leaning against a trunk. "So I think Nick's the type guy who doesn't have girlfriends, he has girls he puts his penis in, and I've been that girl before, and I'm totally cool with it. If that's his deal, sign me up. The way I see it, we're only here for another couple months, so might as well make the most of it. His jeans are so hot. And him getting those things in his head. I love them. They make him more vulnerable, more real. Do you think he's bagging Shug from the Green House?"

"What's the Green House?"

"He hasn't told you? He's been going to the Green House in the morning. You sleep too late. He goes to the Green House to see Shug and these other botanists and this one intern. He doesn't come back till noon."

The Green House? Someone named Shug? Where I'm from, we say *shug* when we couldn't care less about your name and we just want to complete a transaction, like we're selling you a forty. "You mean the place where he gets his plants?"

"Hello? You haven't heard about Shug Tenner, tall as the Statue of Liberty, tats on her shoulder, looks fifty, acts fifteen? She's a botanist. She's working on the cure for melanoma. She thinks it comes from a bean tree. She gave me hoodia, this cactus I'm supposed to eat to suppress my appetite. That was nice of her. She has the hots for Nick. They have a lot in common, I get it, but give me a break, opposites attract. And I am not eating a cactus. One day I stopped in because I saw his station wagon and Shug Tenner was touching him on the shoulder, and when I walked up, he stepped back like three steps, very suspicious if you ask me. I think he wants me, but maybe he's already bagging Shug. He's got that nice-guy mentality, who knows why, nice guys are so pass. He wouldn't want to think of himself as an asshole, and that is what he would be, if he were bagging Shug Tenner *and* trying to bag me."

"What's *pass*?"

"You know. Out-of-date." She meant *passé*. I thought about correcting her, then saw Nick's face in her breasts, Shug's breasts, an archive of breasts, and decided not to.

"Has he tried anything with you?" I asked.

"Did you not see us in the cave?"

Mercedes must have mistaken her actions for Nick's flirta-tion. What was he supposed to do, throw her arm off, ask for his hat back? No way was Nick Burkowitz interested in Mercedes Minnow. Was he? She knew how to work an outfit. She ordered clothes from Anthropologie, Urban Outfitters, BootyParlor.com. Packages crowded the mailroom. I looked down at what I was wearing, a white sweater, a gray T-shirt. Why dress up? I had a boyfriend. What did I need Nick Burkowitz for? So he could have Mercedes, and he could have Shug, and he could have anyone else too, have at them.

Drinking at Sandy's Bar

———

A study of 19,500 adults found the higher the amount of alcohol consumed, the healthier people felt.

—*Journal of Epidemiology and Community Health*

LEONARD AND NICK wanted to know what had happened to us. "We got lost!" Mercedes giggled. They wanted to go to Sandy's Bar. I needed to see what was going on between Mercedes and Nick, not because I liked him, but because I hate being the last one to pick up on things. Nick downed three shots of whiskey. Mercedes spent most of the night telling the bartender about the cave. Leonard moped near the jukebox. Around midnight, Mercedes walked up to Nick and said, "You can't stay here."

"Why not?" Nick said.

"Because I'm leaving and you're coming with me."

Of course he'd leave with her. They were practically physiologically required to fuck.

"You go on ahead," Nick said.

Mercedes stuck out her bottom lip. "Are you sure?"

He nodded. Mercedes dropped off a slip of paper with the bartender and left. Leonard took his coat from the chair and said, "I know, I know, you guys want to get groovy. Now if you could clue

Mercedes into that fact and knock off the bartender, maybe I'd stand a chance. See you later, alligators."

Nick suggested we drive around in his station wagon. I was drunk enough to think driving was a good idea. He tuned the radio to country. He told me the Cave of Common Origins proved one thing: Science is amazing. He told me he'd been raised as if he were going to do bodily injury to himself at any minute. He drove on the road next to the water. I wanted to ask him about the Green House and the woman named Shug, but I didn't want to come off as jealous. We were a couple miles from the Colony. "Deeter is going to town on my suicide gene," he said. "Did you sign on?"

"I got charted. I don't trust science, really. I don't know. I don't want him to build me first and check the plans afterward."

Nick slammed on the breaks for a stop sign. My purse fell from the seat. Its contents spilled on the floorboard. I collected the tube of lipstick, pack of smokes, cell phone, wallet, and Necon 1/35.

"Please be careful."

Nick tapped the gas. "Did I see pills?"

"Yeah, what about it?"

"Birth control?"

"Yeah."

"I'd say that's a form of science."

"You want me to sign on?"

"I'm saying, a lot of things are made possible by someone signing on."

"I'll sign on, then."

"Don't do it for me."

"Since everyone's so concerned."

We parked beside rocks overlooking the harbor. It was gorgeous, like Grayson said it would be. He'd visited Maine with his parents as a kid and this made him the expert on states in the Northeast. I was on birth control for him. Birth control doesn't care which guy you're on it for. I saw two sailboats docked to the harbor and a lighthouse in the distance. Nick told me the lighthouse made the foghorn sound and began explaining foghorns.

"How do you know? Are you some sort of admiral?"

"Are you going to make fun of me all night? Foghorns, you see . . . " were made with deep decibels, and he knew this from his uncle, the navy, and from his love of music. I watched him talk with his hands, chest, mouth, and eyebrows. A deep decibel is louder than a high pitch, he was saying, it reaches farther, and I tried to determine whether Nick would be a deep or a high or a no pitch in bed. Getting guys to pitch their voice in bed is mostly impossible. So be louder, all of you, please. I figure someone always gets to them before me, a stoic and silent woman, a carryover from her mother, a concomitant to keeping timid in the act, and this woman beds the man before I arrive on the scene and trains him as she trained herself, says, "What kind of noise is that?" or some equally ruinous phrase.

I made a pact to be conscientious of whose ear I was talking into, to be conservative with the signals I was sending, and to preserve my deepest decibels for Grayson. No matter that Nick turned Mercedes down. Nick's hand was on my leg, inching up my skirt until his index finger was outlining the area, and I thought of Grayson going to the museum, to the gas station, to Blockbuster. I took Nick's wrist and moved it back to his lap. He kept talking. I wanted to think saucy thoughts about Grayson. What's saucy about Grayson? I pictured him reading the *Times* while the movie *Koyaanisqatsi* played in the background. "For the sound track," he said. It was a cine-poem. I didn't know anything about cine-poems, and this was pretty exciting at first. After multiple and repeated viewings, alongside conversations on why there is no God, and how there is no emotion in Kafka, it sounded like one long, sonorous foghorn. I've found that when I try to think of something, I end up thinking of its opposite. I had not expected to hit it off with Nick. He was over-the-top, and those people usually nettle me. All I had to do was keep my shirt on, show up for my appointments, and hold my breath for X-rays. Nick wasn't wired for solitude. He puttered around town in his station wagon. He went to the dunes or Sandy's Bar or the Green House.

"That's all I know about foghorns," Nick said, putting his arm around the back of my seat. "I got to tell you something."

I waited for him to confess to fucking Shug in the Green House or for him to give me an ultimatum or to say he wanted the best for me or that he was taking his cranios seriously or he, too, believed in God, didn't I hear him talking to Leonard? and he would respect my feelings for Grayson and he was considering my best interests and didn't I want two legs? Didn't I want to go back to his place and screw with my brand-new legs?

"The nurse in Verona called." She was back with her boyfriend. Nick said it without any hint of upset. He looked toward the lighthouse. He bit the inside of his lower lip. "I've never told anyone," Nick said. "Because well, for a number of reasons, she's a nurse and it could ruin her career. Her purse was like a welder's. She had five ways to light something on fire. She's a heroin addict." I knew Nick wanted me to be appalled. I didn't know the girl, so what did she matter? "I'd gone over to her place. She promised me she was clean. It got romantic, you know, and then I stopped because well, I kept hitting against something. She'd hidden something up there."

"What?"

"The syringe."

"With the needle?"

"Do they sell syringes without needles?"

"How would I know?"

"She stuck it up there and forgot."

Sometimes when people tell you something, you wonder what the hell they told you it for.

Nick started the car, as if it had been too much for him, revisiting her to betray her. He peeled out of the parking lot. On the street heading to the Colony he said, "I always use protection, though, always."

Protection Timeline

————

3000 BC   First record of a condom in drawings.

1850 BC   Objects called pessaries fit inside the vagina and obstruct sperm.

600 BC   The herb silphium used as oral contraceptive.

100 AD   Silphium harvested to extinction.

200 AD   Soranus of Ephesus suggests jumping seven times after sex to dislodge sperm.

1844   George Bernard Shaw calls the rubber condom "the greatest invention of the nineteenth century."

1873   U.S. Congress bans every form of contraception.

1898   Margaret Sanger dreams the birth-control pill.

1906   Katharine McCormick, schizophrenic, partners with Sanger.

1918   U.S. Congress says condoms okay again.

1930   Lysol used as contraceptive for the next thirty years. It does not work.

1960   The pill is introduced. Blood clots, women die. The dose is ten times too high.

The Art of Persuasion

―――――

NICK PARKED IN the Colony lot. I was still thinking of the nurse in Verona. What was she wearing, or not wearing, what did they say to each other, did he kiss her lightly on the cheek before leaving, or did he pull out and hightail it? Nick unbuttoned his jacket. The jacket was brown with sheepskin lining on the inside. He wanted to make plans for Halloween. I told him I wasn't sure what I was doing. We walked our separate ways, me north, him south, me reminiscing about the nurse in Verona, as if she were my nurse to reminisce about, and feeling like there was something there, something in Nick's memory of her, that I should pay attention to, but what? He liked women with drug addictions, dangerous women, women who nurtured people back to health? I needed to see a picture of this nurse. Emily Smoak, long-ago best friend, said: "You're only as pretty as the girl before you." Grayson's ex was pretty. What kind of girl did Nick fall for? Nick was hot like Mercedes said and it was no wonder Shug touched him on the shoulder and no wonder the nurse—did this nurse have a name? That was a dead giveaway. Nick had never said her name, which meant she was so powerful in his memory he couldn't even incant her, couldn't drop her name casually in conversation; she was above name-dropping. She probably climaxed like a porn star, walked like a supermodel, and baked cupcakes, and how could

I compete with that? In my bungalow, I checked my messages, Grayson. The phone rang.

"Baby, I want you to come over."

"I'm not coming over."

"Why not?"

"Because." Your ex-girlfriend is too good at everything. Except remembering where she stashed her heroin needle, apparently.

"Why because?"

"You're drunk."

"No, no. I'm not drunk anymore."

"I'm not coming over unless we have an activity."

"There will be an activity."

I was sitting on the blue chair with my legs propped on the ottoman. I thought of Nick grabbing my ankles in a violent manner. "Not that activity."

"Why not?"

"You know why. You don't really want me to come over."

"Don't speak for me."

"There is nothing in the whole huge universe you could say to get me to come over to your bungalow."

"Baby, come over."

"And if there were, *Baby, come over* would not be it."

"I don't understand."

"I'm tired. It's been the longest day, with the cave, and Sandy's Bar, and the harbor."

"Felt to me like time flew."

I wanted to ask him if time flew when he was around Shug the Bean Tree Botanist. When he was talking to Mercedes. "Nick, you don't even mean the things you say. You probably say them all the time."

"It feels like my nucleotides have been waiting since they

were—picture this, Nick's nucleotides wading around in the protoplasm, oozing four million years ago toward you—"

"Mercedes likes you."

"What does she have to do with anything?"

"You played Merle Haggard for her."

"Baby, I'm telling you the story of our nucleotides. I'm cooking you breakfast in the morning."

"You don't have any bacon. I like bacon."

"I'll drive to the store and buy some damn bacon. What are you doing?"

"I'm drinking sweet tea."

"What else?"

"I'm not wearing shoes anymore."

"I'm not wearing shoes either, and even my feet want you to come over."

With Darwin at the Races

————

"DARWIN, I FUCKED up," I said. We were in the center ring at Belmont. I'd had a few mint juleps.

"Should've bought tickets for the stand."

"With Grayson, I mean." We sat on a picnic blanket. Darwin nibbled on oat bread and sipped his drink through a straw. The place was packed with teenagers and college students.

"Do you love him?"

"How am I supposed to know?"

"You just would."

"I like him well enough."

"Here's the deal," Darwin said. "You buy a little boat so you can catch little fish on a little lagoon with some sidekick. Yacht, catamaran, canoe, doesn't matter. Gefilte, trout, snook, doesn't matter. Pick your sidekick. Who's the person you wouldn't mind being in the lagoon with for life? Once you know that, go get him and sit your ass down in the boat." Darwin bit into a slice of bread. He licked his lips. The announcer blared over the loudspeakers. We'd put my money on a chestnut colt that had lost.

Darwin pointed to a woman strolling beside a man. "See that woman in the wide-brimmed hat? She picked the wrong one."

"How do you know?"

"You can just tell." The woman focused on the ground in front of her. The man steered her with his palm on her back. "I know a guy who fucked up. Fell in love young and was reckless. Did some asinine young-guy things. Asked for a threesome with her cousin. She gave it to him. Asked for kink and caboodle. She gave it to him. Made love to the max. But he didn't realize, in the middle of that willy-nilly, she was breaking. I don't mean her heart. I mean something else. Like if she was a tree, he was making little marks in her bark. And eventually he felled her. You have to be good to your tree."

The Dream Director

———

BY THE THIRD week in October, I was getting cabin fever, so I accepted all invitations, even to watch Ping-Pong. Nick and Leonard were playing in the auditorium. Nick killed at Ping-Pong. Between the three of us, we downed a suitcase of beer. Leonard talked about his wife in Fargo. "Ever since Angie turned Church of Christ, with the knitting circle and the prayer circle and the discipleship meetings, I swear," Leonard said.

Nick said he wasn't the marrying type.

"Angie thinks I have spells, and she gets it in her head that when I have these so-called spells there's a demon in me."

"Women," Nick said. Him saying this seemed to seal their friendship.

Every once in a while, between a game, Leonard said, "That Mercedes. She's a looker. Ain't she, Youngblood? Ain't she, though? Makes you wonder what she was like as a little kid."

After the game, Nick didn't even have to ask. I followed him to the door of his bungalow. I put my arms around his waist and rested my head against his back.

"Baby," he said.

"What?"

"They've been in here." We walked into the living room. It looked the same to me. Plants flaunted their green.

"That's what you get for signing on." My feet hurt from wearing a series of heels for Nick. I was freezing. I wanted to get under a blanket.

Nick picked up a letter on Colony stationary from the kitchen table. He read it to himself.

"What's it say?"

"They installed the sleeping pod." Nick flipped the light on in the kitchen, then the living room, the bathroom, hallway, and bedroom, inspecting each room as he walked through the apartment.

"A sleeping pod? Well don't tell me about it. I'm always the last to know anyway," I said.

We stood in his bedroom, staring at the sleeping pod. It looked inviting—a queen-size mattress outfitted with a pale blue sateen comforter and pillows. The bed was two feet off the floor with a metallic headboard. The headboard arched over the bed. A soft hum filled the room.

"Do you hear that?" Nick said. He knelt beside the bed. He took the comforter off. Underneath the comforter, a blue foam mattress. It looked a hundred times more comfortable than the mattress in my bungalow. The mattress in my bungalow sloped low, off the box springs. It probably got that way from people using it as a couch. I climbed onto Nick's bed.

The metallic headboard had speakers on either side. I had never owned a headboard of any kind. Nick sat in a chair opposite the bed. It was much easier to think of sleeping with Nick in a state-of-the-art, high-tech sleeping pod with bass-and-treble speakers. The mattress fit me perfectly. It felt like a cloud. "Nick," I said. "Take my shoes off."

Press Release

———

THE DREAM DIRECTOR triggers sounds and effects, via computer, which alter the nature and content of dreaming. Research reveals that dreams can be brought into the liminal state where ultimately they can be controlled.

The Liminal State

———

The liminal difficulties cannot be evaded without the most disastrous consequence to the body of the exposition.

—*Mind*, 1884

THOSE CONSEQUENCES, FORGET them. Take my shoes off. Are they watching your brain? The chair, the chair, more and some more. Today we are going to learn about the liminal semicolon. Two thoughts conjoined, one and the same thought, separated by, not exactly the same thought. Will it be the same thought the way they see it? Nick I'm not drunk I know what I'm saying. If you want to sleep with Mercedes go sleep with her then. You don't? You *don't?* I didn't know you wanted to sleep with me I figured. I have a boy who through some compounding became a boyfriend. I won't mention him. You're fine, you're not nettling me. You can get up from the chair and join me on the bed, I'm for it. You can take off the straw hat now, I'm for it. You can show off your cranios, I'm for them. Your arms are strong, I'm for them. I'm for the lights on/off, I don't mind. I'm for leaving the leg on/off, I don't mind. Do you mind? Never mind then. Go on. You're right we shouldn't go too far tonight without a condom. This is how we do. Look me in the face and be loud. I'd like to find the secret of life before morning. It tickles. Nick where are you putting yourself below me? Go on I guess. It doesn't work, they say the tongue is the strongest muscle, that's a lie, it's not a muscle it's sixteen muscles and how do you define *strong?* Oh, you know something, you know something, I don't know what you know about that. Teeth, teeth. I've never had it with the teeth—you found me already? I'm thinking of thinking something brilliant with you below me, I'm in the middle of an indimmable, I'm saving the world over here, I'm very busy, go on. I've never had that before. What is it—what is it—yes yes. It feels like a kamikaze, as in *kah-meh-kah-zee*, as in four distinct beats, what do you call it, as in four paratroopers hitting it one after the other, after the other other. I'd like to see your memories of this. I can't think of anything. I quit.

He Sings Country in the Morning

———

I SMELLED BACON and eggs. I lifted myself up on my elbows. The clock on the dresser read 9:07 AM.

"Nick."

He came into the bedroom wearing his straw hat and a towel wrapped around his waist. He held a skillet of bacon by the handle.

"Is the hat necessary at this hour?"

"Baby, I'm making you breakfast."

"Thanks."

"Ain't you just a ray of sunshine?"

"It's nine in the morning." Nick put the skillet on the dresser and attacked me in the bed, going straight for my neck. "That skillet will burn a hole."

"I'm going to evict you from my sleeping pod." He was smiling. As wide as he smiled, it looked like his face was cut in half. It was too early to think of him happy. To think of him high from having gone the long night, a trooper, a troubadour, and not coming once, while I nixed no climax to fairness. Why shouldn't I sleep off the morning? I earned the right to sleep, since I had kept his dick *on* not *in*. Him saying, C'mon. Yes to *on*, no to *in*. The importance of the preposition. So I wasn't cheating, okay I was cheating, but I wasn't having any accidents. I wasn't the best at taking the pill on the dot. I wasn't a pee-test away from a belly bump, having to stop drinking, worse, smoking—whoa—did I want a cigarette at this hour? Possibly. I kept it *on* not *in*. I was being responsible. I opened my eyes. Looked at him with his straw hat, clean face, nice brow. Closed my eyes.

"So what, I'm grumpy." He'd kept up. Drinks strengthened his hard-on, duly noted, underline that, can the man perform when drunk? he can, check, and next, cooking bacon, albeit before noon, but why shouldn't I face the morning?

"If you're not careful, I'll write the Dream Director with a directive. Reconcile my lady, I'll tell him," Nick said. His face smelled like aftershave and bacon. My eyes were closed. I felt his front on my back.

"Let me sleep."

"Has anyone told you you look like Linda Ronstadt with that bottom lip and your bangs?"

"You told me."

"How long are you going to sleep?"

"I have to save someone in my dream."

Nick got up from the bed and walked into the kitchen. A string quartet played from the speakers in the sleeping pod. Grayson liked classical music. "It appeals to my most primitive instincts," he said. Him saying this on the second night we slept together made me think, this guy is a douche bag. I couldn't get the sentence out of my head, and I used it against him; when we argued, I'd be thinking of him saying, in earnest, "It appeals to my most primitive instincts." Number one: Who talks like that? Number two: Do I want to be with the guy who talks like that? Finally, if his primitive instincts were appealed to by Edvard Grieg's *Elegiac Melodies*, then no wonder he couldn't say *suck my dick* with any authority. This was a man who only raised his voice to war and income tax. And still I liked him. Anything I ever fell into began by antagonizing. I think it has something to do with my having been fixed repeatedly. Something not right about you, they said, something not right, fine, you'll survive, but you've got something not right about you.

"Dammit," I said to Nick in the kitchen. "I forgot to plug my leg into the wall last night. Did you plug my leg into the wall?"

Nick appeared in the doorframe. My leg was on the chair where we'd left it. My leg was just sitting there on the chair.

Origins of the First Fake Leg

———

THE FIRST RECORD of a fake leg is in the *Rig-Veda*, now a book, then an oral epic, a thousand years or more, sung not said, passed down from one generation to the next, inked in Sanskrit, copied, collated, and translated: "When in the time of night, in Khela's battle, a leg was severed like a wild bird's pinion. Straight ye gave Vispali a leg of iron." And so we have from the records our first fake leg, on the body of a woman, a queen no less. No one sings the story anymore, and who can say for sure how first they sung it? No one knows how to refrain anymore. Vispali wore a suit of armor, fought on the front lines, lost her leg to battle, was carried to safety. It's not enough to be safe, and our queen was discontent, felt it most in the morning, as if there were more to life than safety, like fighting on the frontlines with her men. She hired a metalworker. His resume listed pots, pans, plates, knives, and the like. The queen approached him, Hinam, or what have you, for his name was not preserved by history; she called for him and said, "Make me a leg." He fashioned her a leg out of iron. She returned to battle.

Origins of the Leg Sitting
There on the Chair

THE LEG SITTING there on the chair comes from Otto Bock, a company, $575 million in sales last year. That leg cost $36,000. Otto Bock, the founder of the company, lived in Berlin during World War I. He saw soldiers come home, legs cut to spare them from gas gangrene, and he thought: "One man's loss is another man's gain." He opened his doors for business. It required a mass supply of Hinams. Across the ocean, Ford cranked out cars for his motor company. People wanted to get around and fast.

The C-Leg was first introduced during the World Congress on Orthopaedics in 1997. It stepped to the microphone and said, "Why have you misnamed me? I will never swim the seas nor dive for sand dollars. I will never feel the sand beneath my foot while walking ankle deep in the water. I will not lie on beaches in Tahiti after taking a scuba dive, nor will I lie on beaches in Panama City after riding a Jet Ski. I will not feel the ocean spray nor the sea mist. I will not be of any assistance helping my person float or backstroke or butterfly. To do so would destroy me."

Nick walked over to my leg.

The night before he had had nothing to say about it. I kept it on for the standing parts, then took it off and sat it in the chair. The upper leg rested on the chair, knee bent, foot on the ground. Nick stared, mouth open.

"Oh," I said.

"What?"

"I just got something."

"What are you talking about?"

"I just understood something I hadn't understood until now."
Nick looked around the room as if the past had encroached upon
us. It had, actually, entered the room through Nick's mouth,
which reminded me of a man I'd been in love with, madly, madly,
he worked at Perkins Library, where he collected pages of the
Gutenberg Bible, and he was married, but I was twenty-two. I
called him Old Faithful. He carried the leg from room to room.
He was considerate and carried the leg between his two arms or
thrown over his shoulder.

"Care to elaborate?" Nick asked, taking a seat beside my leg.
I didn't know how to say to Nick, Honey, someone from my past
climbed out of your mouth, you just vomited a married man, I
wish you hadn't, because now I am thinking not of you, not of
who you think I'm thinking of, instead of a man standing years
behind the both of you, a man who has me now, by your mouth,
thinking of him. What did he mean when he said X? If I had
known Y would Z have mattered?

"It's just that I got something," I said. "Does that happen to
you? Something clicks from the past?"

Nick waited.

"It's not a big deal," I said.

Old Faithful wanted a Real Doll. "I'd buy a Real Doll," he said.
We were having the what-would-you-do-with-a-million-dollars
conversation. I wanted a chef to prepare something other than
sandwiches. I didn't know what a Real Doll was, and he explained,
basically a hooker, fashioned from high-tech materials, with lips
partly spread, and the regular orifices. After lunch, Old Faithful

sent me an email from work with photos of his favorite Real Doll. I was thrilled to see the doll he'd chosen had brown hair and bangs.

"Can I look at it?" Nick asked.

"What?" I said, caught in that space where what one is thinking does not involve in the least the person whom one is talking to.

"Your leg."

"Of course." Why was I thinking of Old Faithful? Hadn't I left him with his wife? Yet, there he was, in the room, as if he'd been there all night.

"Nick, stop that."

"What am I doing?"

"You're freaking me out." Nick was sticking his hand inside the leg.

"I just want to see."

"Give it to me." I stretched forward from the bed, the string quartet still playing. Nick handed me the leg. He handed it to me foot first, and I had it by the calf, but he wouldn't let go. Maybe he was afraid he'd drop it, but so what, I'd dropped it before. I had to remember that Nick didn't know anything about legs, these sorts, legs you could drop, lean against the wall, roll under the bed, forget about, and then put on in the morning. I absolutely hated putting my leg on in front of someone. Or taking it off. When I took it off I became something else, and when I put it on I became something else, and it was the transition, when I was in between things, that bothered me.

"Could you go somewhere?" I said.

"Are you afraid it's not going to work?"

"Why wouldn't it work?"

"Because we didn't plug it in."

I looked at the leg and Nick looked at the leg and then I thought of a time when I hadn't plugged in for a couple days and it still worked. When it lost charge, it vibrated and told me it was losing charge. When it lost charge, it resorted to the hinge mechanism of old-style legs.

"When it loses a charge, it still works."

"So you don't want me to see, is that it?"

I had never had such a long, drawn-out conversation about someone leaving the room. What was the big deal? Get out of the room. I'm cuing you to exit the room, now exit the room. Nick stood there. I thought about putting the leg on, just doing it, but to put the leg on I had to stand up, find the socks—wherever they'd landed the night before—put the socks on, make sure they weren't wrinkled, because if they were wrinkled, then there'd be blisters to deal with at the end of the day, so I'd put the socks on, which would provide the fit, and slide my leg in, and sometimes it made a sound, a humiliating sound, I'm sure it didn't sound that bad to everyone else, but to me it sounded like the most god-awful bodily function that ever existed, and I couldn't have Nick hear it, and I couldn't have him see me work myself into a leg, even though this entire process would take less than thirty seconds. If I knew where the socks were, it would take less than ten. I had a feeling Nick was sticking around because he wanted to show me how okay with it he was. Great for him, but I wasn't okay with it.

Finally, Nick turned and left the room. "The classical music is going to drive me apeshit," he said on his way out.

I found the socks under the chair. I needed to say something, in case the leg made that noise when I put it on, something to mask the noise. "Do you have a hammer?" I yelled to him as I slid my leg on.

"What for?"

"I don't want everyone knowing about us. I need to hang a curtain in my house." I walked in a circle around Nick's room, got my bearings, and joined him in the kitchen for breakfast.

Two Strands Wrapped
around Each Other

―――――

I CROSSED THE quad toward my place with my bra in my purse, my heels in one hand, and Nick's hammer in the other. Eliot was coming from Bungalow East, tossing pistachio shells over his shoulder, and walking toward the lounge.

"You wore that yesterday," he said.

I lifted my head. "Yes," then realizing the need for cover, I added, "Nick attempted suicide. Don't say anything."

"Did he use the hammer?"

"No." This seemed to satisfy Eliot, who had a mouse in his beard. At first I thought it was a bit of fuzz, lint from his sweatshirt, or a cotton ball. But no, it moved, it had whiskers and red eyes.

"Eliot, there's a mouse on you."

"I'm collecting them."

"You are?"

"I caught this one behind the stove. I caught another one in the bathroom."

Over the loudspeakers in our bungalows and attached to a flagpole in the quad, came the voice of the Gee: "The word of the day is *guanine*. As in, *guanine* always pairs with cytosine, and adenine always pairs with thymine. These are nucleotides in your DNA. Your DNA is composed of two strands wrapped around each other."

"I'll be in the lounge," Eliot said as if I had asked. If Eliot wanted to collect mice, I couldn't see any problem there. He seemed lonely. He didn't join us at the bar. I wondered if he was a reformed alcoholic. He spoke in a barely audible monotone. He didn't have the shakes. No one knew how he arrived at the Colony, though there was talk of an ex-wife. I made it to Bungalow North without any more sightings. I hung the curtain, a cotton throw, on the beam beside the bed. I put the hammer on the kitchen table.

Fright

————

ON HALLOWEEN, NICK called, begging me to join him and the others at Sandy's Bar. I'd planned to stay in, eat frozen pizza, and watch zombies on the flat screen. Grayson called and I tucked him into bed with the phone. After waiting half an hour to see if Grayson would call again, I took Darwin's advice and put on the red miniskirt. I sat on the edge of the bathtub to shave my leg. The other leg had a run in the panty hose. I put on fishnet stockings and leopard-print heels with straps. I adjusted the heel height on the fake ankle. I practiced walking in the heels and wondered what it would be like to slip into a pair of heels without having to push a button on my ankle, what it would be like to sit on a lap without thinking—Is the plastic digging into him?—what it would be like not to notice the right side from the left, the real from the fake, the good from the bad, this movie seat from that, what it would be like to sit down on either side without thinking, and what it would be like to never have to explain things to anyone. I looked in the full-length mirror. The calves matched exactly.

Nick was outside the bar in a mullet wig and camouflage.

"Who are you supposed to be?" he said, raising an eyebrow.

"Your escort."

"I'm going for redneck." Nick's wig was tangled. With the wig on, there was no sign of the cranios, but I knew right where they were, and I kept looking above his ears. "I almost punched Leonard."

"Why?"

"I don't think he would've punched back." Nick took a drag from my cigarette. "Baby, aren't you cold?"

"I'm fine." Inside the bar, a group of men hovered around a game of penny poker. There was a pool table, a jukebox, and a cigarette machine. It reminded me of a bar in Durham. It had a cigarette machine that didn't work unless you followed several steps which included inserting twenty-four quarters, waiting for a certain clicking noise, bumping lightly near the manufacturer's sticker, and tilting it to the right. Even then, I'd only seen it produce a pack of smokes on one occasion. But I liked that cigarette machine. It offered addiction and the opportunity to fail.

Our group sat toward the back. Leonard wore two pillows, spray painted pink, on either side of his head. A ribbon tied the pillows to his head.

"I'm an ass," Leonard said, standing up.

Mercedes sat across from him in angel wings. "That's my ribbon. He needed ribbon."

Leonard pulled a chair out for me and said under his breath to Nick, "Don't you have any manners? Get her a drink."

"I'll get her a drink," Nick said without moving. The men stood shoulder to shoulder. Leonard was an inch or two shorter than Nick.

"What are you supposed to be?" Leonard said.

"A porn star."

"I buy it."

Nick clenched his jaw. In one move, he slapped Leonard on the back so hard that Leonard leaned over the table and coughed.

"Are you okay?" Mercedes said to Leonard.

"What was that for, Youngblood?" Leonard said.

"Nick," I said.

"Underestimate your own strength?" Leonard sat down beside Mercedes.

"Anne, you want a drink?" Nick said. I wanted a gin and tonic.

Nick came back with my drink while Mercedes finished telling a ghost story about her sorority house in Portland. She talked excessively and fast. I figured she talked that way because she had to, before she got fat and people stopped paying attention. Her left wing smacked Leonard in the butt cheek. She was talking about doors slamming.

Leonard said, "That's nothing. I got something happened to my sister down in Mapleton."

No one knew the layout of North Dakota, so Leonard showed us with the palm of his hand. "She was babysitting. She was fifteen, so I drove her most places."

I was entranced. Someone was always getting out of prison around Leonard. He had one friend who'd been in for a fight, one for dealing, and one for poisoning his wife. To hear Leonard tell it, these men were good guys. The fighter sold Leonard his Harley. The dealer lived four houses down from Leonard and only sold weed to other fathers on the block. The would-be murderer hadn't gone through with the poisoning, and still they slammed him, caught him on tape asking which prescription drug would put down a large dog. Leonard and his wife, Angie, sounded like the most stable couple in their neighborhood, organizing barbecues, going down to the courthouse to speak on someone's defense, and throwing welcome-back parties in their yard near the train tracks. Nick said Leonard was one of those guys who toed the line Johnny Cash–style. "Leonard hits on you and Mercedes all the damn time," Nick said. "Where does he get off hitting on you right in front of me?" I liked the way Leonard talked. He talked sidelong, lips closed to the right, open for words on the left. They kept him medicated. He called his injections "the juice." He zoomed around on his motorcycle, Montauk one weekend, New Rochelle the next. From his costume, I gathered he had a sense of humor. Nick kicked my leg under the table. He was sitting on the good side.

"Anyway, what happened was, she was babysitting this kid, a real sweet kid, and she put him to bed, and he didn't complain. A little while later he screamed. She walked in his bedroom where they had this life-size clown in the corner."

"A life-size clown?" Mercedes asked.

"Yeah."

"That's fucked up. Clowns are scary. Whatever happened to teddy bears?"

"What did happen to teddy bears?" I said.

"So the kid starts screaming, and she says, 'What's the matter?' and he says, 'The clown moved,' and she explains it's just a stuffed clown and he calms down. She says, 'It's just a clown, don't worry,' and puts the kid back to bed. She goes to the living room and starts watching the flat screen. Then she hears the kid scream again. So she walks back to his bedroom and says, 'What's the matter?' and he says the clown's talking, he's scared of the clown, and she explains it's just a toy clown."

Nick grabbed my hand under the table and squeezed.

"Why didn't she take it out of the room?" Mercedes said.

"Well."

"That's just really cruel."

"A third time, the kid screams, and my sister walks back to his bedroom and pulls the kid out of there and into the living room. He's crying at this point. He wets his pajamas. My sister gets on the phone to his parents. She says, 'Does this happen often? Is there something I should know? Because your kid is really scared of that clown in his room.' And the parents say, 'Get out of the house. Call the police.' There'd been some guy in the neighborhood doing this to kids, sneaking in their bedrooms, staring at them, whispering to them."

"Oh fuck," Mercedes said.

"Bullshit," Nick said.

"No lie," Leonard said. "I picked my sister up from the police station."

"I'm going to have nightmares," Mercedes said.

"Did they catch the clown?" I asked.

"Not to my knowledge," Leonard said.

"Whatever happened to your sister?" Mercedes said.

"My sister?"

"Yeah, was she fucked up over it?"

"My sister passed."

"Jesus," Mercedes said. "I'm always putting my foot in my mouth. Asking the wrong questions. I'm sorry about your sister. I really am. You know, I believe in ghosts, I really do, but ghosts can't kill you. And people can. I'm never like, 'Oh that ghost is going to kill me.' Nick, do you believe in ghosts?" She turned her eyes to Nick. Her breasts leaned over the table.

"Yep," Nick said.

"I'm not as scared of ghosts as I am of people," Mercedes said. "People are fucking scary. I'm not going to sleep tonight. I'm going to stay up all night. Who wants to stay up all night with me?"

"I do," Leonard said.

"Where's Mr. Forgetful Face? He never comes out. Wasn't he supposed to come out? What are you getting into, Nick?"

Sex in the Sleeping Pod

———

EVERY SLEEPING POD I'd seen had trapdoors that shut over the sleeper and encased them up to the neck. Why anyone would pay to sleep in such a pod I don't know. The sleeping-pod industry loves painting their pods black so it looks like their clients are stepping into coffins. If the point of sleep is to go away, to be both nowhere and everywhere at once, then the typical sleeping pod fails. It demands you stay in one position. Nick's sleeping pod didn't deserve to be in the same category. To call it a pod was a misnomer. It looked like a pod with the top half missing. I regretted having packed only three slips. I had a collection of close to fifty, slips from Chanel and Vanity Fair and Frederick's, slips in cotton, silk, polyester, lace, chiffon. Certain slips went with certain nights. For sex in the sleeping pod, I wore a light blue scallop-necked slip. I was wearing that slip on the night Nick fell asleep and slept and slept and didn't wake up for seventy hours. Granted, we'd been wearing each other out, but I've never fucked someone into a coma.

We were celebrating the halfway mark of our stay at the Colony. Or I was celebrating. Nick kept flipping between happy and sappy. "Which way do you want it?" I asked. "Ocean," he said. "If we're celebrating the halfway mark, does that mean we're celebrating only six more weeks together?" The remote control had five settings: Desert, Glacier, Jungle, Mountain. Ocean was our favorite. The mattress turned to jelly, waves crashed from the speakers, salt water sprayed down at random intervals from the headboard.

I feel like I'm in the music video for Chris Isaak's "Wicked Game."

Chris Isaak is a fag.
                    Do you like that song?
                                        No. Keep still.
      Isn't this actually better than fucking in the actual ocean?
      Keep still.
                    I'm trying.
                          It is.
                                        Oh God, I'm almost.
      You're all over the place.
                                        I'm almost there.
Keep still. Wait.

It was difficult for me to wait when we were on Ocean. The combination of waves, the shock of the salt water, and the slipping and sliding made it difficult. Nick took longer than I did on Ocean because he kept sliding out.

Dammit.

I grabbed Nick's belt from the side table and strapped his wrists to the headboard. He could slip around and I stayed on top. I must've fallen asleep after coming. I woke to a spray of salt water in my face and Nick underneath me. The waves had been replaced by a string quartet. When that played, it meant the Gee was at work, in the lab, watching scans of Nick's brain.

"Nick, wake up," I said. Nothing. "Nick?"

"Is Youngblood still sleeping?" Leonard said the next day.

"When's he going to wake up?" Eliot said.

"This is totally unacceptable," Mercedes said. We were standing in the quad. She marched into Nick's place. Leonard scurried to the side of the building to watch. I walked into the bungalow and stood in the doorway of the bedroom. Mercedes was bouncing on top of Nick, straddling him, bouncing, pushing her heels into his calves, saying "C'mon, c'mon."

"Mercedes."

"Yeah?" She looked up, a bra strap falling from her shoulder.

"I wish you wouldn't do that to Nick."

"I'm trying to wake him up." She brushed her lopsided hair from her face. "Oh Jesus, Anne. You're such a little sister. Are you going to tattle?"

The Gee woke Nick the following day. He rolled a machine into Nick's room and plugged into his brain. Other than a headache, Nick had nothing to report on where he'd been, what he'd seen, or whose voices he'd heard. The Gee concluded that, as suspected, Nick had a death drive.

Checking the Mail

———

AS SOON AS Nick woke up, we had to do it again to make sure we could without him falling into another deep sleep. I decided not to tell him about how Mercedes had tried to desecrate him. It was the middle of the afternoon, the first week in November. We did it at my place. During the three days Nick slept, I felt guilty and called Grayson. He said, "What's all this calling about, Annie? Do you have something to say?" It felt like everyone was on my case. The Gee said, "I need a decision. I have observed you for six weeks now. And everything I see proves everything I knew: You can handle this. You can grow a limb at an incredible speed. Your time at the Colony is wasting away." It was the slowest we'd ever done it, missionary style, and Nick kept one hand on the side of my face. Afterward, I turned on the flat screen where the weatherman predicted a bear of a winter. "A bear of a winter," he kept saying. Nick got up and took his jeans from the floor. He wiggled one leg, then the other, into the jeans. I got up and put on clothes and waited for Nick to get out of the bathroom. We walked over to the lounge. I had a package from Grayson.

"Let me see." Nick took the package from me, read the return address, walked over to the trash can and dropped it in.

"Hey."

"Junk mail," he said.

I picked the package from the trash and joined Eliot, who was sitting on the couch. He had his pen in hand, poised above a page in his journal. He and his mouse looked up.

"I'm locked out. Simon's coming. I'm not forgetting anything other than my keys, in case you were wondering. I'm writing a personal life-event journal. Doc's suggestion." Eliot bowed his head and stared at the page.

"Can I ask which life event you're writing?" I sat beside him. He shifted closer to his side of the couch so we had a full cushion between us.

Eliot took his mouse from his beard and sat it on top of the journal. It played with the string from his hoodie. Eliot scratched its head. "What do you think counts as a life event?"

Nick pulled a stack of mail from his box.

"Is everyone getting fan mail?" Nick asked.

I wasn't because I'd made it explicitly clear to the Gee that I wanted privacy. I did not want my name released to the public. All press releases would have to omit me. I looked on with Nick at his letter.

Dear Nick,

Dude, I had a brother who killed himself it wasn't cool. I think my brother had the same thing you had because when he died my Ma and Aunt Patty said they never in a million years expected it and of all people. He was not that type of guy is what they said. He was the captain of the varsity football team at Shelby High and even somehow this girl liked him. She was real upset about the whole thing and I was too but she was upsetter at the time with lots of crying and carrying on. I gave her a Kleenex and she said it was hard to look at me because I was the spitting image. Then she said my brother was her first and they were in love. Maybe but my brother kept a stack of porn under his bed with girls prettier than Tonya and now it's mine. My aunt Patty said I have to be strong for Ma now that I'm the man in the house. I'm writing you this note in second period. Now I am upsetter than Tonya because I found out I didn't make baseball today and it's Devon's fault for sure he would've taught me how to run bases. In second period we learned about you and the Colony and this is an assignment. Don't do it bro (kill yourself). Anyway I wanted to tell you thanks for what you're doing for our country, freedom, and justice.

Your pen pal,
Dylan

Breaking Point

———

I WALKED HOME and Googled myself. I wanted to know if my name had been leaked. I should've been opening Grayson's package, regretting actions, sweeping sand from the floor, thinking of consequences, boiling water for tea. I put the package on the table next to the hammer. The package bothered me there, so I put it behind the coatrack near the door. I slid into that reverie provided by Google. I found my name in a post from one of my students. So I had a presence as a teacher rather than as a guinea pig. I could relax. Many people were on the web and I was one of them. I scrolled down. I was thinking, I love Adam McLane. He will go on to become a genius. He will save nation-states. He wrote: "I feel bad for her. When she sits at the desk in front of the room you can hardly tell a thing. But when she walks, she's like a whole different person."

Later the same day, it got worse.

We were hanging out in Mercedes' bungalow talking about money. Leonard said money didn't matter. His wife, Angie, would spend it all anyway. He said he was tired of being accused of minor infractions that didn't seem like infractions to him. Angie thought he was hardwired for evil. He wanted her to stop thinking that.

"You're not evil," Mercedes said. "What would make her think that?" But Leonard wouldn't answer.

Eliot was keeping his money in cash. He wanted to buy gold bars with it.

"Gold bars," Nick said. "What are you going to do with gold bars?"

"Goddamn," Leonard said.

"What's the matter?" Mercedes said.

"The juice gives me a headache."

Mercedes poured Leonard a shot.

"I'm going to spend mine on new clothes and new front-room furniture for the salon. New beginnings. I'm going to dump my boyfriend. I'm fizzling on him." She looked over at Nick. "Why can't relationships ever end in agreement? Why does one person always fizzle first?"

"Ending in agreement is an urban legend. It never happens," Nick said.

Then they all said what they said. I was sitting beside Mercedes. I kept thinking: It's going to be over soon, what are you going to do? Tell them they're hurting your feelings? Walk out? They don't even know what they're saying right now, but if you cry, if you change the topic, if you do anything, if you move an inch, if you go to the bathroom, if you leave abruptly, then they'll know. People will say things like this, again and again and again and again and again, for the rest of your life, but if you don't say anything, they'll never know, so shut up and don't cry.

Look at that, I thought later in my bungalow, you have mascara all over your hands.

But you did a good job, you did very good, you waited until you were back at your place, you were very good about that, did not shed a tear did not flinch did not allow your lip to quiver engaged in conversation moved your eyes from one person to the next waited and waited and said good-bye see you later good night. You did so good. Urban legends. That started it. No, it started before then, it started three hours ago and the year before that, it started in Mrs. Topaz's class and the class before that, it started with a gene inside my DNA, and if I could pull my DNA out and lay it down it would be as long as a car, and I could step in and drive away. I don't want to remember how it started. Or why it started, like because God knew you were strong and put you on the earth to move about and inspire people, like Paul with the thorn in his side, but Paul never says what the thorn in his side is, so that's not really fair of him, to disguise it in metaphor, so instead of Paul the Epileptic he's Paul the Apostle. How did it start this time?

"Urban legends," Leonard said. "Like the guy with the hook for the hand. The guy got that hook and his girlfriend didn't want to be with him anymore, who could blame her, and he acted okay about it and said "that's okay," and then he went raping and slaughtering people in their cars. Maybe you should get a hook for a hand."

Mercedes said maybe she should get a hook for a hand. Or a scar. Or a cleft lip. Or a defect. Or something really ugly, and when her boyfriend saw her, he wouldn't want to be with her, he wouldn't even be able to look at her because she'd be so *gross* (that was Mercedes), *hideous* (that was Leonard), *fucked up* (that was Nick), yeah, that's what you should do, Mercedes, get *fucked-up* looking, he won't love you anymore.

To the Geneticist

———

Whatever you have to do, do it.

The Proposal

———

But why think? Why not try the experiment?

—JOHN HUNTER, eighteenth-century surgeon

WE WANT TO grow your leg. We want to give you the leg you were meant to have at birth. About that gene, we're certain. We've observed and observed. I've been observing genes since the nineties. I won a Westinghouse Science Talent Award, went to Harvard, then MIT. I work with people at the Department of Energy, the National Institutes of Health, Applied Biosystems, Amgen, Novartis, Insight, not to mention the universities—Johns Hopkins, Arizona, Maryland—you name them, if they have anything to do with genomics, I work with them. I stand by Hippocrates: Above all, do no harm. If I thought there was a fly eye's chance of harm, you wouldn't be here. We're federally funded. We selected you from twenty thousand applicants. That goes to show how many, in your position, are willing.

We chose you due to your unconscionably high blood-cell-count. For some reason, your blood cells reproduce in triple-time, fast-forward, high speed. In brief, you are cellular gold. I am at the top of this field, second to James D. Watson. I've already won the major prizes; here is my vita, take a look. Thusly, I'm not a careerist. I saw your genetic code last May on a quantum cascade laser. These things boil down to recessive and dominant. You happen to have a hardy dominant PRX1 that stunted the growth of your tibia and makes blood in triple-time. The possibilities are monumental. I don't have to tell you we're at war, losing legs, losing blood.

So what we'll do is this. We will go in there, corner the gene, and toggle its properties. We want to grow the leg you should have had at birth from knee to ankle to five toes. The blueprints for the leg are all there. All stored in your body. It's as if your body has been waiting for just this procedure. To grow what it failed to grow. We'll hook you up to the Regenerator, which I will now order, from a select group in Biopolis, that's in Thailand, since you have given me the go-ahead, and we'll begin regeneration. It's not invasive. We'll do it right here on-site. We won't even put you to sleep. You can watch it on the flat screen. We're going in there with a cue and turning you on. It's like a hard drive. Find file. Run. The information is, and always has been, and will continue to be stored in your genes. Think of it like this: The version of me in 1800 didn't even have a stethoscope to hear a heartbeat. By 1900 he could see the heart on an X-ray. By 2000 he could 3-D-image the heart and move around in it and save someone's life. And by 2100, can you imagine? We have every reason to believe you will grow like wildfire. You'll regenerate before you know it. I don't mean to brag, but you're dynamite in my hands. We will be inextricably linked in history. I hope you like me. I almost did it on myself, one night in Santa Cruz; I almost shot my own leg off. Fortunately, I was in love with Stacey Winzel at the time, who was in love with my legs.

The Gee paused to loosen the collar of his shirt. He looked at me, sitting on the steel bed of the X-ray machine. I reached into the pocket of my jeans for a cigarette. I removed the pack and flipped the lid.

"Please," he touched my wrist. "Not inside."

I stood from the X-ray machine and walked to a door under an exit sign. He followed. The door led to an alley out back of the laboratory. The Gee kept his hand on the door. "It locks."

I lit the cigarette.

"Do you think there's something wrong with me?"

He put his foot between the door and the frame, to keep it from locking, and crossed his arms. "That's a relative term, *wrong*; is there something wrong with you, that's relative. Although I see your point."

"I get the feeling other people think there's something wrong with me."

"I'm going to get your jacket." He stepped into the building and returned with my jacket. He opened the jacket for my arms. "What do you think?"

I thought maybe. I thought yes. I thought Adam McLane found something wrong with me, and physicians found something wrong with me, and the team at Cold Spring found something wrong with me, specifically the PRX1, and the textbooks said quietly, "Something is wrong with you. This is what it's called." Nick probably found something wrong with me, and before him, Grayson probably found something wrong with me and before him, standing at the back of the line, Old Faithful. I remember. Old Faithful said he was worried, I was young, but that wasn't it, that wasn't where he stopped. If he had stopped on "you're young" then it would have been fine. Old Faithful said, "There is your *condition* to consider. What if I cheated on you with a two-legged woman?" That was his fear. "How often do you think about cheating on people before you're with them?" I asked. "Not often," he said. "Only with you."

This did break my heart.

I wanted to scream, to point out that he married a two-legged woman, and he was cheating on her with a one-legged woman, so legs obviously had nothing to do with it. I didn't want to talk about myself in the legged sense, what was that, what was he reducing me to? "There's nothing I can do about that," I said. Here was the Geneticist. He had a machine.

I asked: When do we start? What will it make me? Do you have a name for it? How does it work?

The Gee showed diagrams of phases: dedifferentiation, blastema formation, redifferentiation, and pattern formation. It made no sense to me.

"What do I look like on the quantum cascade laser?"

"Striking."

"I am?"

"You're prime property." The Gee looked me in the eyes. It felt like we were having a moment, one in which he thought he knew me.

"You got to cut that classical music off in Nick's sleeping pod."

The Gee's eyes looked to the right as if someone was coming in the door. "Pardon me?"

"You're going to drive Nick to suicide with the string quartets. He likes country music. Don't you know anything about us?"

"Nick's treatment is really none of your business."

"It's just a suggestion."

"Do you have any other suggestions for me?"

"I'd like to smoke inside."

"You should quit."

"I'm not going to."

"I'll see if we can work something out."

"Will there be side effects?"

"It might hurt a little. You might feel some tenderness. You might be on crutches for a couple of weeks. At the rate your cells grow, it shouldn't take more than fourteen days. And don't worry." The Gee collected his diagrams in a folder and then looked me in the eyes again. "Thousands of years ago, regeneration was entirely natural."

In the Prehistoric Time
of Regeneration

The machinery for regeneration must be a basic part of animal genetic equipment, but the genes have for some reason fallen into disuse.

—University College London,
The New York Times, April 6, 2006.

MALAMAR AND MAUD lived peacefully in Mesopotamia until dinosaurs began to attack. The dinosaurs lived on a strict diet of hind and calf. They attacked the legs of Malamar and Maud many times. Each time they lost a leg, they grew it back, lost it, grew it back, lost it again, *dammit*, grew it back. It was exhausting work. When either of them was in the process of growing, they looked at each other and said, "Not tonight." They only had a nubbin. They felt too lopsided. "Don't you dare draw me on the wall like this," they said to each other. One day Malamar said, "Try not to be eaten if you can help it." And with that, he kissed her very large forehead and traipsed out of the cave in search of food. A dinosaur appeared on the horizon. Malamar ran and ran and arrived, by legs, at home. Too late. Another dinosaur had eaten one of Maud's. "Keep it stumped, will you?" Malamar begged. "Every time I come home you're growing. You're five-hundred-and-some-odd legs away from the woman I once knew." Maud considered. She made love to Malamar while the fire crackled and the dinosaurs slept. They'd never done it like that before. They'd always thought, "Legs! We need two of them." They'd been missing a few positions—the Coconut Swing, the Flamingo Fandango. "Fine," Maud said. "I won't grow." News spread to other caves, other Malamars and Mauds, along with a diagram of uniped positions. For a time, the world hopped. And the dinosaurs, as you know, stopped.

After the Dinosaurs
and Before Engel Deeter

LAZZARO SPALLANZANI (1729–1799) studies classics and philosophy, the church funds work in natural sciences. I repeat, the church funds work in natural science, back when the church and science got along, and Spallanzani hikes mountains, walks paths, observes springs for water affinity, refutes theory of vital atoms, takes head of one snail and puts it on body of another. Discovers egg and semen both necessary to make a baby. Artificially inseminates a dog.

A monk named GREGOR JOHANN MENDEL (1822–1884) wants to work with mice, but there is his bishop, the conservative, who bans him from working with mice. The mice will want to copulate, and Mendel is a monk. Mendel chooses peas instead. Let someone else work with mice. And they do. To this day mice are favored over peas, fruit flies, and worms. One wonders what might have been if we worked with salamanders in the twentieth century. Or starfish. Or the sea squirt that can regrow its entire body from one blood vessel.

AUGUST WEISMANN (1834–1914), studies music, takes lessons from a piano teacher with sizeable bosom who introduces him to the butterfly species, develops an interest in natural science, studies medicine instead, dissertates on the synthesis of piss, chops off the tails of fifteen hundred mice over twenty generations, concludes that mice continue to be born with their tails, declares after himself the Weismann barrier.

C.C. LITTLE (1886–1971), a.k.a. "mouse man," loves a mouse, loves many mice, creates a strain known as Black 6, the first genome sequenced. Walks Mount Desert Island with his students, rubs noses with Edsel Ford, cocktails in Bar Harbor, goes to Michigan as president of the university, is dissatisfied, can't put his finger on it, leaves to build a mouse heaven, a mouse hell, depending on if you're him or the mouse, a great big reservoir of mice, at Jackson Laboratory, sells two million a year.

LOLA MAY HATLEY (b. 1930), great-grandmother to first regenerative, her family claims a patch of land near Hickory, North Carolina, born to homesteaders, born to the Depression. Her family sells the land on the river to the state. The state wants for the land a dam. Lola May feeds the men who build the dam. She marries five times, only counts four. Sees the pastor at First Presbyterian in 1989 for reoccurring dream in which "I got things blooming on me."

Badass Dreams

———

IN THE SEVENTH week, Nick called frequently to update me on his dreams. The Gee had plugged into his cranios for the last time, watched the scans of his frontal lobe for the last time, and replaced the seal with Nick's original bit of bone. I was happy that Nick got to leave with everything he came with, down to the bone flap on his brain. His skull was healing. He still had the three bald patches on his head and he wore his straw hat to cover them. The SUI variant, according to Nick, had been corrected, and he no longer had to worry that he would throw himself in front of a train. I was worried because I'd stopped fantasizing about him. Why didn't I? Probably because there was no reason, no opportunity to wonder, Where are you and what are you doing? On days I slept at my place, I woke up with Old Faithful in the stacks at the library. This is ridiculous, I thought. I've got to stop it with this guy. But the more I thought that, the more I wanted to put the guy between my legs. I heard him say, "You can do whatever you want to me." I'd heard guys say it before, but as soon as I said what I wanted, they looked at me like I was crazy, they were suddenly very protective, they had thought themselves open to anything, but really they were open to the usual things. I felt shy when Nick called. I listened as he told me about a dream he titled "Raccoon Assassins." Prompted by Van Zandt's *A Far Cry from Dead.*

"What do you think it means?" I asked.

"I don't know, but Van Zandt was right by my side with bow and arrow trying to shoot down some damn raccoons. It was the best dream I have ever had." Nick was calling four or five times a day. I received most of his calls. Sometimes I let him go to voicemail. His treatment was already deemed a success. As for me, I had no bragging rights. I thought, when I told the Gee I was ready, there'd be research assistants, thermometers, rubber gloves, heart-rate monitors. It had been two days since I'd agreed, and I'd only received an injection. With five weeks left, I worried there wouldn't be enough time. "It will grow fast," the Gee said. The Regenerator had completed the leg of a cat in two days. I tried looking for this cat online—was it a Manx? Persian? Burmese?—and couldn't find it. I had to pay attention to whatever Nick was saying on the phone.

Mercedes waved through the window of my front door.

"I just want to say hi," she said, "Heard it's your birthday."

"Hold on," I said to her, turning my back. "Honey, I'll call you later."

"You just called me *honey*," Nick said.

Mercedes handed me a birthday balloon.

Birth Story

————

A FEW WORDS concerning the people who brought me into the world. Hepsie Hatley is stunning. She's my mom. I've been in the car with her when men roll down the windows of their trucks at stoplights to chat her up. Her hair has the nutrients advertised on shampoo commercials. Her figure is common, 38-28-38, an average figure, perhaps stunning in its prototypical proportions. She reminds people of someone. That's the line most of the time. People mistake her for long-lost friends. They approach and say, "Veronica" or "Martha" or "Karen" or "Elizabeth, after all this time!" I've even heard people argue Mom's identity with her. "Are you sure? You're not from Gainesville? Did you ever live in Gainesville? Is it possible I ran into you somewhere outside of Gainesville?" I used to think Mom was lying. She really was from Gainesville. Her name really was Veronica. I used to think Mom knew these people, had gotten around, had moved across the country, in disguise, several love affairs. I was proud of Mom. People wanted to know her. People thought they had known her, and every time one of them approached, they were happy to see her, as if they'd been hoping for such a run-in for many years. They left disappointed that mom wasn't connected to them.

Dad is six feet two without boots. He keeps a trimmed mustache. He was in the war. He has subscriptions to *Wired* and *The*

Washington Post. He worked for the Department of Defense. He owns the latest gadgets. His socks have holes in them. He's a good-looking guy but not a knockout like Mom. No one's rolling down the window at a traffic light for him. No one's giving him any lickspittle. He met Mom at a party. She'd come with someone else. "Do I know you?" he'd said. He thinks she's perfect. He never criticizes her. "There must be something he doesn't like about me," Mom has said. "I wish he'd tell me what it is." Mom doesn't like Dad's drinking. Mom and I debate whether he is an alcoholic. I say no. Mom says probably. When he gets drunk, he's nice, aloof, and silly. He's an elder at the church. I don't really know him.

My birth story goes like this: "We had no idea, we were shocked, I said to your father, 'How come? Why us?' The doctors told us something was wrong. They didn't have to tell us. It was obvious. I looked at you and I was scared. You were missing a leg. It didn't take a doctor to tell me that. They said birth defects. Did we have a history of this or that? Suddenly I was researching our family tree. Who gave you this? Where did you come from? It wasn't me. I was strict about the pregnancy, no drinking, no smoking, no prescriptions. I followed *What to Expect When You're Expecting*. I remember being very angry that I had not expected this. I called Mother. She said, 'It'll be okay.' But I thought no. It might not be okay. I thought you might die, you might be in a wheelchair, you might never walk, you might not make friends, you might be teased, you might not date. Forget about grandbabies. Doctors said if I got pregnant again, they could test for it and abort." After I'd heard my birth story several times, I finally asked Mom to stop telling it. "I wish you'd stop telling that story," I said. "It's not a nice story to tell your daughter."

Reasons for Birth Defects

On Monsters and Marvels by Ambroise Paré

Contents

Mercedes Wants to Have
Nick's Babies

"IF I'M INTERRUPTING," Mercedes said, handing me the balloon.

"Not at all. That was my mom."

"You call your mom *honey*, that's so sweet. I barely even hear from my mom, much less call her honey. She drinks a lot, but what are you going to do? Like breeds like. Speaking of which, are we drinking later? It's your birthday." Mercedes stepped into my bungalow, taking her shawl off.

"Actually, not until tomorrow." I lit a cigarette.

"Hell, I'm early. I'm never early. I'd be willing to bet that most of my relationships end because I'm late. I had to dump my boyfriend. I was fizzling. The way I see it, I'm turning thirty-seven in January, so I have three years to get knocked up." Mercedes picked up a bottle of Bombay from a shelf in my kitchen. "You haven't even broken the seal. Do you need some help?"

"It's five in the afternoon."

"Do you see the sun? I don't see the sun and that's basically my rule of thumb. What am I talking about? I don't have any rules when it comes to—fuck, were you in the middle of something? Because I could leave, I just wanted to stop by and see—"

Mercedes kept going, but I wasn't listening. She was too young to be a nuisance. I was trying to figure out how someone like her, with the figure and the blonde hair and the blue eyes, made it to thirty-seven without getting seriously involved. No one had to know she carried the obesity gene.

"My boyfriend, the one I fizzled on, he was a painter. We made kaleidoscopes. It was for an erotica benefit through my salon. We took photos of our butts and pasted them together in this tube. It was great because he had Photoshop and so I said, 'Look, airbrush it.' And of course, he said, 'It doesn't need airbrushing.' To which I thought, 'Right answer! You get an A!' Now that I think about it, I don't know what happened to that thing. I guess I'm mooning someone somewhere."

I nodded and laughed. Mercedes kept talking as I paced around the apartment picking up books and setting them back down. I adjusted the thermostat. This went on for a while, until she finally got around to asking.

"What is going on with Nick? I haven't seen him in ages."

"I don't know."

"I told you, didn't I, about my little crush."

"You made it pretty obvious by bouncing on top of him while he was sleeping."

"Oh right. That happened. So you can tell me, I mean if he said something about me, you could totally tell me."

"He hasn't said anything."

"Are you protecting him, being loyal?"

"Let me think."

"Because I can take it. Even if, you know, if he doesn't like me."

"Nope, nothing I can think of."

"Are you sure? Because the other day, in the lounge, I tried to talk to him and he gave me this look—like he didn't know how to answer me."

"Probably just busy."

"Sorry to put you on the spot like that, but knowing you're his friend and all, I thought if anyone knew something, I mean really. You can tell me."

The Robertson Davies Tragedy

———

AFTER MERCEDES LEFT, I picked up the book I'd been reading. I was reading books I might teach in honors English at Durham Prep. You were supposed to have done all the important reading in college, if not by the time of your undergraduate degree, then by the time of your master's in education. You were supposed to have read *The Divine Comedy*, *Moby-Dick*, and I had skipped these because I had neither the patience nor interest to read about the peg-legged captain, the hellfire monsters. Honors English at my own high school had been a cause of distress when Mrs. Topaz, rightly named, calm and soothing, unwittingly chose three novels—Toni Morrison's *Sula* and Saul Bellow's *The Adventures of Augie March* and Robertson Davies's *Fifth Business*—all of which had cripples in them. The worst was Mr. Davies, who had a woman fuck a man and then beat him with his fake leg. This section was of particular interest to Mrs. Topaz, for reasons that remain unknown to me.

"Anne Hatley, you have a prosthetic. Can you give us your perspective?" Mrs. Topaz asked. I hated her more than anyone I had hated before. She was wearing a scarf over a wig, had cancer, was in the middle of chemo, and later, when she accused me of having an attitude, accused me of "acting apathetic," I fired off, "How would you like being in a class full of books on people dying of cancer, Mrs. Topaz?"

During the Davies discussion, I slunk back into my chair and said, "I liked the book," which was not altogether a lie. I had felt deeply for the man, while he tussled with the woman in the bunk, and it was not until she abused him with his own fake leg that I began to suspect Davies of thievery, stealing a very real physical condition and using it to sell his stupid book of stupid fiction. Hadn't he read Maugham's *Of Human Bondage?* Hadn't he seen Byron romance Lady Lamb, Oxford, Webster by way of clubfoot? I hid my face in the collar of my boyfriend's band jacket, which smelled like popcorn, and as soon as the bell rang, I took to the bleachers in the gymnasium to cry. It was then I realized I would always be called upon to give my perspective, people are curious, people want to know, what happened, when did it happen, why aren't you like me, and the life sentence, the sheer relentlessness of it, the idea that these questions would assault me unprovoked and without warning at any given time for the rest of my life seemed unbearable. That feeling showed up again, reading Adam McLane's blog, and sitting on the floor at Mercedes' while everyone laughed, and it was a persistent feeling of shittiness, and it would continue to show up, unless the Regenerator worked. I was a walking pedagogical instrument, and I decided, back in high school, sniffling into Ezra Bowen's band jacket, that fine, if anyone was liable to call on me to teach them about fake parts and real parts and feelings and perspectives, then I'd beat them to the punch and become a teacher, and I'd never, in front of twenty students, call one student out, and make a spectacle of her, and discuss her as if she could relate to a man fucked then beaten by his leg. I'd be the teacher who comes off as calm and soothing, and who is calm and soothing, with an intuition for the weaknesses of her students. I'd know what they could handle, and what they could not, and I'd never ask a question that panhandled their emotions.

The collar of Ezra Bowen's band jacket was by now thoroughly soaked. We'd been together six months, he a senior, me a junior, and it was a relationship neither frigid nor on fire. I was invited to his parents' house, a two-story ranch, though I was not allowed on the carpet. His mother smirked when she delivered this edict: "Now don't go on the carpet because the carpeted areas are bedrooms." How badly I wanted to go on the carpet. I was invited to dinner where I was not allowed to help myself to the green beans. Ezra Bowen's father served us, around the table we went, and holding hands thanked the Lord for Mrs. Bowen's cooking. Then Ezra and I were left alone in the front living room. We knew after the first few months that they would not interrupt us.

They named their son after the book of the Bible where God returns his people to the land of promise after years of exile, and most of the book is spent building a temple. The book of Ezra is written in first and third person, and linguists believe one and the same man wrote both of these parts, the first person and the third person. A man writing about himself in third person must have opposition within himself, must be of two minds, and so it was with Ezra Bowen, one second pawing me near the breast and the next saying, "No we can't, we really can't."

Ezra Bowen was doughy, but otherwise handsome, bigger than the other boys our age. He wanted to be the best drum major Northern High had ever heard, and one day attend Julliard, and make love to me, for we were all about "making love," and it did not occur to either of us that we would accomplish such a feat prior to marriage, both of our households being strongly rooted in templing our bodies. So it was with much surprise that when I met Ezra Bowen after school on the day of the Robertson Davies tragedy, I met him ready to lose my virginity, not just ready but adamant, and I said, "Ezra, if you can't, then it's over," and after dining with his parents, lasagna and sourdough baked fresh, we sat down solemnly on the couch in the front living room, to watch *Lawrence of Arabia*, thereby extending my curfew for two hours, to give us time to figure out how to do it exactly, how exactly to go about it. I had begged a condom off Emily Smoak; I was entirely certain, and we got it done during a stretch of desert, two camels, two turbans.

Happy Birthday

———

FOR MY BIRTHDAY, Nick drove us down Harbor Road. We got on the highway. He was hopped on dreaming. Ever since his long sleep, he'd been having incredible dreams. I kept asking where we were going, and he kept singing along with Johnny Cash. I rolled down the window to smoke. My eyes watered from the cold. Gray clouds lined the sky. We passed a billboard of a woman smiling. "A plan for everyone," the billboard read. Nick kept his hands on ten and two, and knew all the words to "Girl of the North Country." I was wearing the peekaboos and a dress. Nick pulled into a parking space at Fin 'N' Filet. The place had a doorman.

"Looks expensive." I dropped my cigarette out the window. "I thought we were going to Sandy's for a burger."

"On your birthday?" He put his hand on my lower back. "Nice shoes," he said, opening the door to the restaurant.

Inside, a dozen faces turned. The hostess checked the reservation book at the pedestal. Her hair was parted down the middle. She was one of those who straightened it with an iron set to four hundred degrees.

My phone rang. I searched through my purse.

"Don't," Nick said.

The hostess was displeased. The restaurant had two rooms, one with a fireplace toward the back and dark red walls, and an adjacent room separated by French doors. At intervals, a group laugh came from the other room. The waitress sat us between a couple and the fireplace, close to the French doors. The couple, a man and a woman, looked smitten with each other, though they kept talking about Wachovia.

"Baby," Nick said. "A bottle of white?"

The menu was printed on thick paper. It had no prices.

"I don't trust a place that doesn't advertise its prices."

Our waiter brought a bottle and two stems. "Happy Birthday," Nick began, raising his glass. "That I might spend the rest of your birthdays with you. That I—rid of suicide—may forever dream in Technicolor country. That you may walk on one, two, three, four, however many legs you like. That Leonard will become polar instead of bipolar and Eliot will stop flirting with you in the lounge."

"Eliot's not flirting."

"That Mercedes will become the lard ass she's always wanted to be."

We clinked. Again, laughing from the adjacent room. "What do you suppose they're doing?"

Nick leaned over the table and took my hands. "I don't know," he said, studying my nails. "I love it when you paint your nails translucently for me."

"What are you going to eat?"

"And when you ask questions with disdain."

I ordered she-crab soup and pecan-crusted Chilean sea bass. I wanted to get the food as takeout, drive back, and watch the Ping-Pong match: Leonard versus Eliot.

"Babydoll," Nick said. "Here's the deal. I'm going to attend horticulture school at some point; I'm taking the money from here and buying up some land, mustangs, and heifers. I make six hundred a week bartending at The Scout in Madison. We have a farm with a guest cabin, oak and poplar, built by Grandpa Burk, can't see it from the main house. How attached are you to Durham?"

In the pause, I overheard the man at the table beside us drop all pretenses of the bank and say to the woman, "You're pink and sensational."

Nick continued, "Because I don't foresee leaving Madison."

The woman said, "I've been waiting for someone to realize."

The waiter delivered the soup. I struggled with the silverware, bundled tightly in its cloth blanket, and then I lapped the soup.

"Baby, you're hard as a tack."

Nick had something green, spinach maybe, stuck between his teeth.

"You've got something in your teeth."

I showed him where and he used his fingernail between the teeth. The French doors opened. A group of men and fewer women stood in the doorway.

"Shit," Nick said. "It's James D. Watson." He was talking to a woman in a navy dress. The Gee stood behind them.

Watson was much shorter than I'd imagined. "Off the coast of Maine," he said and the woman in navy replied, "We summer in Nantucket."

The Gee saw us, nudged James D. Watson, and whispered something in his ear.

"Certainly," Watson said. "Why wouldn't I?" He approached our table. Nick put his spoon beside his bowl. I kept mine in hand. "I was telling my wife the other day what good recruits we have. You must be the Regen," he said, looking at my legs. "It's remarkable what Otto knocks out these days, quite the fit, of course you can't match skin exactly, and the knees are a smidge uneven. It would be our pleasure to put him out of business. We got legs coming off left and right. It's not like you can prescribe for ten

thousand–plus—excuse me, I've had a nibble and a sip tonight."
Watson placed one hand on the back of my chair to steady
himself.

"Fellas," Nick said. "It's her birthday."

"Happy birthday," Watson said.

"Happy birthday," the Gee said.

The Gee and Watson's wives, or women friends, or colleagues
or whoever, Nick and I were not introduced, slipped into their
coats and said their goodbyes.

"How old?" Watson asked.

"Twenty-six," I said.

"Ah, to be young," he said, winking at me, then turning to the
Gee: "What do you say we take her to the mermaids?"

Onward to the Mermaids

——

NICK AND I followed the taillights of Watson's Cadillac, headed north, Johnny Cash playing. I had been to see the mermaids at Sea World once. I rolled down the window.

"It's about to pour," Nick said.

"I'm going to smoke."

"Ain't you excited to see merms? I am."

I lit a cigarette and inhaled deeply. It was one thing for James D. Watson to finagle genes in actual everyday existence, or to make computerized guide boys for caves, altogether another for him to breed sea creatures for sport.

Nick put his arm on the back of my seat. "Sometimes I get the impression you flat-out don't like me."

The headlights of the station wagon and the Cadillac lit the road. I focused on the outlines of Watson and the Gee's heads. The Gee was driving. They were talking animatedly, one turning to the other.

"I wouldn't be here if I didn't like you."

"It's my wagon then. It's my having wheels."

I hadn't thought about it like that, but with Nick mentioning it, I reckoned that was part of it. It was convenient to have a car, his cooking, necking, and the rest. I checked my phone. I'd missed three calls. Grayson would've objected to a scientific mermaid field trip. He would've cited decency and "knowing our limits." He would've preferred to stay out of it, stay home, write letters of protest, call governors, deliver diatribes on ethics. He was self-righteous. I wondered if he hadn't taken me on as a cause. What better way for him to bemoan humanity's callousness then by seeing it firsthand when strangers approached and asked questions. He was eager to answer for me. And at the same time, "Children," he'd said. "Aren't there risks?" It was the negative part of the question I heard most.

"Wish I knew what you thought about me," Nick said, raising an eyebrow. I thought about him so little because I was with him so much.

"I think you go off on tangents, and while right now I'm in the tangent, I wonder if tomorrow it could be Mercedes or someone from the Green House."

"Baby, I go to the Green House because I like gardening. I'm a gardener. And I care for Mercedes about as much as a slug cares for salt. She's cute but she's no you. I'd push you harder, if we weren't in this situation."

"What's that?"

"This situation. You know the situation." Nick had his eyes on the road. Up ahead, the Gee turned on his blinker. "I'm finished but you're not. You're looking at treatment, some kind of machine from Thailand."

"What do you know about it?"

"Just what I gather from Mercedes."

"What does she know about it?"

"Just that the Gee ordered some kind of machine."

I didn't like the idea of Nick and Mercedes talking about me.

"I can see where the needles enter you. Right on your hip," Nick said.

"Don't get proud of yourself."

"I'm not being proud of myself. I want to know what the hell is going on, but I don't feel like I can ask."

"You can ask."

"What are they giving you?"

"Stem cell injections."

"Does it hurt?"

"Not much."

"What's supposed to happen?"

"It's priming me for the Regenerator."

"When's that going down?"

"Next week."

"See, now how hard was that? So nothing for you yet. But think of it like this. We're driving to see *mermaids*, baby, *mermaids*, and that doesn't happen in Madison, Wisconsin. I keep thinking, 'How does Nick feel about this?' but I keep coming back to, There's no one I'd rather see a mermaid with. I got no dim-dam doubt about it."

"I want to see mermaids with you too, I think."

"You think?"

"I'm not sure."

"You got something against mermaids?" Nick followed the Cadillac past a convenience store and up to a gated entrance with a security guard. The sign read NASSAU COUNTY WATER DEPARTMENT. The guard waved us in and we parked.

"Yee-haw," Nick said.

The Biggest Consensual Human Experiment of All Time

———

NICK AND I followed Watson and the Gee to a tall silo. My toes were cold. I zipped my jacket. Watson pulled keys from his pants pocket.

"He's proud of this project," the Gee said. "Aren't you, sir?"

"Who you calling *sir*?" His hair, what was left of it, whipped back and forth in the wind. He opened the door to the silo and flipped on the lights. We stood on a concrete floor, surrounded by cylindrical walls. The place smelled like chlorine. There was an air mattress, fully inflated, to one side.

"Holy helmet," Nick said. I looked at him. He was looking straight up. Above us, through a sheet of glass, were the mermaids. They swam in gallons of water, illuminated by lightbulbs. The bulbs looked like stage lights, ultrawatted, spaced ten feet from each other and built into the walls of the silo.

"I took lemons and made lemonade," Watson said. "For your sake, and for the sake of sanity, let me say, they are not human. They possess not one iota of human brain matter. They are animals like at the zoo. No one gets his bloomers in a wad over the zoo. At the same time, it wouldn't be wise to say anything in regards to my little aquarium." Watson laughed. Sounded like a cat coughing up a hairball. The Gee shuffled his feet. The room went silent as a sanctuary.

Nick and I stared up into the blue. The animals were chalk white, with fin-arms and chest, a round bauble for a head, and oval eyes.

"These are modified dugongs of the order Sirenia," Watson said. "My mermaids." He sat on the air mattress and extended his legs. "A friend of mine, a gentleman I met at Biopolis, who turned out to be king of an island in the Coral Sea, presented me with a pair. Sent them by boat. I've been raising them ever since. They have remarkable bones."

"Tell the recent development," the Gee said.

"Ah yes, we've been dousing them in thalidomide. They sleep soundly and they are immune to everything."

"Most things," the Gee said.

"Everything thus far, they are immune to."

"What is thalidomide?" I asked.

"Grumbell Company brought it out, put it on the market to help pregnant woman sleep through the night. Perhaps the greatest love story in experimentation. One of the employees from Grumbell took a sample home to his wife. 'Here darling, here my sweet.' She was pregnant with their first child. Took it before it was available to the public. Child born without ears. Severely defected. Died. Ah yes, it's sad, I'll give you that, but what great love story isn't sad? Then, what did we do with the drug? We went ahead and administered it to tens of thousands. Engel, were you alive?"

"Just barely."

"Lucky bastard. You've never seen anything like it. And the quantity. It's not prudent, at a time like that, to handshake and say, 'There's real opportunity here. This is the biggest consensual human experiment of all time.'" Watson bobbed his head, drunkenly, and pointed to a mermaid.

"Look at Poseidon go," he said.

The mermaids swam around the tank. It was harder to see the ones at the top. A larger one had her arm-fins propped on the glass directly above us.

"Come lie down on the mattress. It's first-rate. North Face."

The Gee glanced at his wristwatch. It was a wonder he allowed us to make this excursion, though judging by his reverence for Watson, I guessed he did whatever Watson wanted. Nick stepped to the mattress first. I wasn't sure. I felt like an accomplice. I could see my future self, in a courtroom, claiming ignorance.

"How do I know they're not human?" I asked.

Watson and the Gee looked at each other.

"Do they look human?" Watson asked.

"No."

"They lack the physiological and anatomical structures of humans. They're dugongs. They have remarkably dense bones. How can I explain this to you? It's like the difference between cheese and a diamond."

"Cool," I said.

"What are you going to do with them?" Nick asked. He'd taken the inflatable mattress as an opportunity to press his arm against my side.

"Engel?"

"We're looking at reduced levels of tumor necrosis factor-alpha, anti-inflammation, angiogenesis— "

Watson rose from the mattress, swayed slightly upon standing, and flailed his arms. "We're going to love them. We're just going to love them to pieces."

Fate of the Dugong

———

Scientists believe that only fifty dugong survive in the waters off Okinawa.

—Center for Biological Diversity

ON THE WAY back to the Colony, I asked Nick to stop at the convenience store outside the gates of the Nassau County Water Department.

"What do you need at the convenience store?"

"Cigarettes."

"Baby, you smoke too much."

"I know." Nick turned the car into the Quick Mart, got out, crossed to my side and opened the door. He followed me into the store. The clerk behind the counter eyed me carefully. Nick picked up a six-pack of Natural Light. He played with the key chains on the counter while I asked for Winstons.

"I have to tell you," the clerk said. "My friend Sharon Lash limps and I think you're both so brave. You too, sir. It must take a lot of faith." The clerk was now speaking directly to Nick. I call this the heart-to-heart approach. Able folks love it. It's like they can connect better with their own able kind, so they start talking about me to whomever I'm with in the third person as if I don't exist. The clerk continued, "I just look at someone like your girl-friend and I think of how incredible she is and how many hardships she must've faced. She's an inspiration."

Nick was speechless. When we got out to the car, he said, "What was that?" He took a beer from the pack and opened it.

"I should drive if you're going to drink." I didn't want to explain the clerk to Nick. The first time it happened, the first time I was with a man and called out by a complete stranger, I was outraged. I thought: How dare you interrupt my life and draw attention to the nature of my body when I don't even know you and especially when I'm trying to act cool because I happen to be sleeping with this man and I don't want him to think of me as a girl who other people pity or make brave or whatever. I don't want to be that woman. I'm not that woman. You're confusing me with someone else. I hadn't said a word.

"It's not that far," Nick said.

"I'll drive."

"It's ten miles max."

"Nick, give me the keys." He gave them to me. I adjusted the seat.

Old Faithful had been pitch-perfect. He'd developed his own technique to intercept questions from strangers. He whistled. He inflected the whistle so it sounded like "nuh-uh" or "how dare you ask her that." Sometimes he extended it and whistled the theme from *The Pink Panther* which is a sexy song if you think about it, a song about snooping around, peeping here and there, and getting hot and bothered over a flaw in a gemstone. People typically don't know what to do with a whistle in response to a question. People definitely don't know what to do with a man whistling *The Pink Panther* in a seductive manner to a woman they've just categorized as "limping girl." It was lovely to watch their faces blush and their defenses go up. Afterward, we'd get in my car, his truck, my apartment, the library, and I'd say, "Suppose you whistle to me." I don't know if anyone else can pull it off. Nick was just learning. He would need to find a technique of his own.

"Rev the engine first," Nick said. I revved it with my foot on the brake. "You look upset," he said. "Are you upset?"

"No."

"About the lady in the store?"

"No."

"About the dugong?"

"No."

I put the wagon in reverse and began backing out. "Well I'm upset. Not that it would matter to you. You're a closed garage."

I hit the brakes. "What?"

"Yeah."

"I'm sorry. Excuse me?"

"You've been excused the whole night. I get the feeling you flat-out don't like me. Don't care a continental. I take you to dinner, we see dugongs, pretty almighty if you ask me, and you don't got shit to say. How do you got nothing to say?" Nick's face was red. He pitched his straw hat into the back seat.

"Calm down," I said, reversing out of the parking spot.

"Don't tell me to calm down. I don't want to be like you, calm as fuck, hard as a tack. Do you even have a pulse?"

"I have a pulse."

"Yeah, when I'm fucking you."

I rolled my eyes. Nick saw me roll them, and that was enough, he opened the door and hit the ground.

"What the hell are you doing?" I said without raising my voice. He picked himself up, dusted his shoulders, and came around to the driver's side.

"I'm walking back."

"That's stupid. Get in the car."

"No." Nick stood beside the car, at my window, where in five seconds, I saw the option to beg—get in the car, give me a break, I'm tired, I'm nothing like Sharon Lash, you're tired, it's a long night, we're scared, they're tinkering with your dreams, they're shooting me full of stem cells, we don't know what will come of it, we can work through it, while the clerk inside stares, while I'm hearing whistles from a man who isn't you, doesn't resemble you in the least, sure, we can work it out—and I decided not to.

"Then walk," I said.

"I'm taking my hat." He opened the back door of the wagon, retrieved his hat, and began walking in the direction of the Colony.

The Hitchhiker

———

DARWIN SAT ON the side of the road with his thumb out. I pulled the car to the side. I leaned over the center console to roll down the passenger window. "I almost breezed past you."

A couple of birds flapped around him. They flew in, settled on the dashboard, and pruned each other's feathers. Darwin slammed the door on his beard, opened the door, gathered his beard in a pile on his lap, and closed the door again.

"Where to?" I drove the car off the gravel and kicked it up to fifty miles an hour.

"Tin Pan Alley."

"What's there?"

"Jazz."

"Smart-ass."

"This your carriage?"

"Nick's."

"You know who he reminds me of?"

"You haven't even met him."

"Fanny Owen." One of the birds flew to Darwin's shoulder. Darwin turned and nuzzled the bird's head with his nose. "I dated Fanny when I was eighteen. We dated for three years. Everything I said, she took it. It didn't matter what I said. I said, I'm busy with beetles, I'm reading Shakespeare, I'm addicted to natural history,

I'm going fly-fishing, I'm having doubts about the clergy, I'm pre-occupied with the countryside, I have a hundred species to study, I can't come see you for Christmas, and she took it."

"You didn't go see her for Christmas?"

"No."

"You're a dick."

"Fancy that coming from you. Didn't you evict a man from his own carriage?"

I thought of Nick, when I left him, demanding an argument I could not give him. He'd be pissed when he arrived at the Colony. He'd storm into the lounge looking for anyone. I'd heard about the women he'd been with, there were others beside the nurse, but the nurse was his favorite. She was a country girl whose father had run off. So she kept a man, called him *boy-friend*, and kept three or four others on rotation, just-in-cases, of which Nick was generally number two. He'd figured this out a while ago, made peace with it, and maybe he didn't love her now. "Sometimes it's nice not to be picked," he said, and whether he was saying this about the nurse in Verona or me, I don't know. I listened to him describe her as "full of fits" and "off her rocker" and I said yes dear, yes honey, while I thought, if you spent your twenties stuck on that type of woman, then what do you want from me? By the time Nick arrived back at the Colony, the only people awake would be Leonard or Mercedes, and I tried to stop thinking right then, because I knew just what kind of mood Nick would be in, and I knew just what kind of plans Mercedes had for him.

"He wanted to walk."

"Right."

"What happened to Fanny?"

Darwin adjusted himself in the seat. "I broke with her in

February of 1830. Same month Macaulay spoke before the House of Commons."

"Who's Macaulay?"

"If you have no sense of history, how do you live on a day-to-day basis? I brought something for you, a few papers from the Cold Spring Harbor Laboratory archive, what I like to call bloopers of scientific thought. The world is flat, for instance. Or what Priestly said about oxygen, 'Hitherto only two mice and myself have had the privilege of breathing it.' So you might get a kick out of these." Darwin pulled papers from his satchel, opened the glove box, and left them there.

"How'd you end it with Fanny?"

"She was wearing lace gloves the last time I saw her. She kept her hands clasped in front of her dress. I said, 'Fanny, I've been commissioned to go on a voyage.' Her expression did not change. 'When will you return?' she asked. I didn't know, so what could I say? Six months later, she wrote to tell me she was engaged. *I'm engaged*, she wrote. *I did not want you to hear it from someone else.* Here was a woman who had waited for me and written to me and given me everything she had for three years and all of a sudden she was engaged? I tried to read between the lines. Did she want me to sail across the Atlantic Ocean and stop the wedding? But there was no warmth in Fanny Owen's last letter. Do you get my drift? No one's too attached to who they're with."

Darwin looked out the window. I drove on. It began to sprinkle. "You could've had her if you'd wanted her. You didn't pick her. You must not've wanted her."

"What kind of poppycock hypothesis is that?"

Surprise

———

Surprises are foolish things.

—Jane Austen

I PARKED NICK'S car at the Colony. There was bird shit on the dash. I wiped it with the sleeve of my jacket. Grayson greeted me from the door of the lounge.

"There she is," Mercedes said. She had her feet on the coffee table beside three bottles of nail polish. The room reeked of acetone.

"Where have you been?" Grayson said.

"What are you doing here?"

"Surprise."

"How'd you get here?"

"I flew."

"What do you mean?"

"I flew into New York and rented a car." Grayson moved toward me. I remembered myself and smiled.

"You didn't have to." We hugged. Over his shoulder I mouthed to Mercedes: "What the fuck?" She was waving her nails through the air. She mouthed back, "You're golden" or, "You're rotten."

Grayson kissed me on the forehead and turned to face

Mercedes.

"She lives in Portland," Grayson said.

"I know."

"My aunt lives in Portland. We should visit."

I stared at Mercedes, who wiggled her toes. Grayson adjusted his glasses.

"How long were you waiting?"

"Not too long. A couple hours."

Mercedes screwed the cap on the polish and leaned forward on the couch: "I told him treatment takes a while. Dr. Deeter can be so needy."

"On your birthday? I'll have a word with Dr. Deeter, if you want." I melted a little, though I hadn't been at treatment, and though Grayson hadn't any authority to speak to the Gee.

"Give me the tour. Where do you live?"

Grayson picked up his duffel bag. On our way out the door, he turned to Mercedes. "We're coming to visit you, I don't know, maybe this summer."

We walked hand in hand across the quad.

"What's with all the shells on the ground? Is there, I don't know, a nut tree nearby?" Grayson said.

Inside my place, I looked at him. The entire time I'd known him he'd been the least spontaneous person on the planet. Suddenly, he jumped on a plane. He dressed up. He was wearing a shirt I had ordered for him from a catalogue. That shirt had lived for two years in the clothes-I-Grayson-do-not-wear drawer. He was wearing a red scarf that felt soft on my face. He smelled like Old Spice and Marlboro Lights. He smoked less than I. He could take it or leave it. I was envious and suspicious of social smokers—were they, or were they not, addicted?

"I like what you've done with the curtain," he said, ducking behind the curtain I'd hung near the bed and then reappearing. "Annie," he took off his scarf. "I've had an erection ever since I rented the car."

Did he have to call it an *erection*? Couldn't he say *hard-on*? At least we were making progress. When I first started sleeping with him, he acted as if his dick were magical and required a spell of silence. "Don't say *dick*," he said. "Should I say *cock*?" "No." "Penis?" "No." "What am I supposed to call it?"

He pulled me to him. "Yuck. What's on your jacket?"

He looked at his hand and looked at the sleeve of my jacket.

"Bird shit."

"You got shat on by a bird?"

"Yeah."

"Sounds like a rough evening." He washed his hand and took a paper towel to my sleeve.

"Grayson."

"What?"

"Nothing."

"Are you okay?"

"I'm surprised to see you."

"Good. It was a pain to convince Luther to cover my shift and add to that the plane ticket and the car."

Was he talking money? I thought I could muster the enthusiasm for sex until he started with the money. I foresaw him squinting into his checkbook, adding triple digits, carrying zeros. "I took that trip for you," he'd say. He opened the fridge and poured a glass of tea.

"I remember that photo. You were turned on. It's in your eyes."

I didn't remember being particularly turned on by anything that day. The photo was taken at my going-away party. We were sitting at the glass-topped table on the patio of his apartment. Moments before the photo, Dad, on one too many Schlitzes, had said to Grayson, "What are you going to do, be a security guard for the rest of your life? What about Annie? What are you going to do about Annie?" to which Grayson had replied by popping the top of a Stella Artois. Dad had brought a full cooler of Schlitz. "Can't afford Annie but you can I'll-be-damned afford Belgian beer." Mom pulled Dad aside and gave him a talking-to. They rejoined us with the camera. "Let's everyone smile," she'd said. I had shorter bangs then. Grayson was wearing his cop sunglasses with a blue polyester shirt. That photo made Nick call him "collared." Mercedes had said, "Is that your boyfriend? Look how happy you are." Grayson lifted me onto the sink.

Emergency Plan
for When You Need to Make Love
Without Being There

———

Turn out the lights. This is what God made night for. God said, I can't look at you anymore. I've looked at you long enough. Day and night, He created them.

Adopt a persona. I like Isabelle Huppert, the French star, whose favorite children's stories are *The Little Mermaid* and *The Little Match Girl*. One dies of love, one of cold. Both employ the word *little* in the title, which is what you must do when you make love without being there: you must wane.

Say to your partner: "While we are being wild, I hope you are remembering my childhood."

Your partner will have an onslaught of feelings. It is polite to treat others with kindness and to anticipate their feelings. Some feelings may manifest themselves in the following conversations:

Talk of true love

The time–space continuum

Quantifying love via bizarre metaphor, e.g., I love you more than apples love cores.

Analysis of habeas corpus (Who is keeping whom in captivity)

Who is Keeping Whom
in Captivity

———

Many of the King's subjects have been and hereafter may be
long detained in prison.

— HABEAS CORPUS ACT

"I'VE BEEN THINKING," Grayson said. We were in the bed
under the alcove. His arms were around me. I had my back to his
chest and he was smothering me. I knew that I could not broach
the topic of breakup in such a position. It goes against the plan to
make love without being there and follow it with, "Hey, this isn't
working." I missed Nick. But what if I broke up with Grayson
and Nick lost interest? I broke up with Grayson and it was a mistake? What if I couldn't dedifferentiate? I wanted to ask Darwin
about the official definition of survival of the fittest. Was it simply
plotting whom one would next fuck as an insurance against being
left fuckless? And if not, why then, when Darwin had been married happily to Emma, when I'd thought myself partnered happily
with Grayson, was it not enough?

"I've been thinking about what I sent you," Grayson said.
I hadn't opened the package. I had forgotten. "Maybe it was
presumptuous."

"I liked it."

"You did?"

"Yep."

"Why didn't you say anything?" Grayson sat up to gauge my reaction.

"I was going to."

"I'm relieved. I was worried you'd think it was cheap."

I thought of anything cheap Grayson would buy. Most things Grayson bought were cheap. He was a dollar-store guy. He clipped coupons and bargain hunted at Salvation Army. Last Christmas he gave me burned copies of his Criterion Collection DVDs.

"And after two years, I've been thinking of buying you a ring."

"Are you serious?" I said, regretting I'd said it. I sounded incredulous—like how could he even suggest such a thing?—while it had been my suggestion, standing in the aisles of Kroger, where we shopped for organic spinach, as if it takes two people to pick leaves, but we shopped together, if I was going, he was going, and to the checkout we went. I flipped through bridal magazines, pointed to cushion and emerald and fancy cuts: "What about this one?" I'd met this man, who was now piss-poorly proposing to me, on the steps in front of Perkins Library. I was coming out of the library, it had not gone well in the library, and he was marching on the steps. He nearly ran over me. After he apologized, sorry for knocking into you, after I apologized, sorry for screaming at you, we slept together. It had been a relief to meet Grayson. It meant I did not have to think about the person working in Perkins Library. "Yes," I said. "I'm yours every night." Though when Grayson gestured, or did anything that likened him to Old Faithful, I got teary-eyed and Grayson would ask, "What's the matter?"

I took from Grayson everything I'd wanted from Old Faithful, like spending the night, and sleeping in, and a vacation to a log cabin in the Blue Ridge Mountains. Our first year was one big apologia: Grayson apologizing for not understanding what exactly it was I needed, was I depressed, and me apologizing in secret for knowing, even then, that what I needed could not be found in who I was with. But maybe that would change! Maybe I could fall in love with Grayson ex post facto! That was the idea. I read somewhere that a relationship ends how it begins, on an identical pitch. If that were true, then ours would end in reciprocal apologetic fucking. What had I loved about him? Was everyone a catalyst for the one before?

Grayson would find someone else. There were women in Durham less complicated, such as his ex-girlfriend, who worked at Nine West. She didn't know who I was. She was in a bad mood when I visited. She was tending to several customers. I didn't like her because she appeared in fine form—hips, knees, calves—and because she appeared not to know what she had. "I need the left shoe," I told her. She wrinkled her nose as if she was annoyed. "Because the right foot is fake. So it really doesn't matter if the right shoe fits. Sorry. I should've told you." I heard myself explaining more than I usually explained to shoe clerks. Something about her face was compelling. Her eyes were sort of crossed, not crossed entirely, but you know how some people's irises center inward more than others? She looked high maintenance. She wore matching jewelry and professional highlights. She was wearing strapless sandals. When she turned away, I imagined Grayson taking her from behind.

"Do they fit?" she asked.

After I met her, she started busting in on my dreams. She didn't look anything like herself, but I knew who she really was. She was Grayson's girlfriend, before me, in pigtails. She said things like "I don't love you" and "I have to pretend to," substitution, I get it, but the weirdest dream had us—me, her, Grayson—at a campsite with a roaring fire and preacher. Grayson was passing out pamphlets. I was mortified to be wearing a crossing guard's yellow vest with an *X* painted on it. She was stretched out on the lawn. He introduced us flippantly. She kept playing with the hair at the end of her pigtail. They spent the whole time talking, heatedly, passionately, in whispers, her beside him on the lawn, her taking his thumb in her mouth, and the sermon in the background: "All trees which do not produce good fruit must be cut down and thrown into the fire."

Grayson kept in touch with her. Every once in a while, there'd be a lunch. "I don't understand why you need a lunch," I'd say. "Unlike you, I think of my exes as friends for life." "That's absurd," I'd say. I'd sit at home and imagine what they were talking about. What did Grayson tell her about me? I imagine people say, "She's five four, brown hair, brown eyes, bangs," and when that isn't enough, they add, "She has a fake leg." This explains why people, upon meeting me, looked for the leg. I had the best prosthetist in the tri-state area. The technical apparatus of my leg was shipped from Germany. Despite all these provisions, I spent the first ten minutes smiling and talking emphatically. Grayson had told me that his ex was an aspiring actress. He met her on the set of a college play, *Oklahoma!* or *Guys and Dolls*, I forget. He never described her physically. Just said she "meant a lot."

She got married. We went to the wedding. "You came into the store," she said, which caused a brief balloon to pop over our heads as Grayson put together that I'd gone to her store, that I'd known where she worked from him, and that I'd done this behind his back. "Why didn't you say anything?" she said. What was I supposed to say? One time before Grayson went on a lunch, I told him it made me feel strange because he'd been inside her body. "Annie," he'd said. "What? It's true. You've been literally five inches inside that woman's body. And lunch with her is supposed to reflect a level of maturity? You'll be within five inches of her again, and we know where that got you."

After champagne, cake, a bad deejay, I wanted to go. Grayson discovered his lost acrobatic self and was doing splits to Blondie on the dance floor. I was embarrassed. He was mad in the car because I had not stayed long enough or because his first love had pledged herself to someone else or because I'd gone to see her without him or because the rearview mirror he liked to look in had become opaque. He defended her when I quipped that the bridesmaids' dresses were ugly and the deejay was bad. "She meant a lot to me," he said. Ain't it love, what you don't have?

"Annie, do you want to marry me?" Grayson searched for my hand under the sheets. I couldn't see his face in the dark and I was glad he couldn't see mine.

"Sure."

"You do?"

"Yeah."

"Not exactly the response I was expecting."

"What were you expecting?"

"A little excitement."

"I am excited."

"Annie, what is going on?"

"I love you more than apples love cores. More than gefilte fish."

"Gefilte fish?"

"They come in jars."

"Since when are you buying gefilte fish?"

"Grayson, stop overanalyzing."

"Overanalyzing?"

"I'm tired. I'm having stem cells pumped into my body."

Grayson turned, fluffed his pillow sternly, and slammed his head down. He huffed, puffed, and sighed. When he could not settle, he got up and walked to the kitchen. I heard him turn the tap on and drink. I wanted him to bring the water back to bed. Bring it back to bed, I was thinking, bring it here, and drink it here, and put it by the bed. Don't stand there, clanking the glass in the sink, washing the glass with the sponge, clanking the glass some more. When he came back to bed his hands were cold and wet. A while later, we woke in a jolt to—

"Open the Door I Walked
Eight Hundred Miles to Say I'm Sorry
but You're No Daisy Yourself"

GRAYSON WAS FIRST out of bed, on the ground with both feet, and rubbing his eyes. I pulled the sheet over my head and thought, "What the fuck kind of realistic dreamscape is this?" I heard pounding on the door. I heard Grayson shuffling, and I better stop him, I thought, I better say or do something quick.

"Anne, give me a break," Nick shouted through the door.

"Who is that?" Grayson said.

"He's crazy," I said. "Everyone here is."

"It's not like I wanted to walk."

"Do you know that guy?"

"Yeah."

"Even my feet are sorry."

"What is he doing here?"

"He's crazy."

"Even my big toe."

"Should I open the door?"

"I'll get it." I got out of the bed. I took the sheet with me. I looked for my leg. Where had we left it? I hopped to the kitchen with a sheet around my body. I found my leg in the kitchen plugged into the wall. At least that was good, clear-headed thinking. Grayson stood beside the bed with his hands on his waist.

"Anne, what's taking so long? Open the door."

It took me about ten seconds to put on the leg.

"You're not even dressed," Grayson said. He had managed to find his glasses and boxers. He turned the lights on.

"So? It's three in the morning." I figured I should act as lax and carefree and asleep as possible. No big deal. Nick's here. I opened the door. It was storming outside. Nick leaned against the doorframe with his head on his forearm.

"Finally," he said. "Anne you really ought not let a man—"

Nick looked up and saw Grayson, who had, out of some instinct, picked up the hammer from the kitchen table.

"Whoa," Nick said.

"Grayson."

"What?"

"Whoa."

"Put the hammer down."

"What are you doing here?"

"I came to see Anne."

"Nick, did you have to walk?"

"Yes, I had to walk."

"I thought you had a ride."

"What ride?" Grayson said.

"From treatment. We carpool." Roll with it, Nick, I thought, please roll with it.

"Your car's not here," Grayson said.

Oh fuck, I don't have a car, I thought. In my dreamscape, I had a car, and it was Nick's car, and mine. "It's arranged. Buddy system."

Nick interrupted, "Yeah, yeah, sure. Carpools. She left me at treatment."

"I thought you were riding with Mercedes."

"I don't want rides with Mercedes."

"All right," Grayson said, dropping the hammer to his side. "It's three o'clock in the morning. I'm sure Annie's sorry."

Nick stood in the doorway, inspecting Grayson. "You have different-colored eyes."

Grayson looked perturbed. He put his hand to his brow. In a fight, Nick would win. Grayson had never fought in his life. Nick didn't appear to be drunk, but even if he were, he would still win. Outside, it was raining. Grayson, in his ethical hospitality, might invite Nick in. I tried to think of something, anything, to stop this from happening. Nick was soaking wet. Water dripped off him onto the floor.

"You're making a mess."

"You never told me he had different-colored eyes."

"I didn't?"

"You're the boyfriend."

"Grayson."

"I'm Nick."

"All right, Nick, good to meet you. I've heard about you."

"Really?"

"You're a friend of Annie's. Aren't you from Fargo?"

"Madison."

"Nonetheless. Looks like you need a towel." Grayson went to the bathroom for a towel. While he was gone, Nick mouthed, "Get it over with or I will."

"Here you go," Grayson said.

"Tremendous," Nick said. He wiped the towel down one arm, then another, and patted his chest. He handed the towel to me. I had the towel in one hand and the sheet held to my chest with the other.

"Let us know if you need anything else."

"Can I get some of that tea Anne makes? She makes it so good I can hardly get enough."

Grayson looked at me. I looked down at our feet, at the slats of the floor, at the sand between them. I laid the towel on a chair.

"Annie, put some clothes on," Grayson said.

"Nothing I ain't seen," Nick said.

"Nick's a playboy," I said laughing. "Aren't you?"

"I've had better days."

"The women at the Green House chase him."

Grayson handed Nick a glass of tea. He pulled out a chair from the table and offered it to me. I walked to the coatrack for my purse and searched for cigarettes.

"This late?" Grayson protested.

I lit one, being careful not to let the sheet drop. When I looked down to light the cigarette, I noticed a damp spot on the sheet.

Grayson offered the chair to Nick.

"No thanks."

"Well, I'm going to sit down." Grayson turned the chair out from the table, toward us.

Nick leaned against the stove. He took a swig of tea like it was whiskey.

I ashed on the floor.

"I'm wondering," Grayson said, and I thought it sounded familiar, it sounded like the beginning of a treatise on Kafka's emotions or Rothko's genius and I prayed for these topics, they were topics I'd heard a hundred times, and I wanted to hear them, right then, I was ready for any variation on a Grayson diatribe. "I'm wondering what Annie's told you about me. That's always fun. Finding out, I don't know, how you're portrayed. What has she told you?"

"What has she told me?"

"I bet she says I'm a cheapskate. I am a cheapskate. What else has she told you?" I thought of many things I had not told Nick; many times I'd tucked my tongue in the back of my mouth.

"For example," Grayson said. "I'm remembering you now. You're the one from Madison. Annie called you spon-taneous. That's how she said it: *spon-taneous*. You might not know this about her—because you haven't known her as long as I have—but she has this cadence. She has this beat to how she talks. Sometimes I call her just to hear her say things the way she says them."

I had a cadence? What was this? Where was this coming from? He never complimented. Apparently I had to suck someone else's dick for Grayson to compliment.

"What does she say about me?"

"Let me think."

"There must be something."

"I can't think of anything."

"Nothing?"

"We don't talk about you."

Grayson put his elbows on his knees and clasped his hands. "She must've told you something."

"You're the boyfriend. That's all I got." Nick looked at me. "Should I go?"

I didn't say anything. Nick took the towel from the chair where I was sitting and returned it to the bathroom. He was leaving. He had one hand on the doorknob.

"That's my hammer," Nick said.

Grayson looked at the hammer. His eyes glanced over the bungalow, as if he suddenly realized he recognized nothing, not the hammer, not the appliances, not the furniture, not me, and we could belong to anybody. Grayson gave the hammer to Nick.

"Keep it," Nick said. "I live here."

The Old High Way of Love

_____

It had all seemed happy.

—Yeats, "Adam's Curse"

AFTER NICK LEFT, Grayson took the broom from the wall and swept cigarette ashes from the floor. I stood beside the table and watched as he swept around my feet. He shook the dustpan in the trash. I'd forgotten to replace the garbage bag. "Where do you keep the garbage bags?"

"Same place I always do."

He opened the cabinet under the sink. "What about the shoes? Still wearing them for the same reason you always do?"

I stood beside the table and watched him change the garbage bag and shake the dustpan. Go ahead, I thought. Whatever you're going to do, go ahead. I stood very still.

He leaned the broom against the wall. "I'm playing some music," he said. He shuffled around in his duffel bag, looking for tunes, probably Grieg.

I didn't know what to say. I tried to think of Grayson but all I could think of was Nick walking all the way from the Nassau County Water Department, arriving at the Colony, passing the door to the lounge and walking instead to my door, presenting himself at my door, using his signature wisecracking. Nick expected me to fling open the door and receive him. And if I had? If Grayson hadn't come? Nick wasn't the type to sweep the floor.

I thought: Why are you sweeping the floor when I'm despicable? It's exactly like you've suspected. You have a reason to be self-righteous, entitled, disgusted with the world. The world is disgusting. What are you going to do? He searched through his duffel bag. Moved shirts around. Unpacked and packed. He wasn't going to do anything. I was disgusted with him, and I knew it was fucked up to be disgusted with him, since it was me who'd been caught, and I knew too that I should've told him. I didn't move an inch. I stood still. Grayson played music. It was soft, dark, piano. I decided the best move, the only move I had available to me, the only one I could think of, was letting the sheet drop and climbing onto the kitchen table.

"I'm heading out tomorrow."

"Why?"

"I want to see museums in the city. I can write it off. I want to see the MoMA."

We went to bed. I went first. I picked the sheet from the floor and tucked it into the bottom corners. Grayson puttered in the kitchen. I pulled a slip from under the bed and put it on. The piano slowed and the room was quiet. I spread the comforter over the sheet and arranged the pillows. I crawled into the bed.

"You forgot to plug in." He took the cord from the floor and connected it from leg to outlet. "What would you do without me to remind you?"

He climbed into bed. He waited until I was almost asleep. I was in that place, with my eyes rolled back, that liminal state, and wherever I was headed, the night had not happened. I was lying on my side, facing the wall, when I felt him on my back.

I reached behind and felt for it. I had to find it through boxers and that wasn't right; Nick didn't wear boxers. Oh God, it wasn't Nick. I snatched my hand back. I opened my eyes and saw my hand beside the pillow, saw my ring finger, saw a million nights of Grayson asking permission. Why was he asking? Did I always have to invite him? What did it matter if I had two legs if I had to spend the rest of my life inviting him? I remembered the evening. I saw the evening before me, we had been asleep, Nick had woken us, Nick had stayed, and it was obvious. What else happened? Was Grayson mad? Nothing else. He played music. He was leaving in the morning.

I wondered how he'd do it, if there would be him coming, as he usually did, on my stomach. He was breathing unsteadily. I wanted him to take control. He might do it. He might can. He rolled onto his back. He wasn't going to do anything. He wasn't going to, after all, do anything. I thought, of course, how exactly like you you are, you don't do anything, who did I think you were? You're not the one who does things. I have to do things, suggest them, plead for them, all the words, all the positions, all the recommendations, I do them. You can't possibly take control. Is that it? You rolling on your back. Are we finished? You coward. "Honey," I said. I wasn't sure if he had fallen asleep.

I heard the sheets rustle. He was taking off his boxers. He put his hands on my shoulders. He dug his fingers into my shoulders and turned me on my back. I thought, Of course, yes, where have you been? I've been trying to tell you, it's good, we're good, we'll be fine, this is what I meant. I had no inclination to stop him or start him or help him or pretend. I said nothing. He hooked his thumb under the strap of my slip and pulled until it came unstitched. It made a noise. Then the other strap. He grabbed the slip at the neck and pulled it down. "Where have you been,"

I said. He put his hand over my mouth. He pressed his hand over my mouth while he did it. I felt the pillow under my head. I thought, you can you can. He took his hand off my mouth. His hands were on either side of me. Palms flat on the bed. I said nothing. I made none of my usual flourishes. It was the most there I had ever been for him. His right hand moved. Where was it going? There wasn't anything there to go to. I got up, propped my elbows on the pillow, to watch him. I saw his hand reach for it. Oh not that, I thought, not that, that's not even there, don't do that, it's not even there, it's not meant for anything, who is that, you can't, please, not that. "You're always into it," he said in between. "You're always—always—into it—why aren't you— aren't you—why aren't you now?"

Appointment

———

I WENT TO have my shadow taken. I disrobed in the bathroom and put on the gown. I sat on the bed of the X-ray machine and waited. He would take my shadow and put it to the light. He would point with the end of his Montblanc to various regions of black, gray, and white. Without the light, he couldn't see the X-ray. It's easy to forget this. The inadequacy of the human eye. No one calls it a failure; it's just the way we're made.

The Gee was late. Grayson was in a Hertz rental car on a highway. He wanted to see MoMA. Earlier in the morning, he woke before me, took a shower, and got dressed. He pulled a chair from the kitchen table and set it beside the bed. He was staring at me when I opened my eyes. "Were you going to, I don't know, tell me? How long has it been going on?" He was relaxed and mellow but he had this little catch in his throat. I wasn't fully awake and I was thinking the conversation would go better if I could just smoke a cigarette and put some clothes on and then I'd tell him that true, I was cheating, but that I had these reasons, these valid reasons, what were they again? "What's the story, Annie? Did he have to convince you, or were you just begging for it like you usually are?" There was that catch in his throat. It sounded like a cough wanted to be a laugh. "Yeah, you were begging for it. I know you, and you were begging for it." He didn't sound like himself and it scared me up and out of bed, hopping to the bathroom, where I shut the door. "Were you with him while I was sitting in the lounge waiting for you? Because I thought you felt loose, I mean the first time; the second time, well, I didn't really care what it felt like."

The Gee walked through the double doors. "How are you?"

"Good."

"How did you fare in last night's storm? We call that a nor'easter. It dropped ten degrees in ten minutes. Now that's a bear of a winter." He consulted his clipboard. "You and Nick make it home safely?"

"Yeah."

"No glitches?"

"No."

"Do me a favor?"

"Okay?"

"Don't be destructive in your emotional relationships with fellow Colonists."

"Excuse me?"

"Nick Burkowitz."

"What about him?"

"There's a reason we chose this particular group. And there's a reason we have you cordoned off here."

"I don't know if you've noticed, and I don't mean to tattle, but you don't have us all that cordoned off. Leonard goes to Montauk."

"Leonard isn't a suicide. Nick, on the other hand."

"Nick is the happiest guy I know."

"Are you familiar with LeDoux and Gazzaniga?"

"Who?"

"Joseph LeDoux and Michael Gazzaniga. They suggest that

we're not happy. That we're miserable, wretched creatures who rationalize ourselves into believing we're happy. They suggest that we don't know why we do what we do. We don't consciously decide anything. We figure it out in the dream space, in the unconscious, mainly, and the rest we figure out based on what other people want. So if you were to tell Nick, 'I don't want you anymore,' then he might tell himself that he doesn't want himself anymore. We saw a complete lack of desire in the brain scan this morning."

"You're not supposed to be telling me this. You can't tell me this. What about privacy?"

"A person's health—"

"I'm sure Nick's health is fine. I'm not breaking up with him or anything. I have a boyfriend."

"That's one of many reasons we favored your application."

"Because of my boyfriend?"

"Among other factors. Our brain systems operate without conscious knowledge and—"

"What are you getting at?"

"I'm keeping an eye on Nick's brain and you're impeding the process."

"No."

"Anne."

"What?"

"Please remain on the best of terms with Nick."

"You can't tell me—"

"We would prefer if you—"

"You're worried that I'm affecting Nick's treatment?"

"This morning's scan seems to indicate—"

"People have lives."

"He's upset. Do you know why?"

"I have no idea."

"Interesting."

"Anyway, I have a boyfriend."

"Excellent. That's excellent to hear."

I'd tell the Gee whatever he needed to hear. The guy was giving me the creeps with his candid query into my personal life. I wasn't too worried about Nick. Nick had been in and out of love with the nurse. Whatever blip on the brain scan the Gee saw was reasonable. I just needed to see Nick and make sure.

"The Regenerator is on its way. How are you doing? How are you feeling?"

"Fine."

"Do you have any questions?"

"No."

"No questions whatsoever?"

"I'm depleted."

"To be expected, when you consider the stress along with the pluripotent stem cell injections. It wasn't an early night last night."

"No. It wasn't."

"I'll put you on a multivitamin."

"I'm already on one."

The Gee sat on the stool with wheels and brought himself closer to me. "I'm going to take a few X-rays, before and after shots, that type of thing." He gave me the metal shield for my ovaries and left the room.

"Be still," he said. He didn't need to say it. Each time he took an X-ray he acted like I'd never had one before.

"Hold your breath."

A New Kind of Rays

———

I have discovered something interesting, but I do not know
whether or not my observations are correct.

—WILHELM CONRAD RÖNTGEN,
Nobel physicist, to a friend

THE FIRST TIME Röntgen met his wife, he held his breath. He
met her in a cafe. Her father was Mr. Ludwig, the owner of the
cafe. Her uncle was Otto Ludwig, the poet, critic, loved Shakespeare, found fault with Schiller, which was not cool in his day.
Her uncle published tragedies in five acts, such as *The Forest War-
den*, which begins, "Here comes the music."

Röntgen's family was more humble. His father spun cloth.
Röntgen wore a beard like the rest, deep-set eyes, dark suits and
ties. He came into the cafe and there she was. She took his breath
away. He came again to the cafe. He was clumsy. His students
gave him poor ratings: "He talks too fast" and "He doesn't make
any sense." He preferred to stay home. She did too. A pair they
made. Married. Wanted babies. Couldn't. They lived like this:
Him in the basement with tubes, coils, charges, electrodes, and
cardboard, her upstairs, sick in the sleigh bed. One night he called
up to her. He needed to see about something. She gathered her

petticoats. What time was it? What did he want now? She gave
him her hand. He put her hand in the path of the rays over a pho-
tographic plate. They held their breath.

Swan Lake premiered in St. Petersburg.

The Importance of Being Earnest premiered in London.

The first movie premiered in Paris.

The bones of Mrs. Röntgen's hand premiered in Europe.

"I have seen my death!" she said.

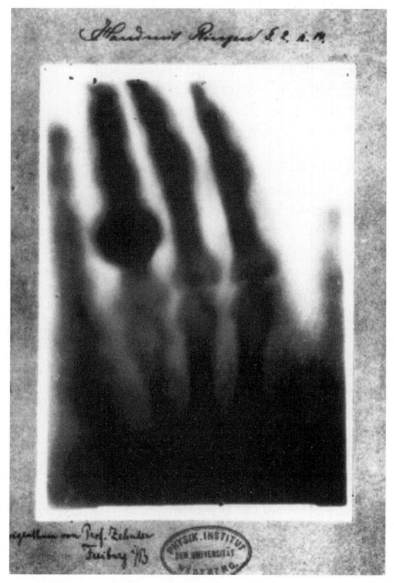

Figure 1. *Hand mit Ringen* (Hand with rings): Print of the first X-ray.

The Stone and the Watch

———

I CALLED NICK and he didn't answer. I ran into Eliot who said Nick couldn't be better. It felt awful to hear about Nick from someone other than Nick. I wanted to interrupt Eliot and say, "Yeah, I know he went out in his station wagon. I noticed it wasn't in the parking lot. He does that. He goes out to the dunes or he goes to that one road next to the harbor. I know him better then you." Instead, I listened to Eliot list the specifics of his last Nick encounter. I spent hours loitering in the lounge, watching flat screen and waiting for Nick to check his mail. I ran into Leonard and he said, "Youngblood's at the Green House." It was as if they'd been put up to say these things to me. On my walk from the lounge back to Bungalow North, I ran into Darwin. He was on his knees looking at a stone and a wristwatch. "What are you doing?"

"I'm trying to figure something out." He pointed with one finger to the stone and then to the wristwatch. He tied his beard in a knot and threw it over his shoulder. I looked around. I could see my breath in front of me. To the far right, near the road, Simon poured rock salt on the cement. Otherwise, the quad was empty.

"If you came upon this stone, what would you say?"

"I'd say, 'Darwin put a stone on the yellow line of the parking lot.'"

"No, no. You're not getting it. Pretend you happened upon the stone. Just happened upon it. What would you say?"

I inspected the stone. It was flat and gray. It looked like several other stones lying in the parking lot.

"I probably wouldn't say anything."

"Precisely. You'd think the stone had been there all along." Darwin pointed to the watch. "And if you came across this watch lying here in the parking lot, what would you say?"

"I'd say, 'Somebody lost their watch.'"

"A-ha! Somebody lost it. And why in the world would you think somebody lost a watch?"

"Because somebody did. Watches don't belong on the ground in parking lots."

"Where do watches belong?"

"On wrists."

"Are we born wearing watches?"

I thought maybe this was a trick question. "Sort of?"

"I wasn't born wearing a watch. Were you?"

"Darwin, can we talk about this over a beer?"

"Help me up." I gave him my arm and we walked toward Sandy's Bar. We walked along the shore beside several overturned boats. Darwin wanted to take a boat out to sea but I was too cold.

"Body temperature," he said. "I do miss that."

We walked into Sandy's and ordered Guinness. "I can't believe you've never heard of the stone and the watch. I was tested on that material. The proctor was a grizzly man who quizzed me over and over, stone, watch, stone, watch. Is there a God? Is there a God? Why is there?"

"A lot has changed since Cambridge, buddy."

"And recently, I tried reading *Much Ado About Nothing*, and I agree, it is much ado about nothing. I find it so intolerably dull that it puts me to sleep." Darwin and I drank our beers. He said he was sorry for going on and on about philosophies, literatures, Fanny Owen; he didn't know what had come over him. He'd been thinking about his college days. "Back then we didn't shack up. Back then an aunt served crumpets. So you can imagine how far along I got with Fanny Owen. Nothing. Hardly anything. Until. Which is not to say I regret Emma."

"Until what?"

"I grew up with Emma, you know, she was my cousin." He hadn't answered the question. Something had happened but Darwin wouldn't say what. I wondered if my opinion of him mattered. Was that it? Lola May Hatley, great-grandmother, matriarch, tells us over and over again, "When I die, don't talk about me. If you got any questions down your throat, better ask them now." When one of us got up the nerve to ask a question, such as "How many times were you married?" she'd hedge the question, she'd hem and haw. She'd been married five times. We lost track of her, briefly, in Korea. It was rumored, in our family, that Lola May married for the honeymoon. She left for Korea on one honeymoon and returned to the States on another. She traveled around the world this way. Now, back at her homestead in Hickory, with all the husbands dead, she kept a conspicuous handyman in a rocking chair.

"Do you fancy any cousins?" Darwin asked.

"That's not done much nowadays."

"I sometimes think I loved Emma best. She was with my brother when it clicked. She wasn't really ever with him, you understand, she wasn't with him in the shack-up way. It was just the intimation that she was with him. That's all it took for me to . . . my brother, rest in peace, had a thing for married women. It was the scandal of our family. He went to Emma and, I don't remember precisely, you'll have to ask her. She intones him by pitching her voice, and he said, Emma, if we could act properly together, as a couple, if we could act properly, then that would spare me the libel, the imposition, of my involvement with Wedgewood's wife. He didn't name the woman. It was just like him to spare her name from mentioning. Emma, who never refused a pauper, much less family, complied. I saw Emma with my brother at the Winter Pageant and I felt like ripping the bloke's head off. I never had such rage. I proposed to Emma thereafter."

A group of fisherman at the other end of the bar settled their account and left. The sun was setting. "How are things with Nick? How's he in bed?"

"Darwin."

"What?"

"I don't want to talk crudely about Nick."

"Yes, we must be civilized."

"I don't want to ruin it by talking crudely."

"You're rather Victorian all of a sudden."

Calling Around

———

DARWIN WENT OUT to sea. I was drunk. I walked home and called Nick. The Architecture Channel played in the background. A group of architects stood around looking at the House of the Future, which had been built for Disney in 1974. The house was fiberglass.

"Thank you for answering the phone. Now get here," I said. "They're going to blow this house up on the flat screen. Get here and watch it with me. They're going to blast it. *Pa-shoo.* Like that. *Pa-shoo. Pa-shoo.*"

"Are you drinking?"

"Absolutely not."

The demolition crew stood around and scratched their heads.

"Sounds like you're drinking."

"You're going to miss it."

They tried a wrecking ball. It bounced off. Jackhammers poked holes through the fiberglass.

"I'm busy."

"You're not busy. I know you and you're not. Why would you say that to me? You're watering plants. Don't you want to see me?"

"Baby, I don't think now's a good time."

"Don't you want to see the House of the Future? Don't you desire anything? How are your plants?"

"I got hyacinth all over the place. I got more hyacinth than I know what to do with."

"Are you hungry?"

"I just ate."

"Don't you want to see me?"

"Baby, I want to. Give it time."

"You used to couldn't wait to see me. Now you've done it. You got what you wanted and you don't want it anymore. Is that it? You don't want anything? I don't want you either. I was calling just to tell you that."

The House of the Future had to be removed part by part by squeezing it into pieces with choker cables. I got drunker. I put on my peekaboos and catwalked the bungalow. I called Grayson at nine. I was drinking gin and tonic and looking in the mirror. It had seemed irreconcilably over once before and that had turned out reconcilable. "Is this going to turn out reconcilable?" I said to his voice mail. "Because I'm kind of trying to build my House of the Future over here." I waited maybe ten minutes for him to call back. When I was his girlfriend, it took less than ten minutes for him to call back. I got voice mail again: "You are an asshole. I hate you. You owe me an apology." An hour later, he returned the call.

Grayson's Response

————

HE SAID HE didn't want to talk about anything he wasn't sorry for. Then he said how could I even begin to accuse him of, to blame him for, when it was me leading him to believe everything was FINE when really I was the one lying. He said it was incomprehensible, unless, unless, was this my version of REVENGE for Abigail because if it was, then he wanted me to know, he wanted everyone to know, his relationship with Abigail was professional, was COMPLETELY PLATONIC no matter what I thought, he had not ever thought of her in that way, he had only thought of her as, he didn't know, receptionist, the woman who greeted him at the beginning and end of the day, but now that I mentioned it, maybe he should think of her as something MORE since I obviously had no respect for him or, he didn't know, myself for that matter, I had no respect for, and no wonder I was acting distant when he visited, and he couldn't believe he had PROPOSED to me, he couldn't believe we were that CLOSE and don't worry, he UNDERSTOOD that I was cavorting around, living it up, wearing my peekaboos, and he wasn't sorry for, what did I expect, what had it been, NOT EVEN two months, and while he understood that people have needs, what was I, a NYMPHOMANIAC, was it really difficult to keep satiated, and though he did not believe in regrets, I was certainly making him a BELIEVER IN REGRETS, because he regretted, he didn't know, everything, he wished he'd never met me, since all I did was give it out, give it out, give it out, some things you can't change, and there really was something WRONG with me. And did the last TWO YEARS mean nothing, was I going to, he didn't know, TELL HIM, or was I going to carry on like NOTHING, and maybe it would've made a difference if I had, he didn't know, tried HONESTY for once in my life and he didn't think it was a good idea for us to be friends.

If Cars Could Talk to Each Other

———

Remember when we stayed in the garage when it rained?

The Renaissance

———

To explain all nature is too difficult a task for any one man or even for any one age.

—Isaac Newton

MERCEDES DROPPED OFF a bag of Cheez-Its and a Hallmark card. She was wearing a sweater, with the block letters *PTK*, a pleated skirt, and black patent stilettos. She reminded me of Emily Smoak, dear Emily Smoak, dearly beloved Emily Smoak, cheerleader at Hickory High, on-again, off-again best friend. How did she smell like that? I saw Emily Smoak with the roll-on bottle of essential oil though she refused to tell me which oil was essential. "Get your own," she said. I saw her roll it on her wrists, up her arms, down her shirt. Emily Smoak bought hers from the head shop where her boyfriend, a lanky guy named Beef Jones, bought his bongs. Emily Smoak was rumored to screw the gym teacher in his Mazda Miata before the bell for first period. That early in the morning? "Emily Smoak is always raging for it," they said. "What I wouldn't give to do Emily Smoak." "I'm calling because I heard you were friends with Emily Smoak." "I'd never cheat on you with that slut Emily Smoak." "Are you going to the party at Emily Smoak's?" "I might have cheated on you with that slut Emily

Smoak." She smelled like musk, vanilla, magnolia, cinnamon, and none of these. I tried a dozen oils and still never managed to smell like her. "I like to think," she said, "that one day Beef Jones will be walking his wife to the Victoria's Secret, getting something to spice up their defunct sex life, and he'll smell a woman who smells like me, and he'll think of me, and remember with deep sorrow and regret how I used to afford him the pleasure of sitting on his face." Emily Smoak was lovely.

"I'm on viral vector therapy," Mercedes said, patting her side with one hand and clutching the doorframe with the other.

"Are you okay?"

"I have to hold onto things. Open the card."

What occasion did the card mark? What did a photo of a puppy dog in a pail of water mean? Why were people confusing? "Thanks."

"I ran into your man in the parking lot." The inside of the card read: *Remember that many others are thinking of you and adding their strength to yours during this time.* "He said it didn't go so well."

"Do you want to come in?"

"I'm just stopping by. I have a meeting with Pierre Faivre in a few. Sponsorship. Anyway, I wanted to say oops about the other night. I tried to cover for you. I could not—for the life of me— figure out what was keeping you. Where were you?"

"I was having dinner."

"He called your cell, like, five times."

"I was having dinner with Nick."

Mercedes smiled. "You whore, you were not."

"I was."

"Hot Jeans? You were having dinner with Hot Jeans?"

"Yeah."

She gasped, took her hand from the doorframe, and covered

her mouth. She lifted off the ground. I looked down and her feet were not touching the ground. She was off the ground. When people go off the ground, they usually come back to the ground, and I waited. I thought maybe time was fucking with me, suddenly the world had become slo-mo, or I was seeing things. When I couldn't wait any longer for Mercedes' feet to be on the ground again, I reached up and grabbed her by the arm and yanked. I yanked her arm as hard as I could. She landed.

"Jesus, Anne."

"What?"

"My arm."

"I was trying to help."

"I have to hold onto things."

"Why do you have to hold onto things?"

"Did you not see me?"

"Yes. I saw you. What was that?"

"It's a side effect. Of the viral vector therapy. They give me something they're calling fugitclonal antibodies."

"Shut the fuck up."

"Anne, you're out of control."

"I'm out of control?"

"You're too funny."

"You lifted off the ground."

"I had the doorframe, then you said that thing about Nick. It was shocking, it shocked the bejesus out of me, and I let go of the doorframe." Mercedes clung to the door with one hand and with the other hand she straightened her sweater, looked down at herself, and then back up at me. My mouth was wide open. "I told you, I have to hold onto things. I got a system worked out. When I'm in the house I hold onto a chair, table, bookshelf, counter, towel rack. And when I go outside, I walk next to a building. If I'm crossing the lawn, I wear my heels. I step down hard so the heels stick in the ground."

"Are you okay?"

"Great."

"And the Gee? What does he say?"

"He suggested wearing a rope with sandbags around my waist. Can you see me wearing a rope and sandbags? Now time-out. What happened?"

I forgot what I was supposed to be telling Mercedes. The woman had just risen on my doorstep. I did not believe in magic. I did not believe in illusionists. People did not rise off the ground unless they were jumping rope, or jumping jacks, or jumping. And they always, always came back down. Mercedes was waiting for me to say something.

"You can tell me about Nick. What happened?"

I was flustered. If the Gee gave Mercedes something that made her lose contact with the earth as I knew it, then what was he giving me? I'd never liked the guy to begin with. I'd wanted him to be a Mister Rogers type, let me be your neighbor, let me look at your genes, let me inject you full of stem cells, please. And with Mercedes floating, I saw his every move as sinister, him as the evil scientist, but he wasn't that either, there was no force involved. Any one of us could leave if we elected to. I thought of the dugongs. The dugongs couldn't leave. They'd been taken thousands of miles away from the Coral Sea and plunked into a water tower. For what? So the Gee and James D. Watson could pump them full of thalidomide. For what? Then I had the horrifying thought that maybe the dugong experiment contributed to my treatment, my future growth of dense bones, but that was impossible. I'm human, they're animal. I thought of the thousands of mice and cats and whatever animals that were sacrificed from here to Biopolis all to bring me ten milligrams and a Regenerator. What was I going to do? Drop out and join PETA? No, I was here, I'd committed to be here, I wanted to be here.

Mercedes said, "You look like you're going to faint. Jesus, Anne. You look white as a ghost."

"It's been a rough couple of days."

"Tell me about it. Don't you worry about me. It's temporary, Doc's honor. Now what's the scoop?"

About Nick I knew I should keep the details brief, but I heard myself talking—while thinking: What is gravity? What kind of doctor prescribes rope?—and talking and talking about how it was more than a fling, how Nick and I really connected, and how I'd been spending a lot of time with him, and the consequence of my saying this was that Mercedes would tell everyone. She'd start, most likely, with Nick himself.

"Are you sure you don't want to come in?"

"I guess for a minute." I offered Mercedes my arm. She walked inside and put a hand on the coatrack. "You don't seem concerned about the other one. He was so cute and so sweet. And you're cheating on him. That's so awesome."

"Awesome?"

"Totally."

"How?"

"You. Cheating on someone. C'mon."

"What do you mean?"

"It's totally not what you're supposed to do."

"You mean it's inconsiderate?"

"Duh, it's inconsiderate. But more than that. For you to cheat on someone is way different than for me to cheat on someone."

"How's it any different?"

"Okay, let me think." Mercedes thought for a while. I was still thinking of her lifting off the ground. I was having a worldview shift. Why didn't Mercedes seem freaked out? "For example, Tiny Tim in *A Christmas Carol*. You don't see him getting any action."

"He was five."

"I know but in theory. If he were older, theoretically."

"That's offensive, Mercedes."

"I'm sorry. I'm always putting my foot in my mouth. I just keep thinking of that cleft-lip girl. Can you imagine anyone wanting to kiss her? It's one of those situations where I'm like—whoever kisses her, she'd better marry the guy. And so for you to not marry him. For you to cheat on him. You're a Renaissance lady. Wait. What does that mean? Am I offending you?"

She'd managed to say sort of the right thing after a slew of very wrong things. I forgave her. She said what plenty of people thought. "You're not offending me. Do you want to sit down?"

"Can't. I'm meeting with Pierre Faivre. He drove in from the city. He thinks I can get sponsorships. Huge, huge. I want to catch up with you real soon, though. I got jock itch a couple days ago from the bartender at Sandy's."

"Jock itch?"

"At first, I thought, Yikes! This is chlamydia. This is gonorrhea. This is my vagina on fire. For the first couple days, it was me spread-eagle, holding a flashlight, and looking into my Estée Lauder compact. Then I went to the gyne and she gave me some Lotrimin. She said it was jock itch for sure. I was like, Yay! Awesome! The point of me telling you is—while I was getting jock itch—I'm pretty sure Leonard was watching in the window. So keep an eye out. Little fucker."

The Bible

———

I PACED AROUND the bungalow and talked to Mom. "Are you eating enough? Sleeping enough?" she asked. Dad got on the phone. "Your mother tells me you're seeing things. Now Annie. Are you hallucinating?" This was Dad's way of ending the conversation. Mom got back on the phone and assured me that they were supportive. Mom thought it was connected to the breakup. I heard Dad yell in the background: "Glad to see numb nuts go." Mom said, "You don't tell fibs, Annie. This is an anomaly."

"Anomaly? Where'd you pick up that word?"

"I learned that word from the doctors when you were born."

"Mom, a woman levitated."

She referred me to the Bible.

"People levitate all the time in the Bible. That's supposed to make me feel better?"

"Why don't you read the entire book of Ruth," she said. "That's a pick-me-upper."

I wanted to call Nick, who wanted to give it time. How much time? I dialed Eliot. "Have you seen Mercedes?"

"Yes ma'am."

"When's the last time you saw her?"

"I'm looking at her right now."

I walked to the window that faced the quad and bungalows.

I waved to Eliot who was waving from his window. He pointed to the side, where Leonard, Nick, the Gee, James D. Watson, and a man with a high-tech camera stood near the middle of the lawn, their faces turned up, hands shielding their eyes from the sun. I followed their gaze to the sky. About twenty feet in the air, adjacent to a streetlight, Mercedes Minnow was doing a cheer with pom-poms. There was a yellow rope in the sky with her, connected somewhere. I followed the rope from Mercedes' foot, past the streetlight, down from the sky, and to near the tops of the heads of those standing around. I walked outside. Leonard sidled up to me.

"She's a looker, ain't she?" Leonard smelled like liquor worn to bed. I thought maybe he shouldn't drink so much while he was on treatment. He sipped from a Styrofoam cup. I saw the yellow rope looped around his wrist. Who here put Leonard in charge? I looked at the rope, loose around his wrist, and followed it up to the sky where it attached to Mercedes' ankle. "She never goes farther up then twenty, twenty-five feet," Leonard said, patting the rope around his wrist. "See that guy in the pants with the camera? He's talking twelve-page spreads, commercials, action figures. You and me got stuck with the wrong genetic gizmos." Leonard patted me on the back and walked toward the guy with the camera.

Nick crossed from his side of the group closer to me. I thought he was going to come and stand beside me. Instead, he looked up at the sky.

Headlines

———

Der erste menschliche Vogel der Welt
—*BILD*

La Colonie Froide de Ressort Défie la Pesanteur
—*LE MONDE*

Jesús Cristo, los Estados Unidos Tiene Sobrehumanos
—*EL UNIVERSAL*

Reporting from the Colony

————

AS SOON AS Pierre Faivre's photos of Mercedes reached the flat screen, vans pulled into our parking lot and towers rose. Technicians climbed out of the backs of the vans drinking from Circle K mugs and saying things like, "Bill, I need a quarter inch." Simon berated one who bumped his van into the Colony sign out front. Patricia's skills did not accommodate simultaneous ringing, faxing, emailing, and signing for deliveries. She abandoned the office, carrying a legal pad, and walked the lawn checking press badges. The Gee could not have been happier. For interviews, he donned a blue blazer with red tie. He spoke of progress and deliverance. He spoke of the virus that delivered the correction to her obesity gene. It became known as the Floating Virus. "Think of it like a postman delivering a letter that changes your life," he said. "In this case, it changes all of our lives."

My appointment with the Gee, and with the Regenerator, which arrived on a Tuesday afternoon through the back door of the office, was left in limbo. I was relieved. The Colony had nicely ruined my love life, and teased my sex life, so I fretted over what other carrot it could hang above my nose and then eat.

Mercedes invited journalists into her bungalow where she provided them with yearbook photos, cheerleading photos, and sorority photos. She plugged her salon and the city of Portland.

She plugged her ex-boyfriend-the-artist's kaleidoscopes and sculpture shows. For the more conscientious media outlets, she talked up her big causes, weight loss and cleft lips, of which she said, "Every lip deserves a kiss." For the less conscientious media outlets, she said Eliot was "a little magoo" and Nick was "a lazy lay" and said about me: "Anne Hatley was probably picked last for kickball, teased a lot in high school, you know? So she's very reserved. She doesn't open up like I do. She'll snap out of it with her treatment though. Oh, you haven't heard?" This was how the media learned the plans for my regeneration. That afternoon, a Wednesday, in the eighth week at the Colony, my privacy vanished. I had microphones and voices at my door asking questions like: "Anne Hatley, what brought you to the Colony? What do you think of the Floating Virus? When do you regenerate?" The door was shut and they asked the questions. They asked the questions, and I stayed quiet, on the far side of the bungalow, behind the curtain, on the phone with the Gee, who promised to install a security gate.

Eliot called to say he was going to desert. "I'm two shakes of a sheepskin from out of here."

Mercedes had DVR-ed a ten-minute segment of Eliot's only lab report from the Cold Spring Harbor Channel, sold it to the networks, and exposed him and his brain to the public. I'd seen it on my flat screen. The networks played the footage, over and over: Eliot sitting on the bed of the X-ray machine. Cut to a commentator on Eliot's posture. Cut to image of Eliot's brain. Cut to commentator on brains in general. Graphics showed two brains: healthy, and Alzheimer's. Healthy brain was purple. Alzheimer's brain was inflamed with green, orange, red, yellow—and very little purple. The channel flashed Eliot's Alzheimer's gene—the SORL1. The gene failed to protect Eliot from some substance, illustrated by an arrow on the screen, which entered Eliot's brain and began wreaking havoc. The arrow moved around his brain. It was hot on the heels of (in the Gee's handwriting) amyloid beta peptide. I watched along with the public as Eliot's brain degenerated. The next day, Thursday, Eliot cracked the door of his bungalow. Dozens and dozens of mice scurried from the crack and darted straightly, diagonally, zigzaggedly onto the feet of, and up the legs of, the journalists and cameramen, who shrieked, cussed, dropped their microphones, and ran off-property. So Eliot had been breeding the mice.

"It is an act of defiance," the Gee said.

Eliot refused to apologize and asked the reporters to respect his privacy. The networks replaced clips of Eliot and his brain with clips of Eliot asking for privacy. Greta van Susteren said, "Take us back to the exact moment you released the mice. What were you thinking? How did that feel?" Pest control came with nets, traps, and buckets. They outfitted the Colony with ultrasonic repellants. It was a massacre of mice. Many lay dead on the lawn. Simon raked them up. Eliot wept. The reporters were persistent. I began to recognize their voices. One man in particular returned to my door three or four times a day to ask for the story. He was not accustomed to begging, was not good at it, and said things, in a thick New York accent, like, "You're going to want to talk to me one of these days" and "We can pay you." I peeked through the window. He wore pleated pants under a long coat. I almost opened the door for a woman's voice, small, squeaky, and polite: "Would you mind if I just asked a question or two? I won't take much of your time." She had black hair kept back in barrettes and she wore a black suit. She looked like the type of woman who broke hearts. I wanted to open the door to her and say, I will answer any question if you will ask it without clothes on.

I drew a message and taped it to the windowpanes of my door: LEAVE ME ALONE. They continued to knock, all hours, and I began staying up later, later, I was awake when the morning helicopters took their aerial shots, and when the morning journalists filmed their on-location intros and outros. I took advantage of the daytime to sleep. It was safer to be awake at night when I could move around without being hassled. I stayed up later and later, and woke midafternoon, and ate a sandwich, and Googled our names, and called Nick.

"I don't know why you're being so pigheaded and won't come over," I said. I was watching him on CNN. I kept waiting for him to mention me during an interview. "People are going to ask, 'Where were you when the first human floated?' and what are you going to say? You were playing Merle Haggard? You were cooking something in the Crock-Pot?"

"You're the one who wants privacy. Hung a curtain and everything. 'I don't want anyone to know,' you said. I walked eight hundred miles and saw what I had to see and asked you to make it right. But you wouldn't. So now you want me to come over, bring the Crock-Pot, in front of all these cameramen, so you can have the last laugh when your man sees it on TV, because you know and I know they're taping, someone is, and then who am I to you—I'm just the guy carrying the Crock-Pot."

"I never said you had to bring the Crock-Pot. You must think I really like your cooking."

"I know you do."

"Don't get proud of yourself, now."

The next day I saw him strutting around the reporters, inviting them into his bungalow, charging them for photos of him dressed in straw hat and jeans and boots, lying on the sleeping pod. He sold his story to *Newsweek*. I kept waiting to read about us through some exposé. When I didn't find anything, I began to feel like he thought we weren't even important enough for the tabloids. If Nick didn't come over after my treatment, when the Regenerator finally arrived, when it was my future on the line, I swore I'd never speak to him again.

That Friday reporters got a call that Castro was about to die. "I'm not going down there," one of the cameramen on the lawn closest to my window said. "That guy is always dying. I spent last year sitting on a barstool in Playa Tarará waiting for that guy to die."

Mercedes got tired of roping up for reporters. She called me: "I keep telling them it's temporary. It is, right?"

"How would I know? Do I look like some sort of authority to you?"

"Dr. Deeter says it's temporary. I mean, whatever, it's fun to do, but I have a life."

"Thanks for outing me."

"Are you upset?"

"No."

"Oh, I upset you. That's cute."

A security company installed gates around the Colony. The gates were black wrought iron. The Gee delivered a speech, wearing his blue blazer and red tie. He thanked everyone for coming and told them, kindly, to go away. No one budged. Then the call came that Castro had, in fact, died. That managed to evacuate the majors. When a few hangers-on would not leave, the Gee employed the Cold Spring Harbor Police Department, men who mainly wrote parking tickets, and who'd never had to escort anybody anywhere. The gates closed behind the last journalist.

Eliot's Mice

———

"IT'S NOT FAIR," Eliot said. He was sitting at my kitchen table drinking tea and flipping through *The Secret Life of Mateo Habenero*. Perkins Library said I owed them $325 for this book. They weren't getting the book back. "Who's Mateo Habenero?"

"He's a poet."

"I guess his life's not very secret."

"What's the matter?"

"Layla says she'll come get me."

My folks threatened to do the same. Mom wanted to drive up when the news broke. "Hepsie," I'd said, "It's another month. I didn't go through all this shit for nothing." "Don't you speak to me with that language," she'd said. Dad got on the phone: "You want to stay?" I felt no pressure to stay at the Colony when the only people who knew about it were my family, Grayson, and the principal at Durham Prep. Now the public was involved. I had fan mail from Aruba and Albuquerque. I had Grayson poking me on Facebook. I poked him back. That was as far as we got. Nick said, "Count on me. I'll be coming round the corner when I come." I received a succession of phone calls where the person on the other line didn't say anything, just sat there, not even breathing, or with the mouthpiece covered.

"Do you know how many mice they keep in labs around the world?"

"How many?"

"Twenty-five million. So I don't see the trouble with eighty-seven released into their natural habitat." Eliot wore a pullover with pockets in the front. He had kept the original white and original black mice. "Do you know how much trouble I went through keeping the parents from the babies? I spent the whole month of October separating them and last week I was building more cages." He kept the mice attached by homemade collars to his finger. They poked their heads out of their respective pockets.

"I'm too old to be on psychedelics," Eliot said.

"Is that what they have you on?"

"Seems like. I'm getting bespattered with slice-of-life memories twenty-four seven."

He scratched his beard. "What are they doing to you?"

"They're injecting me with stem cells."

"Mercedes has the Floating Virus. Leonard gets headaches. Half the time he doesn't even wave. It wouldn't be bad for me if Layla would stop saying, 'We're fucked and you've fucked us and there's no way out,' like she says every single morning, enunciating the *f* words, and with that chip on her front tooth from falling on her bicycle when she was thirteen, the same year she lost her virginity. A story I've heard a thousand times."

With Eliot, you had to let the guy talk. His brain was recycling, burbling, and there was no getting him off track. I refilled his glass with tea.

"She lost her virginity to a guy named Zack in algebra class, who wrote her a note involving a combination of charm and genius, and asked if she wanted to come to his wrestling match. I mean, is that all it took with her? She says, 'We're fucked and you've fucked us and there's no way out' every time I turn the cof-feemaker on. And I look up at her, where she would be standing—does this happen to you?—over the counter in the kitchen, she doesn't even drink coffee, and then I have to think about her chipped tooth, like I already told you, because it was the one dis-tinguishing feature on her face. She's not the type of lady to cause a serious stir, unless you're really looking at her, and inevitably I am the one guy who really likes looking at her. Then I cross-ref-erence that with the Zack guy who sounds like a loser and broke up with her over the telephone as soon as school let out for sum-mer break. And then that gets me thinking about summer, and breaks, and breaking up, and do the seasons have something to do with it? I'm not good in the spring. It was three springs ago caused Layla to say 'We're fucked.'"

"Who is Layla?"

"She's the one with the chipped tooth. And I never could fig-ure out about Zack, because she never talks about anyone else, so I'm always sort of fucking her in tandem with Zack. It makes me, to this day, pissed, because she paints this picture of him being naive and country club, that's all I got, but every time I just want to punch him in the gonads. Even though Layla is not the type who would care about Zack, although he did boink her in a most enviable way, behind the dumpsters at Burlington Coat Factory in Scranton, a store right next to their school. Layla should've become a slut after this. That's the conclusion I keep coming back to, because what girl gets it at thirteen and then doesn't get it again until me. That and my parents are dying."

I did not want whatever Eliot was having. "Everyone's parents are dying."

"Mine are dying their guts out in the lockdown wards of sepa-rate nursing homes in Houston, Texas." Eliot turned his attention to the flat screen. I didn't know what to tell him. I thought about Eliot getting stuck on one phrase from a woman named Layla. I presumed she was his wife, the wife he was rumored to have, and I compared her phrase in Eliot's head to the chorus of phrases in my own.

Chorus

———

GRAYSON: I know you, and you were begging for it.

NICK: I'm the last cowboy from Madison.

OLD FAITHFUL: I'd buy a Real Doll.

DARWIN: You better sport the miniskirt.

NICK: You're all over the place.

GRAYSON: Lube is artificial and fake feeling.

OLD FAITHFUL: You can do whatever you want to me.

DAD: Yes, but what's he doing with his life?

GRAYSON: I'm not buying you porn.

NICK: I'm making you breakfast.

OLD FAITHFUL: I'm masturbating in my office.

DARWIN: No one's too attached.

GRAYSON: My ex lives in Alamance.

NICK: In Verona.

DARWIN: In Shropshire.

DAD: What ex? Your mother was the first woman I met.

Eliot Interrupted: "Anne, if I may, you should eat more. Do you want a pistachio?" He reached into his pants pocket and gave me a handful of nuts. The first one I tried to crack gave me trouble.

"Come to my place. I'm going to cook dinner," Eliot said, standing from the kitchen table and putting his mice on the floor. Their collars were made of fishing line. It appeared as though they were following him by choice to the door.

Eliot kept his bungalow much cleaner than mine. I expected it to smell like mouse piss, but it smelled like Windex. Empty cages bordered the room. His place had the same A-frame shape; he'd left the bed stage center. He'd bought rugs to fit every corner of the space. The rugs were a variety of beige. Eliot pulled vegetables from the refrigerator. The fridge was covered top to bottom and on both sides with photos. I looked at a photo of a junkyard.

"That's Orange Park," Eliot said, slicing celery. "One of my closest friends was this guy who built a park out of orange rinds. You pay, like, $3 to take a tour. Garbage mainly. The guy was like . . . my doppelganger. Know what I mean? You're an English teacher. I figure you get a kick out of vocab, and I got vocab coming back to me left and right, larboard and dexter. I lost track of that guy. It seemed he had the best possible life. Seemed like he said to himself: What do I want? And he wanted a rot park of oranges with welded-metal sculptures and a line of Presbyterians paying to walk through. It was open after church on Sundays. It was in the getting-worse part of town. Project to the right, car dealership to the left. My parents took me when I was ten because I liked collecting junk and because I was not a fan of the NASA field trip. Everything huge and black and up in the air. Like what did I need with outer space?"

Eliot placed a salad in front of me.

"Salads in restaurants aren't clean," he said. The salad was spinach leaves, cherry tomatoes, sweet onions, mushrooms, and sunflower seeds. Eliot turned the stove on and tossed ground beef in a skillet. "I bet you don't like celery. I've only met two people who like celery."

The Regenerator

———

Prosthetics were the solution for the twentieth century.
Regeneration is the solution for the twenty-first century.
—Orthopaedic Research Society

FOR THIS, THE zapping phase, week nine, I walked in the lab,
white boots and wool dress. Patricia led me through the hallway
with doors on either side. At the back of the hallway were large
double doors with rectangular tinted windows up high. Patricia
stopped walking.

"Can I say something?" she said.

I nodded.

"My father lost his leg, diabetes."

"Sorry."

"It went quick. He misses golfing."

I was nothing like Patricia's father, or any of the accidentals,
as I thought of them, who lost their legs in medias res to diabetes, cancer, car, shark, boat, train, war, shooting. We did not
understand each other. They had lost something; I had been born
without. It must be natural to want something back; it must be
instinct. The accidentals had come out of the woodwork since
news of my treatment broke. They wanted to take my place. They

wanted to know what I thought of the stem cell injections. They wanted their legs back very badly. How good they'd been at bending the knee, stepping, climbing, golfing. They wrote letters of sorrow. They disliked the new configuration of parts. They had been prom king, jock, sarge, model, father of three.

The letters piled up. People were simply at the wrong place at the wrong time. The cast would be removed in a few weeks and then what. What were they supposed to do with their lives? Would things get better? Would anyone love them? They had been a person with two legs. They had always been that person. They liked that person. They deserved better than one leg could give them. They'd have to marry someone, just about anyone now, wouldn't they? Anyone that would have them? What about me? Would I have them? (One guy indeed proposed with a ring made of marijuana leaves and a note: *If you don't wanna stroke me, then toke me.*) Did I find myself desirable? How was my sex life? Their letters, the tone of their letters, the optimistic ways they began and ended their letters, "You don't know me," they wrote, "I'm hoping you will . . . " And why should I? And why would I? Their favorite adjectives: brave, courageous, inspiring, fearless, strong. They wanted me to apply these words to them, return the favor.

"You can sit down and take your leg off," Patricia said.

The Gee came in with a bright red contraption on a cart behind him. He placed the contraption beside me and walked to the whiteboard where he wrote the letters n and x and y followed by a series of lines, numbers, and equal signs. He stopped intermittently to sigh. He put down the marker and turned the machine on. It purred quietly, beeped three times, and went silent. The lights on the dash blinked red then yellow then green.

"We're set." He hooked the machine, brand-new from Biopolis, to my leg. "It'll feel like getting a tattoo," he said.

"I don't have any tattoos." Doctors weren't very helpful. "Is this going to hurt?" was another good one. A little. Not much. You might feel a pinch. They misnamed things. Skin-ripping adhesive? We'll call that butterfly tape. He took my half leg in his hands.

"What is it going to do?"

"It will reactivate embryonic development. We're filming for a later date. People will want a statement from you. Is there anything you'd like to say?" The camera lowered from the ceiling.

Statement

——

I THOUGHT OF what to say. I'd lectured on passive and active voice, on romantic poets and modernist manifestos. Nothing had prepared me to make a manifesto of my own. I thought of thanking God, my parents, family, and friends. I thought of making a direct address: "Old Faithful. Are you listening? You were always talking about illusory things, but I never thought I was one of the illusory things. Am I more or less real to you now?" I thought of addressing individual letter writers. To the man in Aruba, who sends photos in Speedos: I have no interest in joining you now or ever. To the polyamorous couple in Albuquerque: Your lady is the roast beef, you are the celery. To the accidentals: I'm sorry I've been rude. It's just I imagine you are asking for more than I can give you. This is usually the case. Just because I'm pushing forward, going through with it, this does not mean I despise life with one leg. You think I'm using pride to cover shame; I sometimes liked it. Look, you caught me, I'm already talking about it in the past tense. I didn't have to try so hard to be different, as your children are this second trying, with hair dye or meth or blow jobs or tongue rings or skateboards or spray paint or after-school tae kwon do. It was, actually, a relief to be different from the start. I am not sure what else to say, now that I have your attention. I really only care about growing the leg and going home and walking down the street. Walking into a gas station without getting compared to Sharon Lash or your father. Do you think I like talking to you about these things? Do you think it thrills me? I'd like to teach without the fear that my students will see me one second and won't see me the next. I want to be introduced as "the woman with brown hair," "the short one," "the quiet one," "the one who's sleeping with your husband."

"Anne," the Gee said, "Are you going to say anything?"

One small step for man was already taken. I looked into the camera and said: "For better or worse." He took my leg and slid it into the red machine. I felt suction on the stump. He pushed a button. I felt a shock, pins and needles, a blazing aftereffect. It lasted seconds.

"Good," the Gee said. "Very well done." He looked into a screen on top of the Regenerator. I lay down on the bed of the X-ray machine, felt the paper sheet with my fingers, felt a chill run up my arms, licked my lips, and heard the whir of equipment, the voice of the Gee. I stared into the lens of the X-ray machine and saw a reflection of my face.

"Take me off camera."

"You're off. Sorry for springing that on you. People will want to know. They're going to want to see it with their own eyes."

"Can I have an indoor cigarette?"

The Gee gave me my purse.

I smoked. "Are we finished?"

"Don't you want to see?" He rolled the cart toward me. I looked into the screen. It showed a table of images. Three squares by three squares.

"The first square is where we started." It showed a black background with red oblong cells. They were fluorescent on the screen. I thought *the cells* rather than *my cells*, and it felt like looking at a textbook rather than an image of my inner workings. Those are the cells in a Regenerator, I thought. That's all those are. Moving across the screen, to the right, the second square showed a couple more red dots, edging in from the perimeter. In the third square, the screen filled.

The Regenerator beeped.

"Good," the Gee said. He pulled a strip from the top of the machine. I felt like I had just been in the photo booth and here were my pictures. The strip was one-third the size of photo booth strips. I half expected to see my face on the other side, at the time of regenerating, my hollow face, from biting the insides of my cheeks. He pulled the strip from the machine and held it, by the corner, between his thumb and pointer. "This is your patch."

"My what?"

"Your patch."

"You're going to have to explain."

"This was very popular with hand amputees a couple years back. You don't have hands, then you can't shake hands. A friend of mine invented the patch so that if you didn't have a hand, you could still have the sensation of a handshake. Wear it on your shoulder for example. Who's to say that a handshake has to take place at the location of the hand? We've been working with the technology ever since. It's very productive for something like your case, where you will be growing the parts of your leg, bone by bone, and you won't have a foot until the final phase. In the meantime, you wear this patch and it gives you the sensations of your foot. Be careful with it, of course. It's your foot's nerve endings. Put the patch on your body. Try it out."

"I don't want to."

"Just try it."

"I'd rather not."

"It allows you to feel."

"I already feel."

"You'll want to practice. Just put the patch somewhere and anytime you touch the patch, it will feel like touching your foot."

"How does that work?"

"It sends a message to the area of your brain that thinks *foot*. You want to start getting used to how your foot feels."

"Where do I put it?"

"For example, on your shoulder. Or anywhere on the body."

"Why would I do that?"

"To become familiar, Anne. To acquaint yourself with your foot."

Common Object Theory

———

I PUT THE patch in the bathroom on the sink. I was not going on any patches. In addition, the Gee sent me home with crutches and codeine. I slept for forty-eight hours. I heard the phone ring. I heard the foghorn. I got up to pee. I heard the word of the day from the speaker on the flagpole. I heard voices in the quad. At one point, the Gee checked in and brought minestrone soup. "You're doing good," he said. I went back to sleep. I dreamt I was in an orchestra pit. I dreamt I had to walk to the Red Sea. Mice were, at various intervals, trying to eat me. When I woke, I had the woolies. I felt a slight burning sensation where my leg ended. The leg hadn't grown. My fake leg still fit. I thought I'd better clean the bungalow while I still could. I stood on the table and dusted the eaves of the low parts of the ceiling. Swept the floors. I was getting ready to mop when I found the package Grayson had sent. It was lying right where I'd left it, next to the coatrack by the front door. I opened it. Soft-core. He'd bought me soft-core. He'd finally gone and done it, gone online or gone to the Hustler store four miles from his place where I had bought mine, and fishnet, and other forms of entanglement. I crawled into the blue chair with the DVD. I felt sick. Right then in the chair with the DVD, I wanted Grayson lecturing on the impersonal world. That's why he didn't like porn. It was impersonal. It was fake. That's why I liked porn. It was impersonal. It was fake. And while watching it, nothing was at stake. I thought of Grayson in Durham at my favorite bar with the cigarette machine. I'd have to go back to Durham, collect things from his apartment, give back things, I'd have to face him, and he'd say something snidely, something like, "How's that leg working out for you?" He'd look down his nose when he said it. He was probably dating with full force and velocity. He didn't wait around. He'd aim the rearview mirror on me later.

I was feeling New Age. The whole universe was connected by nerve ending, ringtone, and poking on Facebook. Anyone could connect with anyone. Someone in the universe wanted to call a woman named Abigail. And somewhere a woman named Abigail was picking up the phone. Don't think like that, I thought, you're practically willing it to happen. Who knows why Grayson calls Abigail. What did I imagine Abigail would say? Hi Grayson, I knew the whole time that your girlfriend was tramping you. She never stayed long at art openings. You can't trust, anyway, disabled women. It's worse than having a missing father. Something really is wrong with them. At least a missing father has shoes you can step into. Some disabled women don't even have feet.

I wondered if I'd slept with Nick as an act of self-protection. Did I do that? I developed a theory, sitting in the blue chair, wearing a slip and drinking a gin and tonic, that all I had to do was mimic down to the last detail some action involving the concrete physical world. I had to engage the concrete physical world through an object, identical in any number of rooms, void of nerve endings, void of pain, an object that didn't care one way or another, like a bathtub. I had to initiate an action with the bathtub, in the hopes that Grayson was at the same time initiating an action with the bathtub, so he and I would be doing the same thing, and so he would be thinking of me. Yes, that is very smart, I thought, while putting on mascara. I ran water in the tub. Someone knocked at the door.

"Told you I'd come around." He was standing at the door with a plant in a pot. "I brought you this."

"Just because I'm trying to grow doesn't mean I have a green thumb."

"Baby, I love it when you're disdainful," Nick set the plant on the kitchen table. It looked in every way like a miniature rose bush, except the roses were blue. Blue roses came from somewhere. Tennessee Williams's *The Glass Menagerie. Blue roses* sounded like *pleurosis.*

"I know what you're thinking," Nick said. "'How come Nick's giving me carnations?' But these are not carnations. They're roses infused with the pigment of pansies." Nick rubbed a petal and looked at his thumb as if he was checking to make sure the color didn't rub off.

I closed the door behind him. I was wrapped in a towel. He put his arm around me. I pulled away. "How are you?"

"Thirty-seconds better."

"I'm in the middle of something." Why couldn't I say, "You took too long. Maybe you screwed around with the cute reporter, or Shug Tenner, or Mercedes Minnow, or maybe all three at once, and maybe I don't care."

"Now water these here roses. At least once a week. But don't drown them, either. What are you doing?"

"Taking a bath."

"I happen to be in need of a bath myself. I happen to be the dirtiest man this side of the Hudson Valley. I happen to be dirtier than— "

"Nick." I took his hand. I walked into the bathroom and he

followed, working his boots off in between steps. We stood facing each other. "You going to get in fully dressed?"

He took his clothes off. I kept the towel wrapped around me as I ran the water and poured bubbles into the water. He stepped in the tub. I took my leg off and leaned it in the corner. I hopped across the tile to the tub and settled in beside Nick. I was waiting for the leg to extend at any minute. What if it grew wrong and then who would? What if I could neither hop nor walk? What if the phone rang for the last time yesterday? Nick said it was good to see me. I said it was good to see him. He asked about the leg.

"I wish you'd act like it's not happening," I said.

The bathtub was too small. Nick put his hands under my armpits to lift me up so he could rearrange himself. "Mercedes told me what you said."

"What did she say?"

"You like me. You think we really connect."

"Yeah."

"You should know better than to tell Mercedes anything. She runs her mouth."

"When did you talk to her?"

"Yesterday."

"Are you sleeping with her?"

"No. Why would you ask me that?"

"Because I thought to."

"You just ask whatever comes to mind." He kissed my hair. I thought about what had happened since I'd last talked to him.

"Eliot's a mess."

"What's the deal?"

"He's stuck on some woman named Layla."

"Maybe that's who's visiting."

"Someone's visiting him?"

"I was talking to Leonard and he said Eliot has female companionship. Leonard made Mercedes some weights."

"What kind of weights?"

"For her feet."

"Oh."

"He filled Ziploc bags with sand, and she wears them around her ankles." I laid on top of Nick in the bath. He kept his hands off me in the water. He didn't know what to do with his hands. He kept bracing himself on the side of the tub.

"Does it work?"

"Does what work?"

"The Ziploc bags."

"Yeah."

"What's that?" He pointed to the side of the sink where I'd left the patch. It was made of flexible plastic and felt like Tupperware. I was supposed to wear the patch on any part of my body. The Gee suggested I wear it on my shoulder. I was supposed to touch the patch and that would send a message to my brain: *foot, foot*, the message would say.

"It's a patch."

"You quit smoking?"

"Hardly."

"What kind of patch?"

"It goes on me."

"What for?"

"Nick, do we have to?"

"I'm interested. I want to know, can't help it."

"It mimics the nerve endings of the foot I'm growing. The thing could grow any minute, any speed. The Gee thinks I'll grow quick due to my cells."

"What's the deal with your cells?"

"They reproduce in triple-speed. They've been giving me stem cell therapy."

"So you'll wear this patch?"

"I don't like it."

"Why not?"

"I don't know. I'm used to what I'm used to." I stood from the bath and took a towel from the rack. Nick followed me to the bed behind the curtain in the alcove. It began to snow. He wanted to know the whole story, the whole story from birth, including what life was like for me growing up, and what led to me coming to the Colony, and was I nervous about treatment.

I said, "It's late. It's already midnight."

He wanted to tell me the whole story, the whole story from birth, and I laid in bed wondering if I was lucky to be there, if that was luck, waiting for the leg to grow, listening to Nick.

"Do you know about Pocahontas?"

"Who doesn't know about Pocahontas?"

"I have a personal connection."

"Was your mom Pocahontas?"

"I'm trying to tell you some family history here, baby, don't you want to know about my Pocahontas connection?"

"Go on." He was related to Pocahontas through a genealogy I couldn't piece together, even when he explained with his hands touching the roof of the alcove, his hands drawing lines toward children and children's children. I spooned into him. I realized with Nick talking that there would be legions of things I would never say to him, and this did not trouble me, nor did it compel me to speak. Only once had I felt compelled to leave no words tucked under my tongue. Said everything, said it out. Then, it was almost like knowing someone. Then it felt like dying my guts out in a separate ward of the universe. It wasn't Grayson either.

Grayson was a cover-up. Grayson was already dwindling from epic to epigraph. One second I was trying to common-object-theory him into the room, the next we were irreconcilably through. It only felt like dying my guts out for one person. He'd come back. He'd snuck in. What excessive sex we had. How for granted we took it. I read somewhere that fucking is liberty in essence. When I suffer him in my head, as I did, as I do, as I did, nothing else. I suffer him in oranges, greens, yellows, and reds. I can be doing anything, with anyone, when the familiars come back, the stacks, the driveway.

Comparison of Legs

———

NO COMPARISON. NICK won by the standards. Walked with confidence. Staggered without looking like a sleaze. Played basketball. Played touch football. Thick thighs, strong knees, defined calves, and feet with especially handsome toes. When Nick stood from the bed, I imagined his legs in high fashion suits, imported fabrics, knees apart under desks made of cherry wood, behind podiums, in front of PowerPoints, on billboards for Abercrombie & Fitch. Abercrombie was near-exactly Nick's style: waffle tees, wrinkled button-down shirts. Sometimes he sided off the bed, put his feet through his jeans, and pulled up the denim without buttoning. He looked like the guys in the catalogue, removed from a field with horse, placed in Bungalow North, pants hanging by his cheeks.

I can't say if Nick's legs or the full effect, the parts or the whole, earned him best in the comparison. Turn on the flat screen and you'll see a pair of legs like Nick's on a body like Nick's. I imagine that's why Mercedes liked them as much as she did. She saw them in *Cosmo*. I imagine that's why Nick liked me as much as he did. These things were never voiced. If voiced the conversation would go something like, "Every woman I've been with has liked my body. The nurse in Verona did. She said so. From her liking it, I began to like it. Really like it. Now you sit across from me every day at the kitchen table, or beside me in the station wagon, or alongside me in the bed, and you make no comment whatsoever on my physical form. As much as you don't say anything, it's like I don't even have a physical form. It makes me doubt what I thought I knew, which is riveting, to unknow something, so I like you."

Old Faithful, let's be clear, he waddled. He walked slowly, one foot, then the other, ho-hum, turned inward on occasion. Overweight? He might've been. Not when I knew him. He liked to run to New China and the Silex Scintillans and the Rolling Stones. He did not know the words *hurry* or *I've made up my mind*. He padded around places. You wouldn't, on the street, think, The way that man walks, I bet he has a wife—and a mistress, fifteen years younger, who comes to the library to blow him. You wouldn't think that from the way he walked. He waddled to the freezer. He drank. I didn't care. He wasn't mine. And then I did care. I climbed on a kitchen chair to be face-to-face with him, and as I stood he sat, his knees facing me, suddenly, defeated, as if to say, "We're doing this again. Are we doing this again?"

Do People Ever Change?

———

(Check the most accurate)

_____People change.
_____People don't change.
_____Please change your mind.

Paths of the Mirror

———

There are mirrors which are concave, which magnify the thing that they reflect: There are mirrors convex, which diminish it. And we in like manner represent the Divine in a false, distorted way. We exaggerate and diminish it till all becomes untrue. We bring forth our own fancies.

— Reverend Frederick W. Robertson, sermon

AFTER NICK FINISHED telling me his Pocahontas connection, he wanted us to change locations, go to his place, do it in the sleeping pod.

"It might start growing, and I don't want to be doing that on Ocean."

Nick raised an eyebrow as if he was waiting for me to continue.

"I'm going to the bathroom," I said. Sitting on the toilet, I wondered if the sleeping pod had been a disadvantage for us. Would he always want to do it on Ocean? I wondered if—in a regular bed with sloping mattress—I would be less exciting to Nick or he would be less exciting to me. Could I enjoy anything while on the verge of growing? I flushed the toilet. When I hopped into the room, I saw that Nick had moved the bed from under the alcove to the center, where he'd always wanted it.

I got on the bed. I wanted to feel like I was back to standing topless at his place. Where had that gone? While his cheek rested on my stomach, I thought I knew where it went. It went into the labyrinth. A wall when Nick laughed with the rest at Mercedes' place and another wall when Nick didn't come running to me, like I expected, after Grayson left, and another whenever anyone said Nick was at the Green House, and sitting on the nearest wall was Old Faithful. I could hear him as if he were whispering in my ear: "What's this guy doing in our labyrinth?" I turned my head to watch it snow.

I wanted very badly to enjoy the kamikaze, to have a multiplex climax, but it didn't happen, and I told Nick to stop because it wasn't going to happen.

"You're scaring it off," he said.

"Maybe it's you. Maybe you scared it off. Go get me a mirror."

I wanted to use the mirror to remember what I looked like. Nick went to the kitchen for it, and it was taking a while so I figured he was in the bathroom. The gin was wearing off and my foot tickled. I scratched my foot, the real one, but that wasn't the right foot. I checked my leg to see if we were growing. Nick walked to the side of the bed and stood there, holding his dick in one hand, and the mirror in the other.

I sat on the bed. "All I can see is the snow outside."

He turned the mirror. There was that scratch in the center of the mirror from when I'd checked to see if it was a two-way. I took Nick in my mouth and I was looking at my face. I felt better because nothing elusive was expected of me. My face was dark and shadowed. I was looking at my eyes, then my lips around him, when something was not right, something was clearly not right, something tasted like plastic, was he wearing a condom? And then my foot felt wet.

"What?" Nick was laughing.

"Nothing."

The patch was on his dick. I said nothing.

"C'mon, it's pretty funny."

"It's not funny. That's my foot."

"C'mon."

"It's not funny."

"Annie."

"What?"

"I was playing around."

"Do not call me *Annie*."

"Anne Hatley."

"Nick. When I go to suck your dick, I want to suck your dick not my foot I don't want to suck my foot I don't even know whose foot that is I'm not even in possession of that foot yet." I sat on the side of the bed looking out at the snow. What the fuck was he thinking? He didn't mean anything by it. It was a joke. But it was my foot, the nerve endings of my foot. Nick held the patch between his thumb and pointer. He was standing next to the bed. He looked like he might say something. I hoped it was good, whatever he had to say. He shook his head and looked down.

He didn't know what to say just like Grayson didn't know what to say just like no one knows what to say. If you don't say something, if no one speaks on your behalf, if the people who speak for you say things like "Prevail through Knowledge" while they pump you full of stem cells and put your foot on a patch, then you better watch it, because those same people are suddenly pinning a gold star to your pea coat. Someone has to say it. What am I doing? And by doing it, what am I agreeing to? If you're missing a leg, well, you shouldn't be, and we have machines to remedy you? I believed the Gee when he said, "Regeneration is the answer." But what was the question? Was my life so bad? It only got bad when a commonly held conviction—she will have a harder time finding someone to love her, fuck her, want her—insisted on entering sneakily, through an urban myth, through some unexpected tunnel of conversation, and said, "I'm the popular conviction. You can commence feeling like shit." Even though I'd proven such a conviction wrong, I still believed in it along with the Gee and Watson and the scientific community and the general public; they must be right, there are so many more of them.

Nick was standing there with the patch in his hand waiting for me to say something. THAT'S MY FOOT YOU'RE HOLDING, I did not scream. I had to go away, somewhere else. It felt similar to one night when I was trying to walk with a new prosthetic. I'd outgrown the old one. I'd developed a "bad habit" of swinging my leg to the right. I picked the new leg up at the prosthetist's office and practiced in front of Grayson, who kept saying, "I see a definite improvement. Looks much better." I was freaked out because the new leg didn't feel like *my* leg. So how could it be an improvement on *me* if it didn't even feel like *me*? I asked Grayson to leave. I called Old Faithful. The only time I dialed his home number. "Make something up," I said. Half an hour later he was standing at my door in pajama bottoms and a white tank. He was carrying a Coca-Cola two-liter in one hand and a DVD in the other. I sat on the couch. He opened my closet and pulled a blanket from the shelf. He arranged the blanket over me and put the DVD in the player, a Japanese movie, subtitled, on mute. A man flirted with a woman working behind a take-out counter. Old Faithful found my hand under the blanket. As soon as he found my hand, I felt shocked into myself. I was wearing the new leg but I wasn't thinking about legs. I played with the drawstring of his pajamas. Sweat collected on his forehead, face, and around his eyes. When I was finished, I glanced at the screen, where the man was tightrope walking from one building to another. "I miss you," he said. He was looking at me as if he knew and I knew that we were stuck, we were completely irrevocably stuck, in love against all better judgment, and neither of us would be okay in the morning. I said, "I miss you like crazy; you're the only person who makes me feel like me."

I wanted to ask Nick to leave. I wanted a cigarette. I was sitting on the edge of the bed. Nick held the patch between his thumb and pointer. "Baby, it was—I'll just—you know how I am. I'm spontaneous. I'll just throw it away."

"You can't just throw it away."

"Why not?"

"It's got my nerve endings on it. God."

"I'm sorry."

"Yeah, well, it wasn't funny."

"I'm really sorry."

"Stop apologizing."

Attempt

————

The laws of the human mind, which are under our observation all day and every day, are no better understood then they were two thousand years ago.

—FLORENCE NIGHTINGALE

I WOKE, IN the middle of the night, freezing cold. The window by the bed was open. At first I thought someone had snuck in. Then I realized someone had snuck out. Nick had been asleep with me and he'd snuck out the window. I looked on the floor for something to wear. I hopped to the window, stuck my head out and looked around. There was the street that led toward the harbor in one direction and the forest in the other. There was Nick's bungalow with the lights off. I looked down, at the snow, mainly because I was thinking what if Nick did leave me in the middle of the night to sleep at his place and if he did leave, then did that mean he didn't like me after what he'd done? I would at least stay the entire night dreaming of other people at his place. I wouldn't need to go sneaking off into the snow. While I was thinking of Nick, at his place, nestled in his sleeping pod, I saw the snow, fresh and untracked. I looked out again to the street and thought, truly, Nick devised a way to walk through snow without leaving footprints.

"Watch out." His voice came from above and I looked up where he was standing with his boots on the roof.

"What are you doing?"

"I'm going to jump."

"No."

"What? You don't want me to—"

"No."

"Why not?"

"I'm standing here, catching my death of cold, and you'll fall smack-dab on top of me and kill me too, so it won't be suicide, it will be doublecide, homicide, whatever, and I'd rather us go to sleep like normal people."

"You don't want me to die, is that it? You don't want me to die because you love me."

I paused to irritate him. I thought if he were irritated he'd climb down and fight it out. When it wasn't enough, I gave the answer he wanted.

"You do? Really?"

He climbed through the window. I closed the window and put on a sweater. The sky was getting lighter. Nick sat in the blue chair and I sat on his lap. He was telling me he felt better; he felt like a million bucks. I felt tingly all over, but it wasn't love-induced, it was something else.

"Oh God," I got out of Nick's lap so he wouldn't see or feel it. I hopped to the bed. I was glad Nick had moved the bed to the center of the room so I didn't have to hop as far. I looked at my hands on the side of the bed. I wanted to look at the place where my leg was growing, but I didn't need to look to know it was growing. I tried to think nonchalantly, that's just my leg; maybe I'll take a nap, in a few hours, breakfast. What had once felt regular, the place where my leg ended, regular enough to me, now felt unknown and terrifying.

"Tell me what's happening," Nick said.

"How should I know what's happening? This has never happened to me before." I don't feel regular. I feel like someone has a grip on my leg and they're pulling as hard as they can. I feel like they're going to rip my hip out of its socket. Could I tear in two? Let off my leg, let off my leg, I was thinking, and then I must've been saying it out loud, because Nick was saying, "I'm not on your leg, baby," and I was arguing with him, yes you are, you're gonna pull too hard, let off my leg, let off.

"I'm calling for help," Nick said.

"No. I want you to let off my leg."

"I'm not on your leg."

"Can you see anything?" I said, sitting up to look at the side of his face.

"It looks like a blister."

"A blister?"

"It looks like a blister on the bottom there. It looks like your leg with a blister forming."

"Enough," I said to Nick, to the leg, to the pressure, to the pulling, to the nerves, to the pain, to the convictions, to the stem cells, to the blastemas, to the past, to the future, to the sudden and terrifying unknown.

"Baby, how are you feeling?" Nick said.

"Turn on the TV."

Nick turned on the flat screen and flipped to American Movie Classics. *The Misfits* was playing. He put his arm around me. I shrugged him off. The feeling on my leg shifted from tingling to pinpricks. A saloon. Two men talking. "Well, that's the way it goes." "It goes the other way too, though. Don't forget that." The leg stopped growing. It felt like someone releasing his grip. The muscles relaxed, the nerves numbed.

"You think I want to watch *The Misfits*?"

"Is it better? Are you okay?"

"I'm scared."

"What do you want me to do? Do you want me to call Deeter?"

"I don't want to call anyone."

How much had it grown? Would it always be this unexpected? I tried to think of symptoms I might've missed. Was it accompanied by a headache? Did I feel light-headed? I wanted to reach down and feel where it had grown, but something stopped me from doing that, I wanted to let that part alone, let it do its thing, and I wondered if I could sleep through it. If it started growing again, would it wake me? No doubt it would. I thought the pain would be local. As if the growing of a leg would pain me only on the leg, instead of, as it did, my whole body. I consoled myself thinking that pain is not a remembered thing, it happens and then it's over, no one walks around lamenting the toothache of January 8 or the charley horse of May 15. I kept hearing snippets from the movie. "Why? What difference would it make?" "Might make all the difference in the world as time goes by." I tried to remember the last time I was in physical pain. I wanted to pinpoint it by date and place. I couldn't think of anything except how it had grown and how it had felt and how it had stopped and how it wasn't going to grow all at once and how it wasn't over and how it would happen again. I asked Nick to tell me a story. What kind of story, he wanted to know. Any other night he would've started on some story unprovoked.

"Tell me a story about a cowboy or a bandit or General Custer."

"General Custer was shot to hell by the Lakota-Northern Cheyenne."

"Start at the beginning. How are you supposed to tell a story starting at the end?"

"You're back to picking on me. That's got to be a good sign."
Nick tried putting his arm around me and this time I let him.

In the morning, Nick carried me to the main office. I hadn't
slept. He had drifted to sleep after the Battle of Antietam. I didn't
want Nick to leave me in the office, but neither did I want him
to stay, so I told him I'd be fine and he walked to his place. I told
Patricia what had happened. She was happy to hear treatment was
working. She was probably thinking of her father. The Gee came
out of his office and greeted me in the main entrance. That had
never happened before. Usually I waited for him in the examining room. He carried me down the hall. I was trying to get used
to being carried, but I didn't like the Gee carrying me. I kept my
face away from his collar and out of the cloud of cologne. When
Nick carried me, it was less repugnant. Guys you sleep with are
allowed to carry you. Finally we were back in the examining room,
where four strangers stood. For the next hour, I reverted to my
childhood self, the one who had no problem removing the robe,
pivoting on the ball of her foot, showing off and answering questions for people in lab coats. They took measurements, notes, and
photos. I wondered if they were stalling in the hopes of seeing it
grow. At one point Patricia stepped in with my crutches. Debates
ensued over stem cell dosages and morphine prescriptions. "I
don't think morphine is necessary," one said. "She's complaining
of pain." "Codeine is sufficient."

The Gee interrupted, "Send her files over to Biopolis. I'd like to
get Xui Ling's opinion on this lateral abrasion and I'd like to know
what he thinks of the blastema sequence. I'll call Watson myself."

I put my robe on, tying it in the back, and hopped over to
the crutches. The thing about crutches is they hurt your armpits.
I turned back to the room, trying to think of something to say
to them, and while I was standing there, they walked up to me

individually and shook my hand. In my experience, doctors don't shake your hand. They tell you you're dying or they tell you what they need to do to prevent you from dying and then they write it down on a legal pad. "Thanks," one said. "We've been working on your case for so long." She parsed her words out as if she needed to use simple language to communicate with me. "It's a pleasure to finally meet you."

Dig Season

———

The bones are just everywhere.

—Norman Gardiner

IT WAS DARWIN'S idea to get out of Cold Spring Harbor. He wanted to go to Montana.

"Triceratops," he'd said. "For real." I had to swear to the Gee that I would only be gone for the weekend. I told him I needed privacy. I told him the agreement didn't have any rules against taking a weekend off. When he continued to argue, I said, "What are you going to do? Lock me in my room?" Darwin and I shacked up on the second floor of a ranch in Southwestern Montana. This was the Badlands. Our quarters had two twin beds and a double sink. We shared the bathroom with some inner-city kids on scholarship. Darwin wore a hard hat to excavate Hell Creek. I stayed in the room, on crutches, reading books on folklore. The owners of the ranch had done well for themselves with a thousand acres of land. They had nonprofit status, grants from the state, certificates hanging in the hallway.

I'd never seen dinosaur bones outside a museum. It had taken a while for me to believe dinosaurs existed. I was raised to believe God planted dinosaur remains on Earth on the fourth, fifth, or sixth day to make Earth old from the beginning. I stuck by this belief through adolescence, until a boyfriend said, "You're kidding, right?" and I felt dumb. "Of course I'm kidding," I'd said. That guy had turned out to be dumb himself, but I took from him the dinosaurs. The front room of the ranch held various bones under glass. Our hostess, Mrs. Lyle, "call me Mama," served pork chops. The inner-city kids wanted to know why I was on crutches. "Accident," I said. They wanted to know what kind of accident, and by the end of the conversation I'd made friends with three tenth-grade paleontologists from South Side Seattle.

"Can I see?" the tallest boy said.

I rolled my pants leg above where the knee would be, if a knee did in fact arrive one day, and it looked promising, a nubbin right there at the end, as if a knee were on its way.

"Where are the scars?"

"What scars?"

"If it's an accident, why aren't there scars?"

"I had them removed."

"That's incorrect," he said.

"It's the truth."

"If you had the scars removed there'd still be a scar where you had the scars removed." For the rest of the day, the tall boy eyed me suspiciously and whispered behind his hand to the others. By the time five o'clock rolled around, I was sitting on the twin bed watching the minute hand and waiting for Darwin to return. The front door opened. I peered down the staircase. Darwin was carrying one giant bone. Mrs. Lyle stopped him in the hall.

"Oh my," she said. "Oh my, that's very big. I don't know if we can let you keep that one. I'll check with Mr. Lyle."

"You can have it. I'm not going anywhere anyway. I'm just going to show it to Anne."

Darwin climbed the stairs, stopping every couple of steps to lean the bone against the side of the wall, beside the portraits of the Lyle family. Darwin wheezed for a second, then picked the bone up, and clunked it up the stairs.

"Where did you get that?"

"Haven't seen bones like this since Tierra del Fuego. Help me with the door, will you?"

I hopped to the door and helped him. He placed the bone between our two beds.

"You think they have room service?"

"I'm sure Mama Lyle will cook you up anything you like."

"Scotch, you think?"

I dialed down to Mama Lyle and she said, "Oh my, I don't know if we do," and found in Mr. Lyle's cabinet barely a shot of scotch. She delivered the scotch on a white wicker tray and made a face about my smoking a cigarette. She made a face, I saw the face, and we exchanged between us a face agreement not to talk about it.

Darwin took a sip of scotch. He was fired up from the excavation. He'd met a man named Norman Gardiner, from Australia, and they'd hit it off. "Norman was root-tooting around with a vertebra when I pickaxed and found this." He couldn't take his eyes off the bone. He'd begun to measure it using the length of his sleeve as a ruler.

"How'd you feel if someone dug you up and measured you?"

"What I want you to think about, Annie," he stopped measuring. He raised the glass of scotch from the tray with one hand, put the other on my shoulder, and said, "Is the price of what you're doing. How much does it cost you? At the end of the day, week, century, are you going home happy?" Darwin drank, licked his lips, and returned the glass to the tray. "Happy is not right. I mean

content. I don't know what *happy* is. I can quote you some Latin—
exporrigere frontem—to unwrinkle the brow; I can quote you some
Moreau, talk about the New Zealanders, the Hindus, the Malays,
the Dyaks of Borneo. I can tell you quite explicitly which muscles
move on a person's face when they smile, but I can't tell you what
in plain terms happiness is. I don't know what I'm trying to say."

He took a rag from his pocket and began to clean the bone.
"My father wanted me to be a doctor. He said, 'You care for nothing but shooting, dogs, and rat catching. You will be a disgrace to
yourself and all your family.' I couldn't do it. This was before chlo-
roform, and I saw the faces, the expressions, and knew I couldn't
do it. As for evolution, what's that? Did that make me happy? As
if I did it single-handedly. And there's the rub. I didn't know what
I was doing half the time. Such and such printed this in a journal
and I took from it what I could and I wrote a response. Such and
such lectured at Cambridge, and I took from it what I could. I get
stuck with 'survival of the fittest.' I hear them. Oh yeah, Darwin,
'survival of the fittest.' I never said that. That's not what I said.
They take Spencer's words and put them in my mouth. It tastes
like chalk down here. I was the world's foremost barnacle expert,
but who remembers that?"

Appointments

————

AS SOON AS I got back from Montana, the Gee started calling every day, at noon and five, and booked me for additional appointments. Each time I went into an appointment, I knew the Gee and his assistants wanted to see regeneration for themselves. I wanted to say, "Look guys, I can't just order it up, it's not take out," but instead I kept quiet, sitting on the X-ray machine, naked under the robe. The Gee sat in his swivel chair. Our time together had not prepared him to have a casual conversation with me. He seemed put off, so we spent the half hour mostly in silence. Luckily, the Gee's female assistant, who insisted I call her Debbie, knew how to talk. In the first fifteen minutes, I knew that she had considered teaching biology at the local elementary school, and she respected teaching, it was a stand-up profession (when she said *stand-up*, I couldn't help but wonder if she was summoning the leg to grow), and that her husband was in the room—he waved from behind the glass partition—and that having two scientists in the house means there are dishes in the sink and clothes that need ironing. As if to prove the point, Debbie smoothed her hands over a wrinkle in her khakis.

"Are you married?" she said.

"No."

"Have a boyfriend?"

"I have a guy I sometimes sleep with. Does that count?"

The Gee looked up from the file he'd been reading, looked at me, and returned to his file. The assistants behind the glass partition couldn't hear us. Debbie's husband poured a cup of coffee. I thought of the other two as Tweedle Dee and Tweedle Dum. They mainly nodded. I thought about how much time had been lost to examining rooms and nodding.

"Do you feel anything?" Debbie said.

"Excuse me?"

"In your leg?"

"If I feel something, you'll be the first to know."

"I just thought maybe you felt something because you had a look on your face."

"We're not necessarily the first to know," the Gee said. "Nick's seen you regenerate. You didn't alert us."

"Sometimes it's not appropriate to alert you." I looked the Gee squarely in the forehead.

"It's always appropriate."

The next day, as soon as I felt the tingling sensation, I boarded my crutches and went to the office. Patricia paged the Gee. She raised her voice and blared into the speakers across the Colony: "Dr. Deeter, come to the office. Anne Hatley is on task! Right this second, I can see it, I can see it. Anne Hatley is on task!" She said it like I was on fire.

In the examining room, Tweedle Dee and Dum didn't know what to do with themselves: They both ran for the same button, a control that lowered the camera from the ceiling, and the taller of the two ran from behind the glass partition to where I was standing, on crutches, in the middle of the room. I'd worn a skirt so they could observe it plainly and I lifted my skirt. So there we were, my skirt up, and the nodders, doing their nodding, mouths open. The Gee came running in, followed by Debbie's husband, and I knew we only had a minute or two. The pain was starting to dissipate. The Gee yelled directives to his assistants, get this, get that, and then I had the Gee sitting in the swivel chair, eye-level with my waist, hands on my growing leg. I didn't think he should touch it, not while it was growing, I hadn't even touched it while it was growing.

"My God," the Gee said.

Then it stopped.

"Where's Debbie?" I asked.

The Gee looked at me as if I'd asked the most asinine question I could ask after regenerating. Was I supposed to say something smart, important, what is truth, what can't we do?

"She has the day off," he said.

Mercedes Interviews
Peter Singer for the Cold Spring
Harbor Channel

———

MM: Welcome to the Mercedes Minnow Lab Report on the Cold Spring Harbor Channel. For this week's report, I'm sitting down with Peter Singer, who is delivering a talk tomorrow night in the auditorium. Mr. Singer. Thanks for joining me.

PS: My pleasure.

MM: So you are . . . a pretty big deal. You are . . . a big-name philanthroper.

PS: Philosopher.

MM: So what does that mean to your life?

PS: To my life?

MM: Yeah, like what does a philosopher do? See, I'm a hairstylist. What I do is make people happy with their hair. I introduce them to products—Paul Mitchell's Super Skinny Serum is my favorite. Hi, Paul, if you're watching, love the product. Love. It. So does a philosopher have a product or clients and, I guess, if not, what does a philosopher do?

PS: As a philosopher, I thrive on debate and discussion, that's what the field is about, and of course sometimes that criticism goes a little bit over the top [. . .] Bioethics is a fascinating field because the biosciences keep moving forward and they keep giving us new possibilities and new choices. For example, as we learn more about genetics, we are going to be able to select our children, and that's going to be a huge ethical issue. We're already seeing at universities like Princeton that the student newspaper carries advertisements offering $20,000 to $30,000 for eggs from students who match a certain criteria.

MM: How much would you pay me?

PS: You mean for your eggs?

MM: Yeah, like I could totally see myself being a donor, if you needed an egg.

PS: I personally do not need an egg.

MM: Okay. Moving on. So I was Googling you and I found out that we're a lot alike. Me and you. Because you like controversy and so do I. I pulled up a letter from Karen Meade in Dublin. Karen writes, "Would you kill a disabled baby?" This is quite a controversial topic, so I'd like us to take a pause before we continue. Pause.

PS: [Silent]

MM: Okay. Continue.

PS: Yes, if that was in the best interests of the baby and of the family as a whole. Many people find this shocking, yet they support a woman's right to have an abortion. One point on which I agree with opponents of abortion is that, from the point of view of ethics rather than the law, there is no sharp distinction between the foetus and the newborn baby.

MM: Okay. One last question: Where do you buy your bow ties?

PS: Not any one place.

MM: Wow. Love. Them. Thank you for joining me. This has been the Mercedes Minnow Lab Report. PTK.

Assembly with Peter Singer

————

Singer is our nation's best philosopher.
—PRESIDENT, United States

Singer is not welcome in Germany.
—CHANCELLOR, Germany

THURSDAY, THE WEEK before Thanksgiving, we assembled in the auditorium for a lecture by Peter Singer. Nick carried me from Bungalow North. The crutches made my armpits sore. Even with the auditorium on-site, I couldn't hop well in one boot on snow. When Nick carried me like that, one arm behind my back, one arm under my knees, and we passed someone, Nick had to turn sideways so I could talk to the person straight on and I didn't like them looking up my legs. Simple conversations became awkward. I preferred to sit on Nick's shoulders, looking at the tops of heads and seeing from the vantage point of a very tall person. Nick sat me down in the third row from the back. I arranged my corduroy pants, tucking the extra fabric under me. Growing the knee hurt more than an oven burn, more than menstrual cramps, and more than butterfly tape ripping off. It hurt more than if you had all three of those at once. The leg was growing conically and looked like a sharpened pencil. It was skinny up top. It looked like the cells, in their rush to extend the leg, forgot to fill it out. It didn't match my other leg or anyone else's.

Eliot sat five chairs to Nick's left with his female companion and the mice in his lap. There were a lot of empty chairs. The women from the Green House sat in front of us. Nick introduced them.

"I'm Dora."

"I'm Shug."

"Misty."

They eyed me and I eyed them back. Dora was the eldest. She wore a white fuzzy sweater with a flower pinned near her breast. The flower sneezed. Dora looked down at it and wiped its petal. Beside her, Shug sat in an off-the-shoulder shirt that revealed an ivy tattoo. She was not the bombshell I'd imagined her to be. Also, she was not a stranger to any kind of pole. Then Misty, whose lips dripped with gloss.

"I've been wanting to meet you," I said, reaching for Nick's hand.

"Wouldn't miss it," Dora said.

"Nick invited me," Shug said.

I might've been annoyed—oh did he, did Nick invite you—if I wasn't in severe pain, which cancels out everything. I felt explosive. I felt like I would not make it through the assembly with Peter Singer when I had an explosion on my body. I wanted someone to take it off. I wanted to take it off. When my fake leg hurt, I took it off and laid it against the wall. I took it to the prosthetist and exchanged it for another. I took a day off from school. I called whomever I wanted at whatever hour. There was no knowing anything with this leg other than pain. I focused on the back of Shug's head, her curly, big hair, and thought, so you're the Bean Tree

Botanist. Her hair turned around, and from somewhere inside the hairdo, she said, "Mercedes invited us to the party tomorrow night. You going?"

"Sure," Nick said.

"Don't know." I looked at Nick.

Mercedes and Leonard came to the door. Mercedes wore Ziploc bags on her ankles, harnessed by pink ribbons, the same ribbons from Leonard's Halloween costume. The gallon bags of sand synched her hose. She was somewhere between float stepping and full stepping. Leonard held her around the waist. They sat in the front row beside the bartender from Sandy's. I focused on the passing of jock itch from him to her to Leonard, who wore a baseball cap. Leonard was going bald but he was not making any concessions to baldness. I took his cap as a sign that he was making progress with Mercedes. Before tonight, he had not cared to cover his head, and now, Mercedes on his arm, suddenly an age prophylactic. Men in their forties who wear ball caps aren't fooling anyone.

The auditorium was ancient, with hardwood chairs that squeaked anytime you moved, teal linoleum, and a popcorn ceiling. Framed photographs lined the walls—James Watson and Barbara McClintock, among others—action shots in the laboratory. The auditorium smelled like Pine-Sol. Simon must've polished the chairs. Down in the front, Tweedle Dee and Dum sat beside Debbie and her husband. A family from the Petri Plate Relay Race sat on the far left. Reporters had not been invited. I counted heads and came up with twenty-two people. The Gee walked to the stage, stood behind the podium, and cleared his throat.

"Welcome to the Colony. I'm Engel Deeter, Lead Geneticist, Prevail through Knowledge." He spoke like he was addressing an audience of thousands. When he delivered the motto, he gestured with his right hand, pointer and thumb making a circle. He raised the gesture to his temple. Three or four people in the audience did it back. "We know you have questions. Let me say that the Colonists are hitting their marks, doing their best, and minor setbacks are to be expected. We're in our last weeks here, and we look forward to showing our final results when Fall Lab is complete. Tonight we'll begin with a few slides, and then I'll introduce our esteemed guest Peter Singer."

Misty raised her hand. The Gee tried to ignore her, but she waved her hand in the air. I pinched Nick's leg and whispered, "These are your friends."

"Please hold your questions," the Gee said.

"How long?" Misty said.

"We'll take questions at the end of the presentation."

"How long is that going to be?"

He continued with his talk.

Misty turned to Shug and whispered something. Dora leaned across Shug and gave Misty a scolding. The three sat back in their chairs. They crossed their legs and swayed their calves and tapped their feet and none of them were in pain. In the front row, Leonard's leg pinned Mercedes to her seat. The Gee showed images of Leonard's ANK3, Mercedes' FTO, Nick's SUI. He paused on Eliot's brain, circling with laser pen various areas, while the audience cooed. He ended on slides from the quantum cascade laser and an X-ray of my femur. It felt bizarre to see the femur inside my midthigh projected onto a screen and to think the femur on the screen was growing in my body. The Gee gave the stage to Peter Singer.

"I've been in some hot water," Singer said, "over a statement I made years ago regarding personhood. The statement was, 'Killing a defective infant is not morally equivalent to killing a person. Sometimes it is not wrong at all.'" I looked at Nick. I said the words back to myself in my head. Singer explained and reexplained and then directed it toward us, as if we were somehow to explain to him what he meant, as if we were complicit. How could that be? Weren't we—Eliot remembering, Leonard keeping Mercedes in her seat, Nick cured of suicide, and me growing a leg—weren't we proof of letting a kid live? I wanted to leave the auditorium, but I couldn't hop out of the auditorium. I couldn't leave the auditorium without causing a scene.

Nick rubbed my fingers, and while I felt him rubbing my fingers, I also felt the mutiny of nerves at the end of my leg, nerves that had not been called upon for years, nerves that were bridging a knee, nerves that knew a foot primitively, nerves in distress. Singer wanted to explain his statement insofar as the future was concerned. This got us into a thorny part of his talk, where he defined time, catapulted time into the number one qualifier of life, cracked a joke to make the audience laugh, and where did the audience think we were? A cocktail party? With Jay Gatsby? Singer discussed how we were further proof of his agenda, namely, that bioethics was the future, and here I got lost, thinking of him as a paradox. Wasn't he advocating infanticide?

"What's defective, exactly, Mr. Singer, because you're wearing glasses," I said. My voice echoed. The women from the Green House looked over their shoulders.

"I'm talking about a person who has no concept of the future."

"People with glasses okay, then?"

"Yes."

"People with glasses okay."

"Did you have a question?"

It was one thing for Singer to beseech us to join him in scientific progress, and another for him to besmirch us in the process.

My leg was burning the hell off, so that was one way to go. I could just stand up and hop to the door. Tell everyone I was having an episode. I hadn't read his books so it was possible—counterargument—that I wasn't quite getting where he was going. Except. There wasn't much wiggle room in a two-sentence thesis. I understood perfectly the words *killing, infant, morally equivalent.* I stood, taking the blanket, taking Nick's hand, and hopped toward the door of the auditorium. If people were gasping, or talking, or whispering, I couldn't hear them. I had ears only for Mr. Singer who was saying: "If you could, I'd like to talk to you about this more. Do you know what I mean by 'concept of time'?"

"I'm pretty busy. I'm growing a leg over here. So I'll just do what I do and you do what you do and you keep me out of what you do. I'm in pain right now. I'm not interested in time. I'm not interested in killing anyone for any kind of reason. Good night, everyone."

What Makes a Human a Human

Oxford English Dictionary

1. You are distinguished from animals by superior mental development, power of articulate speech, and upright posture.

2. You are the nature of humans; that is human or consists of human beings.

3. a. You belong to human beings as distinguished from God or superhuman beings.

    b. Your relatives are humans.

Bible, King James Version

Gen 2:7—And the Lord God formed you of the dust of the ground, and breathed into your nostrils the breath of life; and you became a living soul.

Qur'an

50:16—Now, verily, it is We who created you, and We know what your soul whispers to you: for we are nearer to you than your jugular vein.

Babylonian Talmud

Yebamot 69b—The embryo that made you was considered to be mere water until the fortieth day.

Singer

You have some concept of time.

Are We Going to the Dance Party?

———

THE NEXT DAY I was in no mood for a dance party. Nor was I in the mood to debate what made a human a human with Nick, who'd been philosophizing while he buttered and jellied a piece of bread. "My girl lives on PB and J, clementines, and cigs," he said, licking his fingers. We ate the sandwiches. He said there was no use trying to talk to a man like Peter Singer who hearsed and re-hearsed and whose mind was set. He said he was proud of me for standing up for my principles. He said the little hand gesture they did was gay. He said the important things for us to do were eat, sleep, and our favorite position, standard cowgirl. As for him, he was feeling good: He kept hold of his dreams by the coattails; jotted down, in the morning, various impressions; read a chapter from the Talmud; talked to his uncle about buying livestock; told his mom he'd be home for Hanukah. He had a crick in his neck from sleeping on my shoulder. He said otherwise it looked like we were doing best of the bunch, and that we should celebrate by go-ing to Mercedes' dance party.

"How am I supposed to dance?"

"I'll put you on my shoulders."

"I don't feel good."

"C'mon, I want to show you off." He lifted me from the kitchen and carried me to the bed.

"You got jam on my sweater." The pain felt like a hundred bee stings followed by a gigantic blood-sucking leech. The nerves were dedifferentiating, multiplying, screaming like a death-metal choir, crescendo, decrescendo, and I couldn't enjoy the sex, and the codeine did little for me. The Gee said only to take them when absolutely necessary, so as not to become dependent.

"Let's go to the party. Want to? I'm going to tell everyone, 'My girl regenerates.' How does that sound? My girl regenerates. They saved your slide for last."

I looked down to see how far past the knee I'd grown. I wanted the thing to grow adult-size. "You just need to be patient," the Gee said. "It will mature." So far I didn't like it. It looked conical and pointed.

Nick was hovering: "We should mark inches on the doorframe. Want to?"

"Not really." It was something five-year-olds did. I looked at Nick, who was looking at the leg. "Nick, stop."

"What?"

"It's growing."

"I can see that."

"So stop looking."

Nick kissed the top of my head.

"What are you doing?"

"Nothing."

"You think I want to make out while it's growing?"

"Sorry."

"Go do something."

"What's the matter?"

"I don't feel good."

The leg stopped. Each time the leg stopped, I wondered if it was worth it. When the leg was growing, at least something was happening, so it seemed worth it. I wondered when my sex drive would return. Would I want to do it again in the old high way of doing it without thinking, let's do this so I can try and forget for ten minutes, half an hour, who this person is? The longest I'd had was with Old Faithful. No Ocean setting. Just human settings. Back and forth. Rest and start up. The Marquis de Sade claims there are six hundred sexual positions. Most of the men I've slept with know four. The everlasting night took place in my apartment on Holly Oak Road in Durham, on the fire escape, in the kitchen, and the bedroom. I had no concept of time, so perhaps I wasn't human that night.

"You're wearing lace," Nick said.

"I always wear lace."

"Maybe you shouldn't if you don't want me to kiss you."

"What time is the party?"

"You want to go to the party?"

"Get the red V-neck from the closet." While Nick walked to the closet, I flipped on the flat screen and searched for my femur on the Cold Spring Harbor Channel. I searched for anatomical drawings of bones after the kneecap. I typed things like *anatomy of the calf* and *human bones the knee beyond*. I saw a talus in my future. A talus would be the ankle.

"Can you bend the knee?" Nick asked.

"So far I'm good at extension and not good at flexion. I grew four bones in four days. And look at my patella. My patella is tiny."

"Baby, I want to get you pregnant. I've been having dreams of bassinets, rattles, geometric mobiles, Fisher-Price toys, and that duck on the Yangtze River."

"Dear God."

"Do you know that duck?" Nick was talking from behind the

clothes rack. "I can't remember his name. I'd like to read that story out loud to some children. C'mon, let's get pregnant. You have to admit I'd make a good dad. I'm betting I could get you pregnant on one shot."

"Get my sweater."

He pulled two sweaters from the rack before he found the red V-neck.

"I need a hair band."

He walked to the bathroom. "Leave it down."

"Why?"

"Your hair's long as hell."

I changed into the sweater while Nick used the bathroom. He said it was something special, him going to a dance party, the only dancing he did was back in Madison, at the Lodge, and so he assured me I didn't have to fret because he didn't listen to Mercedes-type music, he was pretty sure he didn't listen to Mercedes-type music, and he liked the sweater, and my hair down my shoulders. He straightened my bangs. He said we'd call it an early night, anyway, we'd tell them we were calling it an early night.

Dance Party with Wine

———

Genes from animals and plants could be spliced straight
into the grape's genome.

— ECONOMIST

MERCEDES HAD INVITED a small group. She was talking in
the middle of the room to the bartender from Sandy's. Leonard
was drinking from a Styrofoam cup in the kitchen. Dora and
Shug danced with a guy who had a handlebar mustache. A few
fishermen stood with their backs against the wall. Music blasted
from a pair of Peavey speakers on stands. The flat screen showed
a playlist of rappers. Mercedes was shaking it to Spank Rock
with the bartender from Sandy's. I'd been trapped in a classical–
country vortex. I started bouncing on Nick's shoulders. He said
something I couldn't hear. The pain waned with *bump that* on
the speakers.

Mercedes saw us immediately. She was wearing a hat that
looked like a pincushion.

"Put me down," I said. I could stand on one leg for half an hour
without losing balance.

"You came!" Mercedes said. "I'm sloshed. Totally, totally
sloshed. Chase got me drunk."

The bartender offered his hand. "What's up," he said. I thought his name was exceptionally cool for a guy who had jock itch and a toothpick in his mouth. It was the first time I'd seen him from the waist down, since he was always behind the bar. He'd seen me full figure, while I'd only known him by the red bandanna he occasionally wore around his head and his long-sleeve shirts with logos. Tonight's shirt featured the silhouette of a curvaceous woman holding a gun. He was wearing tear-away pants with Vans.

"What's up," he repeated.

We stood there looking at each other while Mercedes arranged the pincushion on top of her head.

Nick said, "Do you guys remember that children's book about the duck on the Yangtze River?"

"The who? The what? Get this man a cup of transgenic wine," Mercedes said, kissing Chase on the cheek and wiping the lipstick off with her thumb.

Chase went to the kitchen. Mercedes asked us to forgive her for being so drunk. He came back from the kitchen with two cups.

"What's with the wine?"

"Pinot spliced with pork and blackberry. Chicks dig it. Don't they?"

"I love it."

Nick took a drink.

I wasn't jazzed about drinking porked wine.

"Not too shabby," Nick said.

Chase nodded. He was one of those "I can't be bothered" drunks.

"I bartend in Madison," Nick said. "A joint called The Scout. You ever been to Madison?"

"Nope, I go to the city. After that, what's the point?"

I turned to Mercedes. "I like your headpiece."

"I made it myself. Chase helped hold the foam while I stapled the fabric."

Chase took a swig of his drink. I noticed his hand on the waistband of Mercedes' skirt. I leaned forward, so it looked as if I were checking the place out, to see who had come, and who had stayed home, when really I wanted to know if Chase's hand was inside the waistband of her skirt. It was. Leonard noticed too. When I looked at him, he was talking to Shug the Bean Tree Botanist while looking over her head at Chase.

A fisherman came up to me. "You're like FDR of the Colony," he said as he leaned in. I tried to ignore him. I was pissed because I had done such a good job of focusing on Chase and Mercedes, tracing the trajectory of Leonard's gaze. The tableau got my mind off the patella, the talus, and the leg in general, and the distance Nick and I were from the same place. While I was worried over bone fusion and flexion, he was thinking of ducks on the Yangtze River.

Nick said, "We're trying to relax, if you don't mind."

The fisherman stood. "She's like FDR of the Colony. Nowadays America would never elect a cripple. Back then we broke the Constitution to elect one. Nowadays forget about it. I got a niece with spina bifida. Be glad you don't got that because she can't walk at all, and no one's interested in curing spina bifida at the Colony yet. I saw you walk in Sandy's Bar a ways back, and you walk real nice but she can't walk at all. They love her in Huntington Bay. Have you been to Huntington Bay? I guess they keep you here, mostly. If you ever get to feeling bad, because I know it must be hard—like, why me?—if you ever get to feeling bad, you go to the Huntington Bay Burn Center, and you take a look at some of those people with their faces burned off. You won't last three minutes. I get down on myself sometimes, but then I think there's people worse off. It's like that old saying, I was feeling bad until

I met a man without any legs. My niece is in a wheelchair. That's where she is and I guess that's where she'll always be. Unless the scientists put spina bifida on the radar. How do you go about putting a disease on the radar? Do you know? Did the Shriners help you? The Shriners do amazing things. It's amazing what they can do for the worse off. I hurt a little for you, I look at you, young as you are, and I hurt a little. See me, I got a defect, I only got but four toes on each foot, but you wouldn't know it unless I took my shoes off. I'll let you get back to your friend, but I just wanted to say hello, say I think it's real nice they're making things better for you." He walked toward the kitchen.

"He kept running his mouth and I didn't know how to interrupt him," Nick said.

Of course you didn't, I thought. I felt like a monument that the fisherman had just put a wreath around. So I was worse off than him? The guy with the beer gut and the whiskery face and the stench of dead fish? The guy bumping into the couch on his way to the kitchen? I was worse off than this individual?

Nick was about to say something to me when Eliot and Layla arrived, Eliot first, leading Layla by the hand. We stepped out of the way. I heard Nick ask Eliot about the duck on the Yangtze River. "Ping," Eliot said without hesitating, and Nick said, "Yes! That's him!" I heard Leonard's voice rise, above the music, as he argued with the handlebar mustache over the prettiest land in the country. "Right here in the backyard," Handlebar said. "West of Illinois," Leonard said.

Eliot brought a bottle of tequila for Mercedes. Layla stood awkwardly beside him with her chin hidden in a turtleneck.

"You must be Layla," I said. "Eliot's smitten. We've heard good things." I find it awkward to meet people I've heard about. Or when they've heard about me. What had Eliot told Layla? There's a woman here, short, brown hair, brown eyes. There's a woman here smokes like a chimney, doesn't eat three square meals a day, concerns me. There's a woman here worse off with one leg, so if you meet her try to look waist level or above. Pretend she's behind a bar.

"How long have you two been together?"

"We're not officially together."

"But you were."

Nick could've helped. Instead his attention was taken elsewhere. I saw him mouth something to someone across the room, and I couldn't follow up since I was in the middle of flubbing my introduction to Layla. She had a black bob. Her eyes were light blue. When she smiled, I noticed her teeth were intact. Eliot doesn't love that woman, I thought, because the woman Eliot loves is plain with a chip on her tooth. Then I rationalized that maybe Layla had her tooth capped. She wasn't plain though. Eliot had said she was plain.

The leg started growing and I sat down. Layla gasped. She put her hand to her mouth.

"It's okay," I told her.

She pointed at me and grabbed Eliot by the coat sleeve. Eliot whispered into her ear.

Nick wasn't doing anything except watching.

I rolled the pants up to show them. "See, it's okay."

The fisherman shouted, "She's growing, she's growing." He darted from the kitchen back to the front of the room. Nick put his arm out to block the fisherman from getting too close to me.

Chase said, "Shit."

I sat there, growing for them, not sure what to say, and wishing Nick would say it for me.

"Does it hurt?" Eliot said.

Layla had not recovered from her gasp.

"Not much."

"What does it feel like?" Eliot asked. If it had been the fisherman asking, I would've told him to fuck off, but I felt I owed Eliot an explanation.

"It feels like if you were wearing a latex glove, and poked your fingers through the glove. It feels like that."

Mercedes put her hand on their backs, one back at a time, and led them to the dance floor.

"C'mon party animals, leave Anne Hatley alone. I want each and every one of you out there shaking it."

I loved Mercedes. They followed her to the dance floor, but they kept glancing at me. I rolled my pants down and sat in the chair waiting for the leg to stop.

"Are you okay?" Nick said. I wanted to yell at him, tell him he had to find some kind of better technique to deal with people. Silence would not do.

"Yep," I said. He picked me up from the chair, sat down in it himself, and put me on his lap.

"Are you sure?"

"Nick, shut up." How was I supposed to be sure about anything? How could he ask me that?

The leg stopped and with it my anxiety. So it would not grow right in that moment. I relaxed. I focused on Mercedes. She took the weights off her feet and then I understood the pragmatic purpose for the pincushion hat. She bumped her head against the ceiling to the beat. I thought of how weird Mercedes looked. I said to Nick, "Doesn't Mercedes look weird?" and thought of how weird I looked and compared myself to Mercedes, and the others in the room, most of whom did not look any weirder than any group of people dancing at a party. The problem with the women at this party, even with their mature patellae, their knees pouting for it, their formed taluses in their zipped boots, the problem was that they clung to the men. And these men danced like they might drift off to take a leak at any moment. Mercedes bumped her head on the ceiling for Chase alone, for Chase alone her eyes grew wide as quarters when she touched the ground, for Chase alone her skirt revealed herself when she bumped the ceiling. Dora sucked the neck of Handlebar. Shug made eyes at Nick while bouncing against one of the fishermen.

"Go dance with her."

"I don't want to."

I looked at her legs. I can't tell most of the time what is what and who is who and who means what to whom. But about this, I'm certain. I don't ever want to be the what that prevents someone from who-who-ing. Nick wanted to dance with her. How could he not? I was cone legged. Shug's legs were tan. Her ankles were busily decorated with hemp, butterfly tattoo, and silver chain.

"Why don't you dance with her?"

"She's got a partner."

"I saw you say something to her."

"I'm with you."

Shug was grinding her ass into a fisherman, a different one, not the one who had assaulted me with his spina bifida niece. Shug was bending forward, leaning back, and flinging her hair from shoulder to shoulder. She grabbed a stray breast in her push-up bra and pulled it up.

"I think you should dance with her."

"Anne."

"What?"

"Have you noticed you're trying to pick a fight?"

"Don't be psychological, Nick. I'm just making a suggestion."

"Holy helmet."

"It's just a suggestion."

"Ain't you a ray of sunshine." Nick slid his hands between my legs.

"I feel weird. I feel like Layla's looking at me."

"No one's looking at you."

"Layla is definitely looking at me." She was. I started thinking about Layla's chin, kept tucked in her turtleneck, and was that because it embarrassed her? She took her chin out to sip the transgenic wine. She was probably shy about her chin, poking as it was, sticking out and forefronting her face.

"No one's looking—"

"I don't care if they are or if they aren't." I took Nick's hands from my jeans. "It feels like they are."

We stalemated. Nick was not being honest with himself, with me, since Shug's legs were already grown, long, slender. It was apparent, her knees were pouting for it, toward Nick and me, that Shug had no interest in the fisherman. I looked down at my legs. If I ever had an ankle on my right leg, I would not occupy it with hemp and tattoos and chains. I would let it be just an ankle.

The music stopped. Everyone turned to look at Leonard. "Where's Mercedes?"

Nick jumped out of the chair, which put me on the ground, and I got to my left foot, stood on my left leg, then climbed on the chair Nick had been sitting in to survey the room.

"Has anyone seen Mercedes?"

"She's chucking up in the alley," Chase said.

There was a dash to the alley. I got there last, hopping through the kitchen, and getting elbowed by the fishermen who stood in the doorway. I pushed through them, past Layla and Eliot, past Shug and Dora and Chase, until I was standing beside Nick in front of a pile of vomit. I held my nose. Nick took his hat off and covered his face.

"Party faux pas," Shug squealed.

"I don't see anything," someone said.

Leonard shushed us. He held his hands out to his sides and stared up.

Overhead, Mercedes. At first she was just four or five feet above our heads, and if there'd been a giant among us, he could've nabbed her by the toe of her shoe. She pointed due south, ballerina style, as if she fully intended to pirouette back to us. We spied up her skirt, what Chase had seen, we all saw, a lack of panties, and Leonard said:

"Lord have mercy."

"Dammit, get me down," Mercedes said. There she was, a bit farther away, level with the second story of the bungalow.

"Stay there, stay there," Leonard said.

"Where the hell am I going to go? Give me something to hold onto."

Mercedes was heading toward the roof. For a second it looked as if she might grab hold of a satellite dish the size of a dinner plate, and I knew she could reach it if she stretched out her arm. But she was preoccupied, using her arms like oars, trying to scull through air.

Leonard ran up the stairs to his place and climbed onto the roof. He stretched his hand toward Mercedes. She was a couple inches northwest.

"Leonard, you idiot, can't you grab a stick or something."

"Dude," Chase said to no one in particular.

Nick was looking for a stick on the ground as Mercedes yelled and Leonard jumped up and down on the roof, stretching his hand toward her each time. I thought of the rope and Nick said he could lasso.

"Dude," Chase said. "Where's the rope?"

Leonard yelled down where the rope was—hanging on a hook next to the front door—and Shug went skipping into the house to find it.

"Should we call the police?" Dora said. She got out her cell. We heard her tell the operator: "Our friend is in the sky." The operator hung up.

Eliot said, "The red button."

We all looked at him.

"Go push it," Nick said.

"Mercedes is fucked," Chase replied.

Shug found the rope and handed it to Nick, who tied it and threw it into the air. It was too late, she was too far, she was farther than twenty-five feet, she was farther than the telephone poles, the tops of trees, the roofs of the tallest buildings. It was a matter of direction and wind speed. A high heel fell to the ground. It landed on the road beside the Colony. The other high heel fell. It landed in an evergreen.

"MERCEDES," Leonard screamed from the roof.

We heard a high-pitched little cry.

The Search

———

This was an extraordinary year: For one thing, it had almost
430 days.

— ELAINE FANTHAM, on 46 BC
Roman Literary Culture: From Cicero to Apuleius

THAT SAME NIGHT, Friday night, we had hope, amiable weather conditions, a slight breeze, cold by Southern standards, but to
New Englanders, a mild night for November, a lack of precipita-
tion, a lack of clouds, and the foghorn blared, though there was
no fog. I hopped through Mercedes' place thinking, She'll be all
right. They'll find her. The Gee came in his sports car with the
doors that opened up, and stepped out in his robe, on the phone,
speaking in a rapid, clipped voice. "I can't manage this," he said.
The voice on the other end cleared the airspace over Long Island,
no small feat for the weekend before Thanksgiving, and sent up
search helicopters, and turned satellites to the atmosphere. The
Gee cursed.

If it had been the middle of the day.

Why the fuck not midafternoon?

Why wasn't she wearing the weights?

The flybys lasted into the early morning. The others left: Shug and Dora to their shared apartment on the beach, Chase to the bar for last call, the fishermen to their schooners. Eliot had wanted to stay with us, but Layla was hysterical. She'd gone into a fit with the sound of the helicopters overhead and the commotion of the spotlights. Leonard refused to come down off the roof.

"Leonard, come down, you'll freeze," we said.

"I don't care, I'll freeze then," he said.

I wanted to be close to Nick. Closer to Nick then I'd ever wanted to be, in light of Mercedes' takeoff, and in light of spotlights, and in light of there being too little light with which to search for Mercedes properly. The Gee stood in the parking lot, waiting for Watson to arrive. Nick and I stood in the alley near Leonard. We brought blankets from Mercedes' bungalow and tossed them up to Leonard. He kicked them off the roof.

"She ain't got nothing on but a skirt. How's she supposed to stay warm?"

I smoked another pack of Winstons and sent Nick to the store.

"That bartender is dead meat," Leonard said.

"Maybe she landed on a roof," I said.

"I'll kill him."

Leonard believed Chase was responsible. It was Chase who had his hand in Mercedes pants, which gave Chase culpability for Mercedes' well-being. I wanted to point out that rarely does the person with his hand down your pants take into consideration your well-being. Instead I said, "They'll find her."

Nick returned from the store in auto mode. It was as if his walk to the store had charged him and he suddenly knew exactly what we had to do. "We have to find Mercedes," was his big revelation. He discussed details of the evening with a couple police officers who jotted down his words onto a missing person report while looking at each other baffled. Watson arrived with tufts of white hair tented on his head. "No," Watson said to a police officer. "You wouldn't understand. I'll take it from here."

By 5:00 AM Saturday, I was pacified on transgenic wine. I felt tender toward Nick. At least as tender as I could feel, since the leg was a cone, and it was my cone, and my sidekick had thrown herself up into the air. As soon as Mercedes was in the air, I began thinking of her as my best friend. I began thinking of how she brought joy to my life. I thought it in those words: Mercedes brought joy to my life. The incident revealed a side of Nick I hadn't seen. The under-pressure Nick. He threatened to join the search by helicopter, and I begged him to stay. When he listened to me, when he did not board the helicopter, I thought, Wow, this guy really likes me, and he must not have slept with Mercedes, because if he had slept with her, surely he would be in a helicopter, elevation five thousand feet, instead of standing here beside me. And I thought, Nick will search for me, if I go missing, he will get in a helicopter and ransack the sky.

I drank three glasses of the wine. Nick told me to stop after the second glass but I didn't listen. We stayed in the bungalow with Watson and the Gee and a dozen research assistants who'd set up flat screens, coordinates, charts, and graphs of the sky. We surprised many flocks of birds with spotlights. We honed in on many objects—home, swimming pool, trampoline, pond, skiff, buoy, flagpole, steeple, billboard.

"What's over there?" I asked.

The Gee clicked his mouse to magnify the image. "That's a shed."

"Nick, take me home," I said. "Nick Burkowitz."

"I heard you."

"Take me home and blast me off."

The Gee looked at me.

"What do you know about it? Think you know everything about where everyone is."

Nick picked me up, one arm under my knees—I was in flexion! I was in flexion!—one arm under my neck, and carried me to Bungalow North. My knee was bending! I didn't want to tell Nick. I wanted to keep it a secret a little while longer. Just between me and me. I had a bending knee on my right leg, and I could think *flex*, and it flexed.

"I didn't even know Mercedes listened to rap. Did you know I'm in flexion?" I asked him.

Nick wasn't taking his boots off. Usually, he took his boots off the second we got into my bungalow.

"Why aren't you taking your boots off?"

"Baby."

"Let's check my leg, want to?" I found a rap station on the flat screen and pushed play. Nick followed behind me and turned it down. He stood in front of the screen. I took my pants off, threw them at him, then my sweater. He picked them up from the floor and placed them in the chair.

"You're in flexion. Nice."

"I had no idea she listened to rap. I like rap, but you don't. I can listen to any type of music, but you can't. Look at my patella!"

"I'm going to fix you a glass of water and an Advil."

"I don't want any fixing. Got it? Now please give me a kamikaze."

"You're drunk."

"That is very true. How very true you're always being," I said. I was sitting on the bed in the middle, looking down. My breasts looked bigger. What was going on? I looked at my legs, the better and the worse, and I thought, I know what's going on. I have more body on my breasts too. "What do you think about my proportions?"

"Your what?" He took his hat off and sat down in the chair.

"You're sitting on my pants."

Nick pulled the pants from under him, folded them, and laid them on the arm of the chair.

"What do you think?"

"About what?"

"About my proportions." The album cover on the flat screen lit the room. "Am I going to be a Real Doll? I want to be a Real Doll."

"You are a real doll."

"Oh Nick, you don't even know. Where are my cigarettes?"

Nick stood from the chair, walked to the kitchen, and pulled the cigarettes from my purse. He poured a glass of water and walked back. He sat on the bed this time.

"Thank you," I said, taking a sip of water.

Nick lit a cigarette for himself and one for me.

"You don't even smoke."

"Rarely."

"You shouldn't, because it's bad for you."

"Are you going to be all right if I leave?"

"Why would you leave?"

"Baby."

"Why would you?"

"You're drunk."

"Would you like to see my patella?"

"I see it."

"It is very pretty, don't you think?"

"Yes."

"It is much like a clementine."

"Do you need anything?"

"I need a kamikaze, please."

"Not right now."

"Why not?"

"Because."

"Do you like giving me kamikazes?"

"Yes."

"Are you going to like it if I only have a clementine for a knee?"

Nick held the smoke from his cigarette in his mouth. He exhaled: "Sure."

"I don't know if I will."

Nick leaned forward. I thought he was going to start a kamikaze. I raised my arm and leaned the back of that hand, with the cigarette, on top of my head. I looked down because when I raised my arm it lifted my breast.

"Are my breasts getting bigger? They look huge. I'm not pregnant; I just had my period. Do they look big to you?"

"They do look a little bigger."

"What is that? Is that good?"

"Yeah."

"Where are you?"

"I'm right here."

"But where are you exactly?"

"I'm behind you."

"What are you doing?"

"I'm fixing the pillows."

"No you're not," I snapped. He put his palm on my back.

"I'm arranging them."

I arched my back against his palm and looked over my shoulder at him. He didn't move toward me. He pulled on the comforter and motioned for me to get under it. I nearly burnt myself with the cigarette.

"Be careful," Nick said, dropping his cigarette in the glass of water. He pushed the comforter under me and drew it around my sides. I was still smoking, down to the filter, and he was waiting for me to finish.

"When you're fucking someone do you think about them a lot or do you not really?"

"Here, let me have that." Nick took my cigarette and dropped it in the water.

"Be honest, are you thinking about them or not really? Is there someone you're thinking about?"

"I'm thinking about the person."

"That's really good."

"Why?"

"I don't know."

"You don't know what?"

"What happens to people when you're fucking them."

"Baby."

"I used to not think, not of anything really. I think so much about legs now, what the fuck. It used to not even occur to me to think about them until someone else said something. Now I have a patella and I'm in flexion and I think a lot and I can't know anything for sure about what I was like, and whether it was okay, or if it was always not okay. It's not like you can ever know what you're like in bed. Or what you're like at all. Only other people can. Do you know what I'm saying?"

"Yeah."

"What was I like in bed?"

Nick bit the inside of his lower lip. After a few seconds, he said, "Aggressive."

"That makes me sound mean. What else?"

"You were," Nick paused. "You just did whatever you wanted. You just did it. I've never been with anyone like that. I don't want to make comparisons."

"Then don't."

"You just did whatever you wanted."

"Like what?"

"You were very into it."

"You're talking like we won't do it again. Like whoever we were, we're not them anymore."

"I'm going to let you get some sleep." His voice got softer.

I lowered my voice to match his. "I don't know who you're with."

"I'm with you."

"Is that very true?"

"It's very true."

"But Nick," I said. He leaned his head onto mine. "I don't want to be . . . I was with someone this one time, and he kept saying, 'Let me know if I hurt you,' as if I were made of mica or something. Isn't mica a rock that's really thin and break-apart-able?"

It was a genuine question.

"I'm worried I'm going to hurt more now. People thought I hurt more before, like why the fisherman said he hurts for me, what does that even mean, what a bunch of bullshit. I don't want that guy's sympathy. Or like the lady in the convenience store said what she said. That's universal. You have to find a technique, Nick. But maybe you don't have to, maybe you don't need one, because this works, and I'm walking around on real legs saying, 'Are you made of mica? Me too.' I'm walking down the street, humming *The Pink Panther* theme song, and if someone stops, it will only be to say, 'Are you humming *The Pink Panther* song?' Otherwise, I will not stand out, a-ha, *stand* out. You like standing out. You're a person who likes being known for his presence. On football fields, in greenhouses, on streets. You like being seen. I tried to ignore you once, and you climbed on the roof, and shouted, 'Do you love me?' which is like saying, 'Do you least ignore me?' Meanwhile, everyone takes themselves, their bodies, real seriously and runs around the block, for cardiovascular, and for their neighbors to see, so their neighbors can wave and think, 'That Mitch. He's a health-conscious person. He'll be around forever.' Except no one's going to be around forever. Even you're a Mitch."

"I'm not a Mitch."

"Nine times out of ten, you're a Mitch. I mean you take your body real seriously."

"I do not."

"Yes you do, Nick, that is very true. Everyone does. Everyone thinks theirs is real precious. I think that's why, maybe, when they see me, they get scared and say I'm brave because I remind them that they're something like mica, and they could just break apart at any time. See the fake leg. That knee is actually a better knee than the one I'm growing. If it breaks, I send it off. No surgery. But this knee, the one I'm growing, if something happens to it, I'm totally fucked. See I'm starting to think like them. It's already happening. I'm starting to think differently."

"It's just a phase."

"Maybe it doesn't grow, and then what? I don't want to be alone."

Nick put his arms around me. "Anne Hatley, I don't know if you've noticed, but it seems I can't leave you alone. I'm going to be here tomorrow and make you not alone some more."

What We Fix:
American Plastic Surgery
Procedural Statistics

———

Lips	5,014,446
Hair removal	891,712
Breasts	307,230
Nose	279,218
Hips/Thighs	245,138
Leg veins	222,047
Eyelids	221,398
Scar revision	162,803
Face	112,933
Hands	100,354
Forehead	42,063
Birth defect	31,950
Ears	29,434
Dog bite	28,232
Breast-implant removal	19,939
Hair transplant	17,580
Chin	14,117
Buttocks	4,407
Vagina	1,030

Company

_____

I too began to consider the mobility of the earth.
                               —Copernicus, _On the Revolutions_
                                        of the Heavenly Bodies

SUNDAY MORNING. I was sleeping when the caravans began to arrive. I slept until three in the afternoon, and when I woke it took a couple minutes to remember what had happened to Mercedes. That couldn't have happened to Mercedes, I thought. Did I dream it? I sat up in bed and looked out the window to the quad, and beyond the quad, the parking lot, where cars and trucks and RVs and motorcycles were parked outside the gate. People were getting out of their vans, standing around campfires, looking somber and concerned. It was cold, and anytime one of them spoke, a cloud appeared in front of their faces. I turned the flat screen to CNN, MSNBC, Fox, and every station was playing footage of Mercedes, the original footage they'd shot on the day when she wore her cheerleading uniform and did somersaults in the air. It occurred to me that I could die. If Mercedes could disappear, up, up, up, then I could die, and I wasn't scared about this possibility—it's hard to be scared about death when you've been raised around doctors who thought you were going to die soon and told you as much. I felt casual toward the prospect of death, like all right, but first let me smoke a cigarette.

Nick knocked on the door. From the bed, I yelled at him to come in.

"It's Grand Central again."

"Where's Leonard? Is he off the roof yet?"

"He's with the Harley riders from Montauk. They're taking care of him."

"Sorry about last night."

"You were drunk as a skunk."

"Do you want some sweet tea?"

Nick poured himself a glass. "Your favorite reporter's here."

"I don't even know that guy." I wiped sleep from my eyes and tried to get my bearings. I looked down and I had the beginning of a calf.

"I don't understand," I winced as I tried to step down. It felt like a blister hitting the ground. "I don't understand how they can zap your suicide gene, and grow me a leg, and they can't find Mercedes. Don't they have Doppler radar?"

My cell phone rang. It was the mysterious hanger-upper.

"Who's that?" Nick asked as he watered the blue roses.

"No one."

"Are you being shady?"

"Shady?"

"You heard me."

"How would I have the time? The energy?"

"Are you?"

"I can't even walk."

Nick told me the Harley-Davidson guys from Montauk shared their fire pit with a family of Evangelicals from Jersey. Nick called the Evangelicals "the Evans" and gesticulated with his hands how they'd set up camp—coolers, grills, lawn chairs—next to the Harleys.

"Isn't everyone freezing cold?"

"Propane heaters. They hold vigils."

"She's a prophet now?"

"This is what they're saying. You got the guys from the CFI—"

"CFI?"

"The Center for Inquiry."

"Go on."

"You got those guys mingling in between, rebuffing the prophet claims and giving Kleenex to Deeter, who's bawling his eyes out and calling it allergies."

"I'm tired."

"Your leg hurt?"

"No, it's not that."

Nick swore it did not look like a pencil.

"I know what a pencil looks like," I said.

The Case for Mice, as Demonstrated by Mercedes' Disappearance, and a Mouse Has Never Risen into the Sky, and if a Mouse Did, It Would be Less of a Crime

ELIOT'S OPINION: HE and Layla rode in the Astro off the Colony, into the city, and flew from JFK back to Houston. "I've had enough of this crap," Eliot said. He said good-bye to Nick and Leonard. He gave me his life-event journal. It was blank. He told the Gee he was grateful, but at the same time, he was mad about Mercedes. How was he supposed to remember the red button? He remembered it as quickly as he could. He felt horrible. And he hoped that in future trials, the Gee would find a way so that not every memory came rushing back, like a surge, like a flood, because it had been distressing to Eliot, to remember Zach the wrestler, vocabulary from the SAT exams, and every occasion on which he'd fucked up, especially since he'd assigned certain fuck ups to certain people, and it was embarrassing to discover that he'd fucked up one way with one person and another way with another person and he couldn't figure out which fuck up belonged to which person. Much less who he loved. He thought he loved a woman with a chipped tooth that he'd fucked up with, but this was conjecture, he couldn't actually know for sure if he'd fucked up with her, or if he loved her. "Importance of people," Eliot told the Gee. "A file cabinet could keep better track of which people are important." Later Eliot wrote to apologize to us for not remembering the red button quickly enough. He told us he felt personally responsible for Mercedes' disappearance. He told us he'd met this amazing woman named Layla. They shared a rental house in Katy where the landlord consented to him raising mice on property.

Memorial

————

For I in spirit saw thee move
Thro' circles of the bounding sky.
                    —Tennyson, "In Memoriam"

THE DAY AFTER Thanksgiving, the Evans unloaded a trailer's worth of timber and began building, outside the gates of the Colony, a suspension bridge upward. A member of the city council drove by in his Caddy and said, "You can't build here."

"Why not?" the leader of the Evans said. You could tell he was the leader by the way the others surrounded him.

"Private property."

"Who's it belong to?"

"The Colony."

"Mercedes Minnow is part of the Colony. We're building out of respect for Mercedes Minnow." The city councilman went into the main office and returned with the Gee. I was smoking a cigarette in the quad, a blanket covering my legs, and had an eye on Leonard, who looked wrecked. He talked on the phone in front of the bungalow he had once shared with Mercedes. His friends, the Harley-Davidson riders, had blazed out of town. He asked for a cigarette.

"Angie doesn't get it," Leonard said, coughing as he exhaled.

"Get what?"

"Why I'm upset over this shit."

We were all upset. We had been upset as we sat through the search, and sat through the Gee's apology, and Watson's stiff rhetoric on scientific progress, in which he quoted Kant. "Another utilitarian coyote bastard," Nick said. On Thanksgiving we sat in front of the flat screen in the lounge watching the president say, "Let us give thanks for the brave people at the Colony, who have weathered the loss of their friend. Let us mourn with them. Their loss is our loss. Let us keep strong and united in the face of an inventive developmental science that has already proven to be the salvation of many." None of us felt grateful or saved. The president pinned an American flag to the lapel of Mercedes' mother's jacket. Leonard suffered the worst. The Gee arranged for a research assistant to move with Leonard back to Fargo, where they could finish treatment and observe him at MeritCare Medical Center. This was his last day.

"Angie doesn't get it."

"I imagine she doesn't know the extent of your relationship with—"

"I'm going to punch Chase in the nose."

Leonard looked toward the gates of the Colony where the Gee was proposing a compromise. He said the Evans could build as long as they agreed to disassemble it after twenty-four hours. The Evans vigorously discussed the pros and cons of the offer. They did not want to leave Mercedes' transfigured body in the sky without a way to return.

Leonard was somewhere else. "I used to drive a truck, back and forth between Fargo and Billings. At night, in my cab, I looked down into the car windows and you know what I saw? Lots of lonely people driving between Fargo and Billings. It liked to have put thoughts in my head. After a couple years, I got a thought in my head to marry Angie. She's a firecracker. Red hair. The nails. What do you call them nails?" Leonard held his hand out. His nails were short, his fingers stubby.

"Acrylics."

"I figured it out that she was getting bored. She was bored by the time I figured it out. She started going to the Church of Christ. Something happens when you put a man and a woman in a house and tell them they got to stay there. Something neither love nor worship can cure. She started talking to Frank Jenkins. I don't trust that man farther than I can throw him. She started talking discipleship to Frank Jenkins. So I went looking for something basic in the nights when Angie went to her meetings at the church. I didn't mean nobody harm. Angie said I was going to the demons or I was going to the Colony to drive the demons out. Where's the demons? Do you see them? I ain't seen a demon in my life. Do I look like a demon? I think when people expect demon things of you, then you start doing demon things."

Leonard stubbed the cigarette out with his boot. "I sure do miss Mercedes."

I gave Leonard a hug. When I pulled away, my hair was caught on the button of his shirt. "I got it, I got it," Leonard said as he plied my hair from the button. "Your hair sure is getting long."

The Evans brought ladders from the trailer, hammers, toolboxes, and extension cords. "Plug this in somewhere," the leader said.

Leonard got to his feet, stumbling at first. He was an SOB from sober. He was probably happy to have one more thing to do before he left, one more thing to delay his departure. While he plugged the cord into an outlet on our side of the gate, I remembered plugging my leg into outlets near and far. Grayson remembered to plug in better than I did. I counted on him to lock the doors, bring me a glass of water, and plug my leg into the wall. I was perfectly capable of doing these things on my own, but I didn't mind Grayson doing them for me. Was that love? Letting a person do for you? Leonard stumbled up the steps to his bungalow. The Evans built the suspension bridge with their power drills. It slanted into the sky like a ramp.

Conversation in the Dark

———

Head plumage helps the whiskered auklet of the Aleutian
Islands avoid obstacles in the dark.

— *SMITHSONIAN*

A STORM CAME. Who knows what Nick was doing for me. Earlier in the day, after the Evans finished the sky ramp, their leader
suggested I climb it to get closer to God. I was seeing the leader's face with my eyes closed, as Nick did what he did, and I was
wondering if he'd taken down the ramp. The leader said I was a
miracle. "If I'm a miracle," I said, "maybe I'm closer to God than
you think." He didn't have a retort. He was holding the spokes of
the gate with both hands, leaning his head between the bars. He
said it was my father's sin that brought me into the world deficient
and it was a miracle my leg was grown to the calf and it was my being an adulteress that aggrieved him. He said *deficient*, and as Nick
was doing who knows what I was thinking of the word *deficient*
because I'm called a lot of things but that's not been one of them.
I saw the leader of the Evans, eyes closed, and I made the expected
noises, and thought more about the word *deficient* and how the leg
seemed now more deficient than ever.

"Can I ask a question?" Nick said.

"Ask it."

"I'm not sure I should."

"Why?"

"I'm not sure you'll answer me. Are you serious about me?"

"Yeah, I'm serious."

"How serious are you?"

"I'm serious."

"Are you sure?"

"Yeah."

"Good to hear."

"Was that the question?"

Nick sat beside me. We had no place to lean our heads since he'd moved the bed to the middle of the room. I reached for my cigarettes.

"Please don't smoke."

"Why?"

"We're in the middle of something."

"I can smoke and pay attention." Nick put his hands behind his head. I lit the cigarette. The wind knocked tree branches against the window.

"I just got a chill," Nick pulled the sheets up.

"I can't move to Madison."

"How'd you know I was going to say that?"

"You've been saying it."

"I never asked you to move to Madison."

"Well, I'm not going to."

"Let me ask it. You should let me ask before you answer. Pretend like you don't know what I'm going to say." Nick put his lips on my neck. I stretched my neck back and inhaled on the cig.

"Anne Hatley, will you move to Madison?"

"No."

"Anne Hatley, will you move to Chicago?"

"No."

"Will you move to Saint Louis?"

"No."

"Terre Haute?"

"Where the hell is Terre Haute?"

"It's in Indiana, baby."

"Nick, what is the point of this?"

"It's making the city of Madison feel better. At least you're not begrudging the city of Madison. I guess I'll have to move to Durham."

"I don't think that's a good idea either."

"You don't?"

"What about your land and the cabin behind your parents' house?"

"They got land in Durham, don't they? Who says they don't?"

"Nick."

"What is your suggestion?"

"I think we should visit each other."

"Visit?"

"I don't want to force this."

"Forget I even asked."

"I don't want to make decisions in this state. Who's to say when we're out of here?"

"We're leaving December 15. It's on the handout."

"Mercedes Minnow is on the handout and you don't see her leaving December 15."

"Forget I even asked." Nick got up from the bed, taking the comforter with him. He paced beside the bed for a while, then crossed to the window and ran his hand across a leaf of the plant he'd given me. "You are willfully murdering the roses."

With Darwin at Applebee's

———

"THIS IS MY favorite eatery," Darwin said, sliding into a half-moon booth. He brought his birds with him and they fluttered onto the table. He brought a satchel. An older couple sat in the booth beside us. The woman was wearing pearls. The man wore a coat with suede on the elbows. Gray-headed, both of them. Darwin pointed to a black-and-white photo hanging in a frame. "The ladies' crew team of Sag Harbor. Look at sourpuss on the far right. What are you doing, sourpuss? There's a date in the corner. Can you read it?"

I leaned toward the wall where the photo hung. The date was blurred in silver ink, impossible to read. In my two decades of experience with Applebee's, I had not once studied the photos on the walls.

"Einstein to your right, Jackie Chan to your left, a Viking ship attached to the ceiling, and a trombone in the corner. What else do you want from an eatery? How far along are you?"

"You make it sound like I'm pregnant."

"Your hair is growing like a weed."

I looked down. My hair was to my waist.

"How far along?"

"My final appointment is this week. I have the talus of an ankle. First it looked like a pencil, now it looks like a bat. I hate it." I was surprised to hear myself say I hated the leg. I had not committed to such a statement in my head before I said it. Earlier in the day, I'd stuck the talus in a shoe. It could pass for a leg. An emaciated leg. But I couldn't walk without a foot. I began thinking of artificial feet.

"Give it here."

I pulled the leg onto the booth between us. I tucked my hands under the knee. I wasn't used to the leg working on its own. If I had been wearing the prosthetic, I would've needed to tuck my hands under the knee to pull the leg onto the booth. The knee worked without my hands. It was a matter of brain and muscle coordination and it astounded me. I still had to think *move* to get the knee to do it and I wondered if everyone thought *move* and *stay still* and *move* and *stay still*. Probably they didn't have to think as much. I rolled the jeans up. Darwin inspected the leg. He brushed the tip of his beard against the skin around the ankle.

"That tickles." I concentrated on moving the leg, without my hands, until the knee was in flexion against the booth.

"It should tickle."

"I can't wait to wear skirts again."

"What are you waiting for?"

"It's too cold."

"Are you self-conscious?"

"Of course I'm self-conscious."

"After the Colony. What then?"

"I'll go back to Durham."

"And Nick?"

"He wants me to visit."

"Don't do that, Annie."

"Do what?"

"Don't be a visitor."

I took the lime from the edge of my glass and squeezed it into my drink. The waitress came to our table with her manager.

"Sir, we can't have birds in our family restaurant."

"These are family birds."

"I'm sorry, sir."

"I'll be damned," Darwin said. He cupped the birds in his hand, slid out of the booth, and walked the birds outside.

I ordered coconut shrimp with sweet-and-sour sauce. Darwin said he wasn't hungry.

"I've been storing things to tell you."

"Why? Are you going somewhere?"

"I'm going back to the sand trap." Before I could argue, he put a finger to my lips. "Let me do the talking. Number one," Darwin leaned over the table. "You're keeping something from me. I don't know why you'd keep something from me of all people. Who am I going to tell? The archdiocese? Number two. I am coming across more and more bloopers. I can't even call them bloopers anymore because they're atrocious. Did you read those papers I gave you? Those papers came from the archive across the harbor, and it's not pretty. Those papers belong to the very institution into which you are incorporated. They make my son Leonard look like the devil. Lastly, are you going to eat that shrimp?"

I shook my head. I knew that Cold Spring Harbor Laboratory had been a different operation at the turn of the century, a time of phrenology, mesmerism, and water bathing, a completely bogus time. Since then our guys sat down together, roundtable, and discovered the genome. Since then our guys bred dugongs with extremely dense bones and built a greenhouse and harvested bean trees and cured various strands of cancer.

Darwin wrapped the shrimp in a napkin. "My finches thank you." He sat back in the booth and looked through his satchel. He placed a thick manila folder on the table.

"What's this?"

"Files from the archive. My son's involved. They mention my name. My name! They went around collecting defectives like barnacles."

"Where'd you get them?"

"I stole them."

"Darwin."

"What? This is the scientific outfit to which you are incorporated."

I skimmed the files Darwin pushed toward me. "What do you want me to do with these?'

"I thought you should know. If you had read the papers I gave you, then you'd already know what they proposed for cutting off so-called defectives, and you'd already know that Alexander Graham Bell, the magnificent telephone yokel, was completely behind such a project, and you probably do know more than me about the twentieth century. I am becoming more and more concerned about nineteen forty-two. Don't tell me. I trust that you are taking these things, these years, into consideration. Are you?"

"Do you mean eugenics?"

"Right, my cousin's neologism."

"It's been disproved."

"Disproved?" Darwin stood from the table. He looked around at the other booths. "Disproved?"

"Darwin, sit down."

He left the table, walked to the window, and stared out to the parking lot, went to the bar, ordered a double scotch, the whole time playing with his beard, tugging on it, scratching it, and finally braiding it. When he came back to the table, he said: "Newsflash: You are *eugenics*. Eugenics comes to us from the Greek *eu*, meaning *good* or *well*, and the suffix *genes*, your genes, your birth, as in *generate, generation, regeneration*. Eugenics is simply improvement of the human race through intervention. The scientific outfit to which you are incorporated believes themselves to be *intervening* to *improve* you. Am I talking to myself over here?"

"We don't call it that anymore. We call it genetics. That eugenics stuff—it's been disproved; it's antiquated. We've moved beyond that. We have the Universal Declaration of Human Rights now. We have checks and balances."

"So they call it genetics all of a sudden and it's *disproved*? What is this—the name game? It's the same thing, Annie. Call shit any name you like and it still stinks. Are you wearing a blindfold over goggles?"

"Of course I'm wearing a blindfold over goggles. I'm in the middle of growing, here, Darwin, so excuse me if I don't get my panties in a wad over terminology."

"All right, fine for you, but Davenport cites me in his research. Me! If he's going to incant me, he should at least incant me truthfully! I am the most important person of the century. I heard it on satellite radio, Charles Darwin, most important person of the twentieth century. If they're going to laud me now, they should at least know what I stand for. Am I in favor of expunging the defectives from the face of the planet? Most certainly not! Is that what everyone thinks? I like jazz! I like improvisation! You haven't even read the files yet. Read them."

"I'll read them later."

"Davenport calls one woman too wild and another too light fingered. What is the world if not wild and light-fingered women?"

"I don't know."

"Have you even heard of Davenport?"

"Who's Davenport?"

"Do you know Alexander Graham Bell?"

"Yes."

"Why do you know him and not Davenport?"

"Because I use telephones. I don't have any use for what Davenport's pushing."

"You are living at his incorporation."

"It's not his anymore. And stop calling it an incorporation."

Darwin nabbed our waitress. "Do you know Davenport?"

"Does he work here?"

"See what I mean, Annie, it's like he never existed."

"Okay, Darwin, I wouldn't trust the waitress at Applebee's with being the beacon of history."

"Who would you trust?"

He calmed down and sipped his scotch. He closed his eyes. I didn't want to think about the word *eugenics* or the history of eugenics or the files in Nick's glove box or the files sitting on the table in front of me because my leg looked like a baseball bat. It was embarrassing. I overheard the older couple:

"How many people have been inside you since me?"

The woman replied, "I already said."

The man didn't believe her, and there ensued a discussion of who had cheated on whom and at what point in the relationship and for how long.

"Annie, back to number one," Darwin's eyes were still closed. His lips looked dry. "Why are you holding a candle for Old Faithful?"

"It's not easy to talk about."

Darwin opened his eyes and stuck his hand out. The waitress came by and he ordered a gin and tonic.

"I loved him. That's all."

"I got that much," Darwin said. "Why are you crying?"

"I'm not crying. My eyes are watering."

"Annie, for Christ's sake," Darwin said. "Have yourself a cry. Lean on me and get it out."

"I can't get it out," I said. "It's not a stain." I scooted closer to Darwin.

"Goddammit, where is he? I'd like to meet this guy and give him a piece of my mind." Darwin peeked over the top of the booth as if Old Faithful were in the restaurant.

"It's not just him; it's a more universal feeling. I get the feeling people think there's something wrong with me."

The waitress came with the drink, and while I was taking a sip, Darwin dug around in my purse, found the cigarettes, and lit one.

"We can't smoke in here."

"Fuck 'em," he said, holding the cigarette under the table. "Start from the beginning."

I leaned against his shoulder. "You would've liked him. He worked in the library. Third floor. I studied there so I saw him a lot. He was older. He was always dropping books and spilling coffee. He had a sad, vacant look on his face as if his soul had been evacuated. I didn't know then that I had already begun to fall for him. You have to talk to someone to fall for them—don't you?"

Darwin snuck the cigarette from under the table and I took a drag.

"So I wasn't worried, because you have to talk to someone, and beside, he wore a ring. I know what you're thinking. People act like they don't want anything to do with a predicament such as mine, yet they are all the time trying to get themselves in one, like where's the door? Just show it to me."

"I'm not saying a word." Darwin hid the cigarette under the table.

"He was keeping late hours at the library to avoid his wife. He was always picking lint off his shirt. The first time we talked he cracked a joke. Oh God, he's funny, I thought. I hadn't thought he'd be funny. I thought he was going to be sad and serious. He surprised me. It wasn't sparks and like that. It was more like I wanted to throw up. I'd go to the library jittery and nauseous. He was very smart, he knew languages and translations and the classics, but mostly he was funny. He'd read to me in a British accent, 'Vanity of vanities saith the Preacher, vanity of vanities; all is vanity. What profit hath a man,' here he'd take a breath, as if he really wanted to know, as if this was the big question, and when he picked the verse up again, he dropped the accent, 'What profit hath a man of all his labor?' I kissed him on the bottom lip. He pulled back. 'Is it because the door's open?' Then everything started. I meant it to be a fling. Before him, I thought I had to have a boyfriend, an official guy to officially show up and to officially show the world that I was not who they wanted to pity. But these official guys, they never really did anything for me. I could never feel like myself around them. Old Faithful wasn't fulfilling some type of requirement. We were just undeniably for each other. We cracked jokes and made fun of people in the library three nights a week, five nights a week. We wanted to know everything, maybe too much, every detail. How did he get so funny and how did I get so self-assured and how come the sex was so good and where were we from and while we were there how did we live without each other? January, February, March. April, May, June. It was the most honest I'd ever been. Through all that time, I thought he didn't care about the leg. I mean he *cared* about it. He knew what to whistle. But I thought it didn't affect how he thought about me. Then, suddenly, one day in his office, he kept talking about leaving his wife, it was serious, and he kept coming back to my leg, and what if he cheated on me in my condition—*condition*, he used that word—and I felt like a whole different person, a person who had a *condition*, and I felt like he'd been secretly, covertly worried about this the whole time he was with me. Vanity of vanities. So the very thing that bound me to him, thinking for once I'd found someone who liked me regardless of my *condition*, who I could say and do anything with, I could be myself and not worry, all this ended up not true. It wasn't true that he didn't think about it. He just didn't talk about it. It wasn't true that love conquers all. Love doesn't. In the morning, one person has a *condition* and the other doesn't. No one should feel like a condition, as if their entire life, how people see them, revolves around a microscopic chromosome. It's not fair. And don't give me the bullshit about finding someone who *looks beyond* that. What am I supposed to do? Be so happy, so appreciative when I find someone who looks beyond me? I don't want anyone to have to look beyond me. Where would they be looking? If that aligns me with your papers, then fine. If that means I'm in support of the cures the Gee works on, fine. I don't want to be this anymore. Old Faithful was very funny, but there was nothing funny about losing him. I thought we were of the same sense, connected in time and space, perpendicular rather than parallel, if not now then later, *conditionless*. The thing is he keeps being the thing. It's worse since I've been here. He was my best friend. That's all."

Waiting on the Leg
and Reading the Files

———

Please see the Appendixes.

Genetic Counseling

———

Truth in medicine is a goal which cannot be absolutely reached.

—MAZES, ninth-century Persian physician

ONE WEEK LEFT. I was trying to walk on the ball of my foot when the Gee knocked on the door. He held a clipboard under his arm as he took a kerchief from his pants pocket and wiped his nose. He kept saying *phenomenal* as he blew his nose and walked in a circle around me. He returned the kerchief to his pocket and sat down at the kitchen table. I sat beside him. He took my leg in his lap. He took the dimensions of my thigh, knee, calf, and ankle, writing them down on the clipboard with his Montblanc. Something caught his attention.

"What?"

"Nothing," he said. "Let me take your vitals."

He placed a thermometer under my tongue. I leaned forward, in my slip, as he put the stethoscope to my chest. I was 99.1 degrees. He bumped me on the knee a couple of times with the triangle tool.

"What do you think?"

"Your PRX1 is phenomenal. We're already working on

therapies in the lab. We've come a long way. From Durham to Cold Spring. From Thailand to Cold Spring. From Rochester to Cold Spring."

I gathered he was from Rochester.

"Look at you. When would you like to go public? How about this afternoon?"

"I don't have a foot yet. My leg looks like a baseball bat."

"We need to go public."

"But I don't have a foot yet."

"Let's see, it's Friday and it would be wise to hold a press conference on Monday. That gives you the weekend. How does Monday sound?"

"I'm not in charge of the foot. The closest I am to a foot is some nerve endings on what looks like Tupperware."

He stood from the table and pushed his chair in. I watched as he turned away from me and looked out the windows of the front door. I wanted to grow the foot for him right then and there. I would've grown the foot already if it were a mind-over-matter thing. I would've grown the foot to sleep easy at night without waking to check on myself. I had an agenda for the day I finished growing: identify my natural walk, wear a pair of garters, do Nick Burkowitz with sincerity. Was I being rude to ask the Gee to wait? Could he tell me with absolute certainty the foot would grow? And if he could, then why wasn't he telling me? He walked to the table, pulled the chair out, and sat down. He took my leg in his hands and patted me on the calf.

"I need you to trust me. According to your charts, it will grow."

"I have a few charts for you."

The Gee removed his hand from my leg. I reached across the table for the folder from Darwin.

"Where'd you get these?" the Gee said.

"Doesn't matter."

"Uh-huh," the Gee said, lilting up. "It does matter. We run a tight ship here and if you think you can steal documents from—"

"Shouldn't they be public knowledge?"

"They are public knowledge."

"I never knew about them."

The Gee thumbed through the papers. "How often do you snoop for case files?" He closed the file and put it on the table.

"I want you to clarify your intentions. You've shown me umpteen diagrams but you've never clarified your intentions. Are you going to fix everyone? What does *fixing* mean? What needs fixing and what doesn't? I'd like to read a report on how far is too far and how much is too much. I'd like to see some lines drawn. I don't see enough lines being drawn around this place. I'd like you to prepare a report on where you draw the line."

"We have ethics committees."

"Oh yeah? Where are all these ethics committees?"

"They exist, Anne. Just because you don't know about something, you think it doesn't exist?"

"What about you? What are your ethics?"

"Look," he said, taking the folder from the table, "I'm not going to press charges."

"Press charges?"

"For stealing documents, Anne. I'm not going to press charges. I'm sending Jack Ballantine over tomorrow to interview you. I'll see you on Monday."

"Yeah? You're just going to walk out and not answer me on ethics."

"I want you to act—if you can—a little bit more grateful. Here's your last check." The Gee dropped the check on the table and left.

Interview

———

JACK BALLANTINE ARRIVED the next day at noon. He swayed his hips, hands in pockets, while he talked about all the famous people he'd profiled. I was wearing white boots with my red mini-skirt and a sweater. I felt Mercedian. The only problem was balance. The boots had two-inch platforms, and while I could manage them in my fake leg, I hadn't quite got the hang of heels with two legs, one foot. I kept tripping.

Jack Ballantine flung his hand out.

"I'm fine," I said. "I'm doing remarkably well."

He kept looking at the boots and my legs. I poured a glass of tea and judged the distance to the chair in the living room, drew a line with my eyes on the floor to the chair. I only had to walk to the chair with the sweet tea and Jack Ballantine's eyes following me. I walked head down, concentrating, because even though I didn't give two licks about Jack Ballantine, he was the one writing me up, presenting me to the public. This would be a lot easier if you'd let me take off this leg, and put on my old one, relegated to the side of the room, lying horizontally next to the wall of the alcove; in that leg I could walk for you without thinking, and I'd be so self-assured while I did it that I'd make you forget who I was for a second, and you would slip into thinking me like anyone else, and I'd be happier to answer your questions, except, I know you, Jack Ballantine, and you'd want me to think there was something regrettably wrong with me, and eventually, if I were wearing the old leg, you'd turn to me, your hand perched under your chin, as if you'd just had a very deep thought, as if you were the first person to have thunk it, and you'd ask, "But wouldn't you prefer two legs?" Here they are. Do you prefer them?

I walked as gracefully as I could and sat down. He asked questions and I answered the questions. He took photos and uploaded them to the flat screen. In the photo I chose, I'm sitting in the chair with my legs crossed, the good knee over the knee with its fruitlike appearance, as if you could squash it with your finger and it would hold the impression, like a clementine. I'm sitting there, smoking a cigarette. I'm thinking Jack Ballantine is a blandiloquent fop.

"I'll call you when the interview runs," he said. I saw the interview, literally running across screens, across pages, across desks, and I thought how very inescapable language is. One never can get it right. My favorite writer said to an interviewer, "I've never been able to talk about my life actually. As soon as I start talking about my life, I start lying straight away. To begin with, I lie consciously and very quickly I forget that I'm lying." Here are the questions:

When did your parents know there was something wrong with you?

What is your earliest memory? Is it of a hospital?

What was your problem and what was the prognosis?

Is it hereditary?

What was high school like for you? Were you teased?

At what point did you realize that you weren't like other teenagers?

When did you lose your virginity?

Do you need a bottle of water?

Where did you attend college?

When did you first hear about genetic engineering? What was your initial reaction?

What is a regular day like for you?

You once, irresponsibly, threatened to have children. Now that you can have children, do you intend to?

Legs are often associated with archetypal beauty. Do you believe your legs are beautiful?

Do you find yourself more desirable?

Who is your favorite geneticist?

What advice would you have for someone who is considering regeneration?

Going-Away Present

———

THE LONGEST DAY, Saturday, veins crisscrossing the ankle, more waiting, and Nick had a going-away present: "Nothing special," he said. "Be ready at seven PM sharp." The Gee called for an update on my progress. What progress? "It might take another day or two," he said. After that I checked my email.

"Hi Annie, What do you want me to do with your stuff? I think I left *Koyaanisqatsi* at your place. I would like that back at some point. I saw images of your femur on the news last night. Listen, I'm worried about you. I think they should provide some kind of therapy for you. My mom knows someone here locally in case you want a recommendation. Maybe we can get lunch some afternoon when you get back to town. I started seeing someone. Try to refrain from telling me you told me so. Take it easy."

I had become a lunch.

I started looking for the news clip Grayson had seen, and I found myself as the lead story on most of the dot-coms. REGENERATIVE TO TAKE FIRST STEPS MONDAY. The news was being updated hourly with commentators from Biopolis to Kansas City. TMZ named me "Bitch of the Colony" and showed a photo of me peeking from my window and giving Jack Ballantine the finger.

I checked the ankle again. I didn't want to put the ball of the foot inside anything, in case that prevented it from growing, so I called Nick to cancel. He was adamant, 7:00 PM he was taking me somewhere, barefoot. I was pinning my bangs when he knocked on the door. The bangs kept getting in my eyes and I was twisting them back. Nick insisted I finish in the car.

"Where are we going?"

"You'll see."

"I found us on TMZ. They called me a bitch."

"You are kind of a bitch."

"Nick."

"In a good way."

We turned left onto Harbor Road and crossed the bridge to the other side of the water. The sun was setting. We turned down Bungtown Road. So this was where the rest of Cold Spring Harbor slept and ate and worked. We passed a white colonial building with three columns. We passed a bell tower with the letters C and A and T and G engraved in stone.

"Anything you want to do in our last week?" Nick said.

"I just want to hang out with you."

"Holy helmet. That's the first sweet thing you've said to me."

He took my hand. It felt like the last week of summer camp. We'd promise to write, call, visit. It's not that we'd be lying. But one of us would get an email and not respond for two weeks, and the other would take that as a slight and not respond for a month. Or one of us would not return a call. We'd want to call, but we just wouldn't. Suddenly we'd think we had nothing to say to each other, and instead of calling just to say, "Hey, I don't have anything really to say other than I miss you," we'd assume the other person already knew. This is one of the great tragedies of human nature.

We'd get on with our lives. Isn't that how it works? We'd fully intend to "keep in touch" when we said it, even if it was an impossible phrase: From two thousand miles away, from your farmhouse in Madison, from beside the next girl, keep in touch with me. I thought maybe Nick and I should make one of those things, a pact, let's see where we are in six months, a year, if we miss each other, then one of us should move. I was about to suggest such a pact when I started doubting it. Never mind that. If someone wants to go, they go, and if someone wants to follow, they follow, right? We stopped to let a couple cross the road. The man had his arm around the woman's waist—they were keeping in touch.

Beyond them, the Green House. Nick was driving me to the Green House. It was beautiful, a cascade of glass, panels and panels of aquamarine glass, the size of a warehouse, and part of it appeared to be built on the water.

"Is it built on the water?"

"Yes, ma'am," Nick said, driving the station wagon up to the entrance.

"Does this have something to do with Shug?"

"Well," Nick said. The last person I wanted to see was Shug the Bean Tree Botanist. "She helped me get clearance for tonight." Nick stepped out of the car and told me he'd be right back. I watched him walk to the front of the Green House. It was getting dark and he looked small compared to the expansive structure. He punched a code into a keypad. Two plates of glass separated, one rolled to the left, the other to the right. He walked back to the car and put it in drive. We drove into the Green House.

"This is pretty," I said. Nick got out of the car to close the doors behind us. Trees loomed over the car, their trunks twisted, some of them oozing sap, all of them with bright green foliage. How did they get so green? We inched along in the station wagon on a path of mulch. I asked Nick to stop driving. There was a map to the right of the car. It looked like a mall directory. I got out of the car. The mulch scratched the heel of my foot and I asked Nick to pick me up. He carried me to the map of the Green House.

```
┌─────────────────────────────────────────────────────┐
│                                                       │
│  THE ARBOLIS                      AQUABOTANICAL       │
│                                      PHARMACY         │
│                                                       │
│                         Row                           │
│                                                       │
│  AGING                   A                            │
│  CARDIOLOGY              B                            │
│  ENDOCRINOLOGY           C                            │
│  GASTROENTEROLOGY        D                            │
│  GYNECOLOGY              E                            │
│  NEPHROLOGY              F                            │
│  NEUROLOGY               G                            │
│  ONCOLOGY                H                            │
│  OPTHAMOLOGY             I                            │
│  ORTHOPEDICS             J                            │
│  PSYCHIATRIC             K                            │
│                                                       │
│                          L    EAR, NOSE & THROAT      │
│                          M    RESPIRATORY DISORDERS   │
│                          N    EPITHELIAL TISSUES      │
│               X                                       │
│           YOU ARE HERE                                │
│                                                       │
└─────────────────────────────────────────────────────┘
```

The map was overwhelming. I felt dizzy. I looked from the map to the top of Nick's head, where the stitches from his cranios had been removed, and now he had three circular scars, covered by hair. We walked down the row of epithelial tissues, and he said these plants dealt with replicating human skin. The tops of their leaves, rather than green, were flesh toned.

"Put me down," I said. "I don't know if I like this going-away present." I walked to Row L where flowers, like the one Dora had pinned to her sweater, were sneezing their tiny flower sneeze.

In the car, Nick kept asking if I was okay and saying he thought I would like the Green House, considering all the ways plants were being used in biomedicine. Over to the right was *Capparis tomentosa*, part of Leonard's treatment, and over there was *Ginkgo biloba*, part of Eliot's treatment. Wasn't it incredible to consider the genomic attributes of botany? Nick's lingo and tone sounded like the Gee and the voice of the woman in the cave and Craig Venter, words like *genomic* and *attributes* inflected with optimism, and was I the only one worried about the tiny flower sneeze? I looked at the rows and rows of plants, short and tall, thick- and thin-stalked. I was dizzy and everything was moving too fast. When did this happen? Nick said the plans for the Green House were drawn up after the success of Taxol, an anticancer drug developed from a yew tree. Some of the plants traveled all the way from the Amazon, from the riverbeds of the Euphrates. He named this and that plant, this and that species, pointing through the window, "Do you see? Do you see?" I took my jacket off. We passed the wing of the Green House that went over the water, and I leaned out the window to see if there were dugongs below us. I saw glowing seaweed.

"Why is it glowing?"

"Bioluminescence," Nick said.

"What do plants need to glow for? I hope we don't start glowing. What would be the point of that?"

We were driving back toward the Arbolis. Nick parked the car and came around to my side. He put me on his shoulders. We walked to two trees with a roof between them. Nick took his boots off and started climbing.

"Can you climb this with me on your shoulders?"

"Baby, you're light as a feather."

"Can you see okay?" The sun had gone down and it was getting dark.

There were notches cut into the tree. We were seven or eight feet off the ground, and I was scared Nick would miss a step.

"Get down," he said.

"Down where?"

He pointed to the thing I had thought was a roof. It was a leaf.

"I'm not getting on that leaf."

"It's the strongest leaf in the world. *Alocasia robusta*."

"I don't want to get on a leaf. I'd be just as content to get back in the car."

"Just get down there." Nick held me by the waist. I decided to go headfirst for the leaf, with my hands out. When I put my hands on the leaf, it didn't give like I expected. But I stayed close to the trunk of the tree. Nick walked on the leaf and sat down. He motioned for me to come out. I was scared that I'd fall through, scrape against the bark of the tree, need epithelial tissue from the plants, crack a bone, need a dugong to replace it, get lost, need bioluminescence for someone to find me. I crawled toward the center. He pulled me to his side. The grid of the Green House lay below us, trees, ferns, blue roses, hyacinth, honeysuckle. We sat there looking at the plants, and beyond them, the water, which looked black except for the occasional electric blue squiggle, and the lights on the other side of the harbor. Two of those lights belonged to us for not much longer. I looked up, Nick was kissing me, and I saw through the glass, the sky.

"It's really pretty," I said.

"There's something I think you don't know," Nick said.

"What's that?"

"You're real pretty."

"Right." It sounded like a line, something Nick had used before and would use again, something like "keep in touch."

"Believe me," he said.

Practice

———

The longer you look at an object, the more abstract it
becomes, and ironically the more real.

—Lucian Freud

ON MONDAY MORNING I practiced walking. Nick had gone
to his place to shower. I only had to walk the length of the quad,
to the flagpole, and stand still. I only had one foot to do this on,
in my white boots, with toilet paper stuffed down around the leg,
to fill the boot out, to make it look more real. I was getting the
hang of walking when I fell against the fridge. I took the boots off
and got back in bed. I'll just sleep through it, I thought. I kicked
the sheets off, pulled the sheets back up and tucked them under
my chin, then kicked the sheets off again. My real leg, the leg
that had always been real, the leg that supported me from birth,
did not know what to do with itself. The knees bumped together
and the ankles crossed each other. I stood from the bed and put
on garters. The hose had a black seam running down the calves.
The problem was with the grown calf. It was below par. Too thin.
I tried to focus on something pleasurable. What is pleasurable? I
thought. And to whom? The phone rang. I answered with: "Nick,
I'm almost ready."

Silence.

"Who is this?"

"Don't hang up."

I felt rigid. "You're the one who hangs up."

"Listen. I'm sorry. I'm an idiot. I'm sitting here in my office feeling like an idiot because, the thing is, I love you and I should've—"

"You can't—"

"You can't tell me I can't."

"You can't love someone only after they have the right leg count. That's not love."

"Hey."

"What?"

"It's not like that."

"Yeah? Then what's it like?"

Going Public

——

NICK AND I stood at the door of Bungalow North. I asked if there were many people outside, and he said there were. I kept asking him questions to hear my voice because I was scared and hearing my voice makes me feel better because my voice is something I recognize. Nick said he would lend me his straw hat if I wanted him to. He said I had to remember that all the people outside supported me, had come from far and wide to see me, thought I was a brave lady—stop—what's the matter, Nick wanted to know. I just want to be the lady. Okay? Nick said we better get going. We better get going then, I said.

The door opened and the crowd collectively sucked their breath into their bodies. They stood in the road next to the gates. I recognized a few of them. The guy with the handlebar mustache had a prime spot front and center with Dora. I looked for Shug but didn't see her. I looked for Chase and found him standing off to the side with his nose wrapped in bandages. I saw the leader of the Evans with his followers surrounding him. I saw men and women, short and tall, cramming their faces between the bars of the gates. It looked like they were the ones locked in. The Evans had not taken down the memorial to Mercedes and people were perched on it to get a better view. The ramp reminded me of a lifeguard's chair. People squatted at various levels where they could look down onto the quad. Vendors who had been selling soda and beer turned to watch. Kids who had been screaming bloody murder back and forth stopped their screaming. Parents who had been chatting with each other collected their kids close to them and put arms in front of their chests. One family—the family from the Petri Plate Relay Race—held a painted sign that read WE LOVE ANNE HATLEY. I looked at the daughter, a girl in a gingham dress, whose lips were blue from eating cotton candy. Policemen who had been focused on crowd control turned their attention to the quad. It was quiet.

Inside the gates, cameras rolled on dollies alongside reporters. I had a lot of hands to shake from my doorstep to the flagpole where the Gee waited. First I shook hands with the research assistants—the Tweedles and Debbie's husband and Debbie, who whispered, "Go get 'em" in my ear—and John Hobart, senator from New York; Nita Lowey, House of Representatives; Vic Trinidad, Merck; someone from Amgen, Novartis, ABI, NIH; the letters and companies and affiliations blurred together as I shook their hands. I didn't have to think about walking as much as I had to think about looking these people in the face and holding a smile. Finally, we were one man from the flagpole. James D. Watson. "You, my dear, look radiant," he said. I didn't feel radiant. I felt numb. I felt everything numbly. It was weird then because I felt numb and throbbed at once. I wanted Nick's straw hat. Some sunglasses. I wanted to wait another day. So I could step, two feet, into my boots and bask in the admiration of these faces. When I reached the center of the quad, the crowd cheered. They had been waiting for me to walk the length of the sidewalk, and now they could exhale and ruffle the heads of their children, and later step into their vehicles, slam the doors, and drive home pleasantly, smiling at each other and knowing that if they lost a leg, heaven forbid, but if they did, it wasn't the end of the world. Sure, at first it would be an expensive procedure. But everything costs something.

The girl in the gingham dress was sitting on her father's shoulders. He had one hand on each of her legs. She waved at me. I looked down at my white boots, and my legs in the boots, and felt shaky. I stood beside the Gee, who wore his blue suit and red tie. He put his arm around me as he spoke into a microphone. I heard him say, "I give you Anne Hatley." Part of me was thinking, what does that mean—to be given to a crowd—and another part of me was thinking, I've got a leech on my ankle.

"It hurts," I whispered to Nick.

"What hurts?"

"You have to make him stop."

"Make who stop?"

"My nerves."

"What's the matter, baby?"

"Make him stop."

The Gee heard me and said in a whisper, "Five minutes."

I leaned into Nick and squeezed his hand. It was not a matter of emotion or attitude; it was pure physical pain. I recognized it. Everyone was looking at me. I forgot how words went together. I thought discordant things like beggar of kamikazes and what difference does it make and vanity of vanities and what are the wives of Durham doing and when did Nick and I build our labyrinth and who will want to stay still, stay in the canoe, stay mortared to me now? How long until everything is hyacinth? Grin and bear it, I thought. I focused on the girl in the gingham dress and thought if I could return to her age, if I could devolve, if I could sit with Darwin again, if I could desire, if I could be the first figure drawn on a cave wall. Grin and bear it, I thought, and I was sad that so much had to be borne for so long.

After a minute, ten minutes—how long had it been? where was my concept of time?—there was nothing I could do. I knew what was happening. The zipper on the boot snapped. I felt the paper I'd stuffed into the boot fall away. I heard the crowd screaming again. It was not a cheer. It was not a scream of joy. It was a collective scream of horror. The father of the girl in the gingham dress put his hands over her eyes. He stared blankly at me. I looked up and saw Nick's face and wanted to say a million things, like I forgot to tell you, you were the best part about being here. When you weren't at my place, I looked for your boots by the door, and when you went off to the Green House, I looked for your car in the parking lot. When you wouldn't speak to me, I walked around the Colony looking for you, asking after you. I don't trust anyone, really, because anyone might walk up to me and tell me about their niece, their father, their friend, and how bad they feel for me, for me being worse off, for me in my condition. So I built my labyrinths. I like having a plan. I like knowing what the plan is and who's in it. So what's the plan? I'm messy, I'm unwieldy now, my leg is growing too long, too fast, too long, but our labyrinth is short and navigable. We haven't done anything to totally fuck up our labyrinth—have we? Maybe I didn't act right toward you, because I don't know what right is, and I've been wrong, and it looks like I'm getting wronger. "I'm scared," I said to Nick. "Don't fizzle on me." He was behind me with his arms under my arms. "I'm still with you," he said. I felt the arteries and muscles and blood vessels of the leg. It grew and grew and grew. Who would stop it? Why wasn't anyone doing anything? It grew and it did and it did. The girl in the gingham dress cried while Nick held me under the arms and the cameras rolled. This is what happened. Remember me, to your fancies.

Appendix I

Files on Twenty Defectives

1. Her father was a drunkard who wandered into a backwoods town twelve or fifteen miles from a railroad and wanted to get rid of his baby girl. He succeeded in trading her for a dog.

2. She dislikes school and avoids going.

3. She has fair intelligence, but married a worthless, drunken man, her own cousin.

4. She has married an apparently normal German.

5. She has nine children. They have frequently had town aid. When the whole family had scarlet fever, they refused to be fumigated until forced to and then took some clothes to the woods and hid them.

6. She has the physical defect of a congenital union of the second and third digits on both hands and feet.

7. She insisted upon his walking to the store for gifts.

8. She is almost an idiot.

9. She is almost continually on the street of the country village.

10. She is known to keep a house of ill repute.

11. She is very peculiar and rolls her eyes upward in an abnormal manner when she talks.

12. She married a laborer from a family that is below par and has two more children.

13. She, too, had difficulty in talking plainly.

14. She was a "wild" girl when young but finally married an ordinary laborer and lives with her mother on the old farm.

15. She was considered mildly insane at one time.

16. She was frankly glad to send him off to the war, hoping he would never return, but he did. She worked very hard to keep her family together even after she was crippled.

17. She was "light fingered" and untrustworthy.

18. She was placed in a children's hospital.

19. She was removed, and also three younger children who had been brought into the world since the first experience with this couple, but nothing was done to prevent the parents from furnishing more dependents.

20. She was wayward and hard to control.

—From *The Hill Folk: Report on a Rural Community of Hereditary Defectives*, by Charles Davenport and Florence Danielson (Cold Spring Harbor, NY: Press of the New Era, 1912), 45–55.

Appendix II

Q. What is the most precious thing in the world?
A. The human germ plasm.

Q. How may one's germ plasm become immortal?
A. Only by perpetuation by children.

Q. What is a person's duty to civilization?
A. To see that his own good qualities are passed on to future generations provided they exceed his bad qualities. If he has, on the whole, an excess of dysgenic qualities, they should be eliminated by letting the germ plasm die out with the individual.

—From *A Eugenics Catechism*, American Eugenics Society (1926).

Appendix III

Means Proposed for Cutting off the Supply of Human Defectives and Degenerates

    I.   Life segregation

    II.   Sterilization

   III.   Restrictive marriage

   IV.   Eugenic education

    V.   System of matings

   VI.   General environmental

  VII.   Polygamy

 VIII.   Euthanasia

   IX.   Neo-Malthusian doctrine

    X.   Laissez-faire

Which of these remedies shall be applied?

Shall one, two, several, or all be made to operate?

What are the limitations and possibilities of each remedy?

Shall one class of the socially unfit be treated with one remedy and another with a different one?

Shall the specifically selected remedy be applied to the class or to the individual?

What are the principles and the limits of compromise between conservation and elimination in cases of individuals bearing a germ-plasm with a mixture of the determiners for both defective and sterling traits?

What are the criteria for the identification of individuals bearing defective germ-plasm?

What can be hoped from the application of some definite elimination program? What practical difficulties stand in the way?

How can they be overcome?

—From the Dolan DNA Learning Center, Cold Spring Harbor Laboratory, Document 978, www.eugenicsarchive.org.

Dec 27, 1912
Eugenics Record Office
Cold Spring Harbor, L.I.

Dear Dr. Davenport,

You have started a great work, of vast importance to the people of the United States and to the world, by the establishment of the Eugenics Record Office; and I can assure you of my hearty cooperation as one of the Board of Scientific Directors.

Alexander Graham Bell

From the Dolan DNA Learning Center, Cold Spring Harbor Laboratory, Document 431 (excerpt), www.eugenicsarchive.org.

Nov 11, 1922
Major Leonard Darwin,
Cripp's Corner,
Forrest Row, Sussex, England.

Dear Major Darwin;—

Thank you for your kind letter of November first. I am arranging to have two copies of the sterilization book sent to you.

I gathered from contact with geneticists and eugenicists in Austria and Germany that so far from eugenics not being recognized that the German Government is about the only one that has asked and secured the cooperation of leading scientific men (certainly members of leading scientific societies) to cooperate with the Government by constituting a committee to which should be referred all legislation of eugenical import.

Apart from the international society of Dr. Alfred Ploetz in Munich, the liveliest society dealing with eugenical matters is the Deutsche Gesellschaft für Vererbungswissenschaft of which Dr. H. Nachtscheim, Landwirtsch. Hochschule zu Berlin, Invalidenstrasse 42, Berlin N.4, is secretary.

With kind regards to Mrs. Darwin, as well as yourself,
Sincerely yours,

Chas. B. Davenport, Director.

From the Dolan DNA Learning Center, Cold Spring Harbor Laboratory, Document 440, www.eugenicsarchive.org.

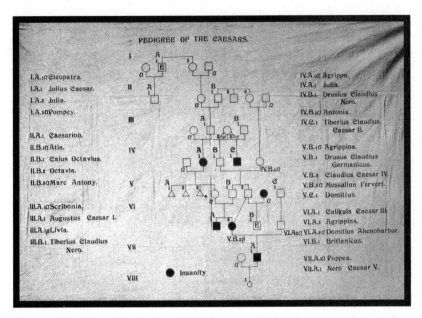

Figure 2. *Pedigree of the Caesars*, 1921. Courtesy of the Cold Spring Harbor Laboratory Archive.

Figure 3. *Eugenics Tree Logo*, circa 1925. Courtesy of the American Philosophical Society.

Notes

"Ceremony in Honor of James D. Watson": The epigraph for this chapter comes from the television series *DNA* (2003), produced by David Dugan.

"Modern Science (Some Things I Know about It)": Darwin often closed letters to Emma with "Believe me." The Darwin Correspondence Project was an invaluable resource, and their archive can be accessed at http://www.darwinproject.ac.uk/.

"Goal of Cold Spring Colony": This might echo in the goal of company 23andMe: Genetic Testing for Health, Disease & Ancestry. 23andMe was cofounded by Anne Wojcicki, wife of Google's Sergey Brin. Google invested $3.9 million in the company. Their website is https://www.23andme.com/.

"Nick's Place,": The ANK3 gene (Leonard's, in the novel) is discussed in Ferreira, O'Donovan, Meng Ya, et al.'s "Collaborative genome-wide association analysis supports a role for ANK3 and CACNA1C in bipolar disorder," in *Nature Genetics*, August 2008.

    The obesity gene (Mercedes') is the topic of Catherine Paddock's "Obesity Gene Discovered," in *Medical News Today*.

"Interview with the Geneticist": I give thanks to my colleague Michael Sehorn in the Department of Genetics and Biochemistry at Clemson, and to Shelton Wright for many conversations on the topic of genetics. A fact sheet with additional information on gene therapy, with specific reference to the Cavazzana-Calvo research group, can be found at http://www.genetics.com.au/pdf/factsheets/fs27.pdf/.

"*The New York Times* Responds to the Declaration of Independence": The excerpt from *The New York Times* comes from an opinion-section article by Yuval Levin: "A Middle Ground for Stem Cells," *The New York Times*, Jan 19, 2007, http://www.nytimes.com/2007/01/19/opinion/19levin.html/.

"Cranios": Eliot's gene—SORL1—is hypothesized to be linked to Alzheimer's. Nick's suicide gene is invented.

"Field Trip": The idea for the robotic boy in the cave was based on the article "Flexible 'E-Skin' Could Endow Robots with Humanlike Sense of Touch" by Kate Wong, in *Scientific American*. The Craig Venter quotes come from James Shreeve's *The Genome War: How Craig Venter Tried to Capture the Code of Life and Save the World* (New York: Ballantine Books, 2005).

"The Dream Director": The title of the actual press release for "The Dream Director" was "Artist Shapes Dreams During Gallery Sleepover." The full press release was accessed at http://www.dshed.net/studio/residencies/clarkbursary/documents/press_release_july.pdf/.
The project, which is ongoing, is by artist Luke Jerram, whose website is www.lukejerram.com/.

"Origins of the First Fake Leg": This chapter was informed by the Disability Social History Timeline at http://www.disabilityhistory.org/timeline_new.html/.

"Origins of the Leg Sitting There on the Chair": This chapter was informed by the Otto Bock Company website: http://www.ottobock.com/.

"After the Dinosaurs and Before Engel Deeter": These biographies are not entirely factual; for more information, see "Mousework" by Terri Peterson Smith, in *Invention & Technology* 23, no. 1.

"Reasons for Birth Defects": Contents excerpted from *On Monsters & Marvels* by Ambroise Paré.

"A New Kind of Rays": The Röntgen biography draws from his page on the Nobel Prize website: http://nobelprize.org/nobel_prizes/physics/laureates/1901/rontgen-bio.html/.

"The Stone and the Watch": This chapter explores Paley's *Natural Theology*, which Darwin argued against in formulating his ideas on evolution. More information can be found in *The Case for God* by Karen Armstrong (New York: Knopf, 2009).

"Headlines": Translations provided by Lee Ferrell and Luca Barattoni.

"The Regenerator": The epigraph comes from the article "Body Regenerate Thyself" in *Biomechanics*, August 2007, http://www.biomech.com/full_article/?ArticleID=108&month=8&year=2007/.

"Statement": Information on "the patch," called "FILMSkin," available at the websites http://www.ornl.gov/info/ornlreview/v40_2_07/article14.shtml/ and http://neurodudes.com/2007/02/02/amputee-controls-feels-bionic-arm-as-her-own/.

"Dig Season": Norman Gardiner is a real person. His quote, along with details about the excavation site, are from "Digging Up Dinosaur Bones in the Fossil-Rich Badlands," *The New York Times*, September 11, 2005, http://travel.nytimes.com/2005/09/11/travel/11dino.html/.

"Mercedes Interviews Peter Singer for the Cold Spring Harbor Channel": Peter Singer's response to the question "What does a philosopher do?" is taken verbatim from an interview on ABC's *Talking Heads*. Video is online at http://www.youtube.com/watch?v=-lu9sc4FWLw&NR=1/. Later in the interview, Mercedes mentions Karen Meade, who posed the question, "Would you kill a disabled baby?" Singer answered in a profile of him in the *Independent*.

"Assembly with Peter Singer": Quotes from the United States president and the chancellor of Germany are invented; though it's true some factions in Germany are not fond of Singer. See *The Hastings Center Report* 21, no. 6, p. 20: "Singer's positions are murderous. The right to free speech does not extend to the public propagation of murderous positions."

"What We Fix": Plastic surgery procedural statistics collected by the American Society of Plastic Surgeons' department of public relations. Statistics on "vagina" surgeries were last available in 2006 and have since been removed. http://www.plasticsurgery.org/Media/stats/2008-US-cosmetic-reconstructive-plastic-surgery-minimally-invasive-statistics.pdf/.

Acknowledgments

Thanks to Wendy Kline, author of *Building a Better Race: Gender, Sexuality and Eugenics from the Turn of the Century to the Baby Boom*, for many conversations about the eugenics movement. Thanks to William H. Moore for his work on discrimination and political violence.

The writing of this novel was supported by Clemson University and a Fulbright Fellowship. Thanks to the following people who read this novel a lot and talked to me about it extensively: Jon Baker, Brock Clarke, Okla Elliott, Adam Frelin, Anne Horowitz, Brigid Hughes, Julia Kenny, Bo McGuire, Charles McLeod, Liz Vogel and Thomas Yagoda. Thanks Mom and Dad.